Crazy
IN
LOVE

A SECRETS OF SUBURBIA NOVEL

IVY SMOAK

Crazy
IN
LOVE

This book is a work of fiction. Names, characters, places, and incidents are fictitious. Any resemblance to actual persons, living or dead, events, or locales is purely coincidental.

ISBN: 9781942381198

2020 Hardcover First Edition

To all the Hallmark Christmas movies I've watched.
This is nothing like them.
You've been warned.

CHAPTER 1
Friday

I gave everything to my husband. My heart. My soul. My bank accounts. And piece by piece he took it all until our lives were so intertwined that there was no escape. It was a great plan. To diminish me to nothing without him. To make me feel like there was no out. There was just one problem with his plan. He had a secret. A secret that was about to tip the scales back in my favor.

The hotel doors slid open as I approached. How many times had I dressed like this on a cold winter night? Thigh-high black boots that did nothing to warm me when my upper thighs were so exposed by my short skirt. Combine that with the plunging neckline of my blouse, and I looked exactly the way my husband wanted. *Easy.* I'd never usually wear something so revealing, especially when the evening air was so crisp. But my husband loved role-playing. It was something I could get on board with as long as I was allowed to use my actual first name. There was nothing creepier than him looking me in the eyes and calling me another woman's name when my legs were spread for him. Especially now that I knew the truth.

The high-heels on my boots clicked across the hotel's entryway as I made my way over to the bar. There were Christmas lights and garland strung around the hotel. It was subtle and tasteful, unlike the local mall that looked like Santa's elves had thrown up Christmas cheer everywhere. God I hated Christmas now. My husband had a way of sucking the joy out of everything.

I took a deep breath as I entered the bar. The ghosts of Christmases past didn't need to make an appearance tonight. There was already enough to worry about.

I knew I was early, but I preferred getting a good vantage point and the upper hand. Tonight I'd have to immerse myself into my role a little better. I listened to the chatter around me. Apparently there was a convention going on in the hotel for some team-building exercises. I'd just be one of the many attendees. Sweet, innocent, and oh so very single. And what better team-building exercise than spending the night with a team member? It was perfect.

I slid onto a stool at the bar and ordered sparkling water, ice, and lime in a glass that would usually be reserved for an actual gin and tonic. The bartender didn't seem to mind my strange request. He just smiled, probably because of my low neckline, and placed the glass down in front of me. Next time I saw him, I'd have all my money back, and I could leave him a generous tip. As it was, my date tonight was the one paying for my drinks. And I had a feeling he'd be leaving a shitty tip.

I nursed my fake drink, knowing that liquid courage would have helped. But I couldn't let a single thing slip tonight. I had to be on my A-game. Because I was about to take the first step towards getting my life back.

My eyes kept gravitating toward the hotel entrance. He was late. The bar was getting increasingly more crowded by the minute. And the more time that ticked by, the more nervous I got. Maybe this was a bad idea. I finished my second sparkling water and realized that I needed to use the restroom. I silently cursed and slid off the stool. Not actually drinking was endlessly boring, and now I was going to lose the element of surprise. I finished up in the bathroom as quickly as I could and walked back out.

I saw him before he saw me. He was sitting on the other side of the bar with a leather jacket. It was definitely him. Tall, dark, and handsome. He looked just like my husband. *How ironic.* I smiled at my own joke.

But my smile fell as he leaned in and whispered into the woman's ear beside him. I felt jealousy surge through me, just like I had the last time my husband had done this in front of me. He thought he could get away with it. As if I wouldn't confront him? I thought about the wedding and engagement rings sitting on my bedside table back at home. How would he react with me flirting with another man? Would he get as angry as me? I looked down at the counter. *Probably not.* And even if he still cared, he wouldn't soon enough. That was the whole point. I ran my fingers down the condensation on my glass.

"Why are you glaring at me?"

I looked up. He'd walked over and was now staring at me rather accusingly. "I wasn't." I hadn't been glaring at him. Had I? I took a sip of my drink.

"You're shutting down my game."

I laughed. "What game?" He wasn't supposed to be flirting with other women tonight. I had worn this ridiculous outfit for him. He was supposed to be flirting with me and only me.

"Wouldn't you like to know." He sat down in the stool next to mine. "You really shouldn't leave your drink unsupervised."

He was the one that should be worried about that tonight. Not me. "I'm a very trusting person." I wasn't. Not anymore.

"I don't know what kind of places someone like you usually hangs out, but if you're such a trusting person, trust me…this is not the kind of bar you leave your drink unsupervised in."

I looked around at all the smiling faces and tasteful Christmas decorations. This bar was upscale. Classy even. What on earth was he talking about? "This place seems nice to me."

He shrugged and took a pull from his drink.

"I think my company paid good money to have our workshop here."

"Workshop?"

"Team-building." I smiled. "Which is ridiculous because I loathe everyone I work with."

"Is that so?"

"Devastatingly so." I put my hand out. "I'm Ensley Hill."

"Noah Thompson."

Interesting. I wasn't sure what kind of game he was playing tonight. But he sure as hell didn't know mine.

Instead of shaking my hand, he grabbed it and kissed my knuckles. His fingers trailed up the inside of my wrist and I shivered.

Well, at least we were on the same page there. I had him where I wanted him. Now I just needed to escalate things before the bar got even more crowded. My husband loved when I was forward during these sessions. Hopefully tonight would be no different.

"I have to wonder," I said, dropping his hand and leaning closer to him, "if this is a bar filled with such heathens, why on earth are you here?"

"Isn't it obvious? I'm one of them." His eyes twinkled like it was the best pickup line ever.

News flash. It wasn't. And this wasn't a dingy bar in the middle of the city. We were in the suburbs for goodness sake. Here I was thinking I was bad at role-playing. But he took the crown.

"Does that line always work? You hang out here trying to pick up women from these conventions regularly?"

"Only when they're as beautiful as you."

I laughed. A real, belly aching laugh. I wasn't sure if he was trying to make me jealous or make me smile. Yes, he was gorgeous. But his game was garbage. Still, I leaned in closer. "And does that line usually work?"

"I don't know. You tell me, beautiful. I've never used it before."

My smile faded. When was the last time my husband had called me beautiful? The word falling from his lips twice was hard to ignore. What if my plan wasn't as flawless as I thought? Something about the way he was looking at me made me feel like it was time to abort my mission. Just because I had been hurt didn't mean I wanted to hurt him. "It's not awful," I said.

He laughed and called the bartender over to refill our glasses.

When he wasn't staring at me, it was easy to remember the coldness in my husband's eyes the past few months. Even easier to remember what he'd done and had been doing for months now. He flashed me his perfect smile and all I felt now was resolve.

My husband needed to pay for what he'd done. I had a plan and I wasn't one for not following through. Hell, I'd married him even when I'd had cold feet. That was commitment, even if I regretted it now.

Now all I needed was a distraction. Originally I thought I'd just knock my own glass onto the floor. But I found myself being distracted by his lips. One kiss wouldn't hurt my plans. If anything it would make the night progress a little easier. Faster even. And I needed to be out of these stupid clothes and happily asleep in my own bed. Alone.

I ran the side of my foot up his shin. "My company spared no expense and even got us all single rooms here. No awkward roommates."

"How convenient."

"For who?" I ran my finger along the rim of my glass. "You?"

He put his hand on my thigh. "More along the lines of us."

Us. There never was and there never was going to be an us. "There are a lot of men here I could take up to my room. Prove you're worth a night with me."

He cocked one of his eyebrows. "How great is a night with you?"

I leaned forward so my lips were against his ear, like his had been against another woman's half an hour earlier. "You'll never forget me."

"Is that so?" His breath was hot in my ear. And then it traveled down my jaw line until he was staring deeply into my eyes.

"I'll ruin you for life." It was a promise. And not at all a sexual one.

His lips brushed against mine gently at first. But I wasn't doing slow. I leaned in and kissed him hard. For a second I almost forgot to slip the pill in his drink. But only for a second. When his hands moved to my waist, I plopped the small white pill in his glass. I tried to count down from ten, knowing it would take some time for the pill to dissolve. I started to lose track when I buried my fingers in his hair around seven. And I completely lost track when his hands slid to my ass around five.

I pulled away after far too long, completely breathless.

"Maybe I'll be the one that ruins you."

I was already ruined. Wasn't that obvious? I downed my drink. Fortunately he did the same, because I didn't know how I was going to convince him to finish it when I had promised him something far better upstairs.

But I thought he'd slowly drink it. He'd downed the whole thing in two seconds flat. He'd be getting loopy any minute now, and I wasn't strong enough to carry him out of here. "Let's go up to my room."

He didn't hesitate. He placed some bills down on the counter. A great tip considering the fact that my beverages hadn't been alcoholic. I smiled to myself. Originally I'd thought I'd have to return after I got my money back to give the bartender a proper tip. But now there was no need. Which was probably good, because it would be rather daring to show my face again at the scene of the crime.

"Isn't it the other way?" he asked as I steered him toward the front doors. He started to turn around but then looked genuinely perplexed.

Oh God, don't fall asleep yet. "Change of plans. I've always wanted to have sex with a stranger in my car."

He nodded and followed me outside like a confused puppy. An adorable lost puppy. A puppy that was about to pass out.

I grabbed his hand to lead him toward my car.

His steps slowed and became wobblier.

Not yet. I could see my car in the distance. We were so close. "Almost there," I said, but I was pretty sure he didn't hear me. He was staring up at the sky as I pulled him through the parking lot.

A couple walked past us. I tried to keep my eyes straight ahead so they wouldn't engage. But we were in the suburbs, not the city. And with the suburbs came nosey housewives who couldn't mind their own business.

"Is he okay?" the woman asked.

"Fine. He just had a few too many drinks," I said with a laugh and a roll of my eyes. "I'll get him home safely."

The woman smiled. "That better not be you tonight," she said to her husband and patted his chest.

"We could always get a room instead," her husband said.

This time I rolled my eyes for real as I steered my lost puppy toward my car. Almost 50 percent of marriages failed. He'd probably already been in one of those rooms with another woman. *Pig.*

When we finally reached my car, my pig was practically putting all his weight on me. I pushed him against the back door, hoping he'd stay on his feet.

"It's so beautiful," he said, his voice slurred now. "Almost as beautiful as you."

I tried to ignore his words as I unlocked the door. Why did he keep saying stuff like that? This was supposed to be easy. Each compliment made me rethink everything. But it was too late now. "Get in the car," I said.

"Look." He pointed to the sky instead of following my very simple directions.

I followed his finger. The sky was ignited with stars tonight. They seemed even brighter than usual. I remembered my first date with my husband. We'd stopped just like this outside the bar in our college town. Except then we'd both been drunk. And I made the biggest mistake of my life by falling for him. Tonight I wasn't going to make the same mistake again.

I opened the car door and practically had to shove him inside. "Put your seatbelt on."

"You put it on," he grumbled.

We'd never had kids. But I imagined this was how they would have behaved. I sighed and reached over him.

He caught my arm and pulled me against his chest. "So you've always wanted it in the car? What is it...the threat of getting caught that turns you on?"

He was practically falling asleep in front of me, his voice low and slightly slurred. But the question still sounded sexy falling from his lips.

"Yes."

"Hm." He tucked a loose strand of hair behind my ear. "I'm tired," he said with a yawn. "Are you tired? Maybe we should take a nap first. And then I'll make all your dreams come true."

It was too late for that. I pulled away from his touch. "That's a great idea." I finally managed to buckle him in.

When I climbed into the driver's seat, he was staring over at me, his eyelids drooping.

"Ensley, did you..." he laughed. "You did." He shook his head. "What did you give me?" He rested his head against the back of his seat. "Something strong," he said. "Why?" His hand dropped onto my leg like a dead weight.

I didn't have to respond because he yawned once more and closed his eyes. I looked down at my watch. Three minutes faster than I had planned. But he was safely in my car, numb to the world. Phase one was complete.

I wasn't sure why, but instead of starting the car, I found myself reaching out to touch his face. His stubble was rough against my palm. I ran my thumb along the lips that had just kissed me. I thought I'd feel bad. That some sense of remorse would kick in and I'd stop this plan. But I felt nothing. Nothing.

I'd loved my husband once. Mad, deep, all-consuming love. Maybe a part of me still did. But I'd found that hate was a much stronger emotion than love. Because I hated him so much more than I'd ever loved him.

I removed his hand from my thigh and started the ignition. My husband was unfaithful. I knew he'd been planning on leaving me for her soon. Or else my bank accounts wouldn't be all zeros. But I'd caught him before he'd had a chance to escape.

My husband had slowly ruined my life. So it only made sense that I ruined his too.

CHAPTER 2
Friday

I kicked off my boots and quickly changed into a pair of baggy flannel pajamas that I hadn't worn in years because my husband hated them. They were in fact ridiculous...ridiculously cute. And oh so very comfortable. My husband was clearly insane for not liking them. I completed the look with a pair of pink slippers before practically skipping out of our room and down the stairs. No more satin nightgowns. Or lace anything. God I hated lace. Nothing was as itchy as lace. I imagined throwing all my lace lingerie in the fireplace and watching it go up in flames. *Maybe tomorrow.*

Tonight I had a few more things to cross off my list. I pulled my cell phone out of my pocket...another benefit of the flannel pajamas. There were huge pockets to store my phone, my snacks, and even my taser.

I plopped down in my husband's favorite chair and dialed 911.

It only took a few seconds before someone picked up. "911, what's your emergency?" the dispatcher asked.

"Hi, I'm not sure if it's technically an emergency yet, but..."

"Ma'am, this line is for emergencies only..."

"Right." I cut her off. "Sorry, I think it's an emergency, but I've watched my fair share of crime shows on TV and I know you're not supposed to report things until someone's been missing for 24 or 48 hours, depending on the show." I sniffled, hoping she'd think I was crying.

"Ma'am, is someone you know missing?"

"My husband. He left for work this morning but never came home. And I called his office and they said he never showed up."

"And what time does he usually come home?"

"Usually around 5:30. 5:45 at the latest. I'm worried sick." I sniffled again. The action hurt because my nose wasn't in the least bit runny.

"It's only 10 o'clock. Maybe he went out for drinks or something?"

Something like that. "No, he always comes straight home. And I've tried to call him a hundred times." I pretended to sob, but it sounded more like a hog squealing. *Oops.* I'd have to practice my fake crying tonight.

But the dispatcher's voice softened like she believed I was terribly upset. "I can get an officer out to speak with you right away."

Wait, what? "Right now?" I glanced at the hand cart I'd used to pull his body out of the car and through the house. And then my eyes landed on the deadbolt on the basement door.

"Yes, ma'am. Someone will be out in fifteen minutes or less."

Shit. All the crime shows said they'd wait at least 24 hours. A cop couldn't show up right now. I was supposed to go to the police station tomorrow night. I had it all planned out to the minute. They were never supposed to come here. Ever. "Are you sure that's necessary?" I asked.

"Of course. If you truly believe he's missing?"

"Mhm." My voice was oddly high pitched. "Would it be easier if I came down to the precinct?"

"Not at all necessary. An officer is already en route."

Holy hell. I stood up and ran over to the hand cart. I needed to get it back in my garage. There was also duct tape and rope on my kitchen island. My stomach churned. *I'm going to end up in prison.* "Thank you," I said.

"We'll find him," she said very calmly.

Probably because she heard the panic in my voice. But I wasn't panicking over my husband. I couldn't care less about him. He wasn't going anywhere. I was panicking because I thought I'd have all morning to practice my distraught face. I looked happy and cozy in my pajamas...not at all like a scared-to-death housewife. How had I already messed up my plan only an hour and a half in?

"Stay strong," the dispatcher said.

"You too." *You too?* God, I was going to ruin everything. I hung up before I could say anything else stupid...like a confession.

After putting the handcart back in the garage and shoving the duct tape and rope under the kitchen sink, I double-checked the deadbolt on the basement door. Locked. Everything was secure. I could do this. I looked down at my pajamas. All I needed to do was change.

As soon as I entered my bedroom, I saw my reflection in the floor-length mirror. I was still wearing my blonde wig. If anyone at the bar remembered us from tonight, they'd identify me completely wrong. A blonde and her drunk beau from the team-building conference. The cops would be spinning in circles for weeks. But not if they showed up and I was still wearing it like a kidnapping novice. The pros made all of this look so easy.

I pulled off my blonde wig and threw it into the closet. Maybe the pajamas worked. I looked innocent and scared. Innocent was good. I pulled my hair into a messy bun, leaving a few strands out to make me look more frantic. *Look scared.* I made a face in the mirror that could only be described as joyful. Because that was how I'd been feeling up until several minutes ago. Joyful. But my plan was falling apart right in front of my eyes. Damn it, I was totally screwed.

The doorbell rang.

I cracked my neck and rolled my shoulders as I made one last attempt at a scared face. My eyes grew big and round. My bottom lip trembled. *Perfect.* I could do this.

I ran down the stairs, my phone in my hand like I'd just been calling all of my husband's friends instead of working on my facial expressions. But as my hand reached out to open the door, I realized I wouldn't have to really act. My joy had quickly been replaced with these anxious nerves butterflying around in my stomach. I just wasn't worried about my husband's whereabouts. I was worried about the police unlocking my basement door. I was worried about being caught red-handed.

The doorbell rang again and I opened it, shoving my worries aside.

Because standing there was none other than Detective Damien Torres. The nervous butterflies in my stomach were replaced by fan-girl butterflies. Everyone knew everyone around here. But I wasn't excited because I'd seen him around town a few times. I was excited because Detective Torres had worked a local case I'd been following closely on the news. A case that had helped give me confidence that I could get away with the perfect crime. It was also a case that proved Detective Torres was terrible at his job. I couldn't believe my luck. Tonight couldn't be going any better! I tried to hide my smile.

"Hello, Miss. I'm Detective..."

"Torres," I said, cutting him off. He was just as handsome as he was on TV. "I know who you are. I mean, I've seen you on the news. You were working on the Violet Clark case. You were partners with Detective Tucker Reed. Is it true that he ran away with her? That they fled the country together before all those bodies were pulled out of the lake? Did she really murder all those people?" I looked behind Detective Torres like his partner would be plastered to his side. But he was all alone.

Detective Torres lowered his eyebrows as he watched me.

I swallowed down the rest of what I knew about him. I wasn't supposed to be excited to see him. And my excitement was getting the better of me - making me look like a crime show junkie instead of a worried housewife. A sympathetic wife with a missing husband who I loved dearly. "Never mind, it's not important," I said. "All that matters is that you're here to help me find my husband. It's all I can think about." But God, I wished that I was meeting Detective Torres under different circumstances where I could ask him every detail about his last case. Violet Clark was kind of an idol of mine. After all...she'd successfully gotten away with murder.

He nodded. "I need to know everything about the last time you saw your husband. Who you've reached out to. How long he's been missing." He pulled out a notebook. "Can I come in?"

Part of me had been hoping I could just tell him everything on the front porch. I looked past him at the cookie-cutter houses on the lane I lived on. I wasn't sure which was worse - a detective on my front porch, igniting gossip around the whole neighborhood, or a detective inside my house.

In my house. Definitely in my house. I was a kidnapper! "Actually, could we go for a walk? I feel like I need some fresh air or I'm going to lose my mind." *Don't talk about losing your mind in front of a detective!* I cleared my throat as I grabbed my jacket. "I mean, I just need some air to clear my head. I've been cooped up all night fretting."

"Yeah, that's fine," Detective Torres said as I shut the door, not leaving him much of a choice.

Classic Detective Torres. I was already outmaneuvering him. As we walked down my driveway, I was vaguely aware of him staring down at my pink slippers. And even more aware of the fact that I was wearing my comfy pajamas in front of a local celebrity. I shoved my hands into my coat pockets and turned onto the street.

Maybe I imagined it, but I swear I saw neighbors peeking out their blinds at the two of us walking down the street. Normally it was easy to see inside their windows at night, but all their houses were aglow with Christmas lights, casting weird shadows on the glass. But I could feel them staring. Judging. I tried to focus on the person standing next to me. I couldn't avoid the gossip now. I was already two feet in. Two slippered feet in. "So what were your questions?" I asked.

"How long has your husband been missing?"

"The last time I saw him was this morning before work. Everything seemed normal. He wasn't acting strange at all. It was just a normal workday. But when he didn't come home tonight, I started calling friends and family. Apparently he never showed up to work today." The lies came so naturally. I was basically already a pro.

Detective Torres jotting something down in his notebook. "Is there anyone you haven't reached out to yet?"

"I've talked to everyone I could think of. I've been going crazy all night." *Again with the lunatic talk.* If I kept saying things like that he'd lock me up before our walk was over. "Crazy with worry, I mean. I'm not crazy. You can ask anyone." *Stop talking right now.*

I swore I saw a flash of a smile on his lips.

"What time does your husband usually come home from work?" he asked.

I pushed my hands into my pajama pockets, brushing my fingers against the taser. How likely was it that Detective Torres would pat me down? I tried to run through the odds as I answered his question. "5:30ish." Maybe a 10 percent chance of a pat down? He had no reason to suspect me of any wrongdoing at this point.

"I noticed that you're not wearing a wedding or engagement ring. Is that why you're hiding your hands?"

"What?" I pulled my left hand out. *Shit balls!* I forgot to put them back on after my role-playing. Now he had a reason to suspect me. "My diamond is expensive," I said. "I never sleep in it. I took it off when I changed into my pajamas." What the heck was going on? Detective Torres was supposed to be a terrible detective. How had he noticed that I wasn't wearing my rings? My stomach churned. Maybe he was a better detective than I was giving him credit for. Just because he made one mistake...

"And you were getting ready for bed instead of looking for your husband?"

I'm going to jail. "I've been looking all night. And I'm exhausted. Mentally and physically. I doubt I'll be able to sleep...but what else can I do tonight?"

He stopped walking. In the middle of the street. Like a dumb pedestrian instead of a detective. "Ensley, do you know where your husband is?"

In my house. "No." I kept my voice even. And I found myself gripping the taser in my pocket. I could still get away. I could tase

Detective Torres, run back to my house, and drive away into the night. I could forget about my past. I could forget about vengeance.

"You didn't want me to come into your house. You're not wearing your rings. Right now all signs point to you."

"What?" *Oh, God. How the hell did he put that together so fast?* I was seconds away from confessing everything. How long would I go to prison for a simple kidnapping anyway? Maybe I'd just get a slap on the wrist because I'd never broken the law before. And if Detective Torres reacted poorly to my confession, I'd just tase him and run away. Easy-peasy. I gripped the taser tighter in my hand and was about to open my mouth when Detective Torres smiled.

"Sorry. I had to ask," he said. "You clearly know all about me. So you know that I already let one guilty woman get away. I don't plan on making the same mistake twice."

"Of course." I breathed a sigh of relief. He was just being cautious. I let go of the taser in my hand and gave the speech I had planned for tomorrow: "Detective Torres, I have no idea who would possibly want to hurt my husband. All I know is that I love him. I love him so much and I'm so scared." I did the sniffle thing that I'd mastered and my eyes even grew a little watery from the cold.

"We'll find him. I promise."

As excited as I was to meet Detective Torres, I didn't believe his promise. He'd been plastered all over the news the last few weeks, but it wasn't exactly a glowing portrayal. His suspect had gotten away. His partner had helped her escape. A promise from Detective Torres wasn't worth much. Which was good news for me. I couldn't have asked for a better detective on the case. *My case.* Now I just needed to decide if I really did want to get away with murder.

CHAPTER 3
Friday

I slid the deadbolt and the basement door creaked open. Before today, I'd only been in the basement ten minutes tops. I hated basements. They were underground and creepy for a reason - to store things that should never see the light of day. Which was why it was the perfect hiding spot.

When my husband and I first moved in, we didn't even need to store anything down here because we had so much closet space. But as the years ticked by, there was some overflow that had wound up in boxes down here. Christmas decorations, old clothes, and memories I no longer needed.

I tiptoed down the steps. But it wasn't necessary. He was still fast asleep. If he wasn't gagged and tied to the wooden chair, I would have said he looked peaceful. I pulled the cord above his head, illuminating his slumped body even more, then placed the icepack I'd brought down on one of his thighs. If I'd had more I would have put them all over him. I hadn't meant for him to fall down the basement stairs. Truly. But his shoulders had slipped out of my hands and gravity had done the rest. At least he'd been unconscious. He'd have a few bruises, but it didn't seem like any-thing was broken. I'd taken a peek under his shirt to make sure.

Although I had been a little distracted by his six-pack earlier. Maybe I needed another look... I reached out. *Stop.* I folded my arms across my chest to prevent them from wandering. I was a kidnapper. Not a pervert. The only reason I was even attempting to look at his perfect abs was because it had been a while since my husband had been intimate with me. I bit the inside of my lip as I stared at him. *Asshole.* It was tempting to kick his shin. To slap him awake. To take away his ice pack. He deserved those bruises. Hell, he deserved to be thrown down the stairs on purpose instead of an innocent, accidental tumble.

As I stared at him, I started to wonder if it had been an accident. Had my fingers slipped, or had I wanted him to fall? I reached out again, this time touching his face. He'd said I was beautiful. Something I hadn't heard in years. But he was the beautiful one. Chiseled jaw line. That perfect 5 o'clock shadow. Slightly shaggy hair that fell effortlessly on his forehead. These tiny little crinkles around the corners of his eyes caused by laughter.

I let my fingers fall from his face and touched the corners of my eyes. I had the same small lines. I'd started to notice them last year before I turned the big 3-0. I was beautiful once. But not now. I looked down at my pajamas and slippers. I looked like a hermit. The kind of hermit that never wore lace.

But I wanted him to think I was beautiful. I wanted to remember how he'd looked at me before all this. Because he'd wake up soon and there would be no going back. Maybe I'd reconsider burning all my lingerie. How fun would it be to torture him while looking amazingly chic? I smiled. Much more fun.

I continued to stare at him, his light breathing calming me. I knew I needed rest, but it was like I couldn't look away. He was tied up in my basement. I did it. I was as good as all the perpetrators in crime shows. Better even.

I'd already crossed four things off my list. First was the one I'd thought about the most - the kidnapping itself. Then I successfully hid him. Then I called 911. And thanks to the fact that

TV shows spewed lies, I was ahead of schedule because I'd already talked to the police. I was killing it. A laugh fell from my lips. *Killing it.* I was hilarious.

Not only was I hilarious and great at this, but I also got the best detective on my case. And by the best, I actually mean the worst. Best for me, worst at his job. I'd have all my answers by tomorrow night, just as planned. I'd be long gone before anyone put the pieces together. And I'd be the best criminal in this town. Maybe I'd even wind up on the news by Christmas.

My husband was going to regret everything he ever did to me. I leaned down. "Poor sweet, Noah," I said out loud. "Of all the cities. Of all the bars. You just had to walk into mine." I was wrong before. Role-playing was so much fun.

I moved the ice pack to his other thigh. There. He was practically all fixed up. If he needed anything else, it would have to wait until he was conscious. I looked around at all the spider webs in the basement. And I shivered from the draft. I sighed. He was such a diva even when he was silent. *Fine.* I opened one of the boxes on the ground and pulled out a light blue blanket. A blanket that was never used. I ran my hand along the soft fabric and looked back down at the box. Everything in that box was the start of all our problems. I placed the small blanket around his shoulders before kicking the box to the side. A baby rattle that was never touched jingled against the rest of the contents and I tried not to cringe.

The blanket looked ridiculous on top of his broad, leather-jacket-clad shoulders. I frowned. Well, not that ridiculous. He somehow pulled it off. I stopped myself from removing his super uncomfortable looking jeans. There were lines and I needed to be careful to stop crossing them.

I stepped away from him. Now I could sleep peacefully knowing that his bruises had been taken care of and he was warm enough. I wasn't a monster. I pulled on the cord above his head and retreated up the stairs. Deadbolt back in place. *Check*. Front and back doors locked too. *Check*. I locked my bedroom door behind me and stared at the empty bed.

And then I stared at the ceiling while I tried to fall asleep.

And stared.

And stared.

I'd kidnapped him. I'd thrown him down the stairs and tied him up in my basement. And I'd molested his abs. I reached over and pinched myself to make sure this was real. *Ow*.

I was officially a criminal. There was no going back.

I wasn't sure if it was that thought that kept me awake. Or the possibility of him escaping.

Or maybe it wasn't either of those things. I flipped the light on my bedside table back on. When I was little I had been terrified of the dark. I slept with a nightlight until I was a teenager. I continued to stare at the ceiling that was fully lit now. Maybe I was still a little afraid that the darkness would swallow me whole.

CHAPTER 4
Saturday

Every inch of my body was sore, like I'd just run a marathon. Not that I'd know. Just the idea of running that many miles made me want to fake an injury to get out of it. I groaned and reached out my arm, expecting to feel my husband stretched out beside me. But my fingers came up empty. Silky sheets and no husband.

I yawned and slowly opened my eyes. His side of the bed was still perfectly made. Had he not come home last night? I sat up and looked around the room. His clothes weren't tossed carelessly on the floor, waiting for me to pick them up. And the shoes he refused to take off at the door like the asshole he was weren't anywhere in sight. I couldn't even smell his cologne that made me want to gag.

I touched my forehead, the action making the muscles in my arms sing. What the hell happened last night?

And then I heard a noise. It almost sounded like...screaming?

Oh. No. I threw the comforter off me as I scrambled out of bed. A part of me had hoped it had all been a dream. A bad, horrifying, wonderfully exciting dream. I felt my lips curl into a smile. I'd actually done it? Oh my God, I'd actually done it!

Oh. Yes. I threw my arms up in the air. *Ow.* Lifting him had not been easy. He was one heavy asshole. Inconsiderate like always.

He screamed again.

Shit. I ran out of my bedroom, down the stairs, and slid open the deadbolt. I finally had the courage to go through with my plan. And I wasn't about to have him ruin it by screaming bloody murder.

"Help!" he shouted. His words were a little more clear now. But still muffled. He must have somehow gotten the gag partially out of his mouth.

How the hell had he done that? I'd watched so many videos on how to properly...

"Is someone there?! Help!"

I started to walk down the stairs. "I need you to take a deep breath and calm down," I said. *Shut up, shut up, shut up.* Could our neighbors hear this? The last thing I needed was for nosy Sally to show up on my doorstep wondering what I was up to.

"Calm down? I don't know who you are or where I am but I'm tied up! Please, please for the love of God help me!"

Wait, what? My feet stopped at the top of the basement steps. He did know who I was. He did know where he was. What the hell was he talking about? "What do you mean you don't know where you are?" I called down the stairs.

"I mean I don't know where I fucking am! Untie me!"

Why did he not know where he was? Unless...how hard did he hit his head last night when he fell down the stairs? Did I break his skull? Had he been bleeding?

"Help me!"

I needed a minute to think. "Stop yelling. I'll be right back to untie you." I closed the door and slid the deadbolt back in place. Was he serious? Did he really not know where he was? Who I was? If that was true, he had serious memory loss. The smile returned to my face.

He started screaming at the top of his lungs again.

I needed to stop that. But first I had an opportunity I couldn't pass up. This was better than I could have ever asked for. I must have given him a concussion or something. I mean...by accident of course. He didn't know where he was. He didn't know who I was.

I ran back to my room and quickly did my makeup and changed out of my pajamas. My husband hated those PJs. And I couldn't shake that hate.

I put on a pair of tight jeans, a sweater with a low neckline, and my thigh-high black boots from last night. As a finishing touch, I pulled my blonde wig back in place. I might be able to get through this whole thing without him even knowing me.

His shouts drifted into the bathroom.

If he'd stop screaming. Before heading back downstairs, I pulled out a box of random things I'd been meaning to donate from the top shelf in my closet. It only took a few seconds to find what I was looking for. I lifted the reindeer mask they'd handed out last year at my neighborhood's annual Christmas light competition. It was like a masquerade mask, only more ridiculous because it had antlers instead of feathers. I pulled it over my wig. For some reason dressing up made it easier to be bold. I'd found the same thing last night when I'd worn the wig. Or maybe it was just a blonde thing. As far as I could tell, blondes did have more fun.

I made my way back downstairs, unlocked the deadbolt on the basement door, and walked down as gracefully as possible. The click of my heels on the wooden steps finally made him stop yelling for help.

When I reached the cement floor, he was staring at me. Well, taking me in. His eyes scanned me from head to toe.

"Untie me." He wasn't screaming now, but his voice was firm.

The ice pack and blanket I'd given him were both on the floor. I tilted my head to the side as I stared back at him. The gag was all the way out of his mouth now. But he was still firmly tied to the chair. "We both know I can't do that." I took another step toward him.

"I absolutely do not know that."

I kept my lips in a straight line even though he was being funny.

"What do you want? Money? I'll get you however much you want if you let me go, sweetheart."

Sweetheart? *Condescending jerk.* "I don't want your money." I wanted my money back. And I wanted him to look me in the eyes and confess he was sleeping around. I just wanted the truth. Was that so hard to ask? Apparently so. I picked up the blanket and folded it. There was no thank you for taking care of his wounds or keeping him warm last night. He looked hostile. His nostrils were practically flaring.

"Then what do you want from me?"

I didn't respond. I placed the blanket back in its forgotten box. The sound of the rattle jingling jarred me again as I put the box back on the shelf where it belonged.

"Why does it feel like my ribs are broken?"

I didn't respond.

"Is this a kinky sex thing? Does this get you off?"

I definitely didn't need to respond to that. My mask was sophisticated. And classy, even if it was Christmas themed. *I should have just worn my pajamas.*

"Untie me, you fucking bitch."

Well, he didn't think I was beautiful anymore. He preferred another b-word now. And he seriously needed to relearn some manners. Did he not realize that he was the one tied up? I could do whatever I wanted to him. I was in control. For the first time in my life, I had all the power.

"What would you like for breakfast?" I asked, ignoring everything he'd said. "I went shopping yesterday afternoon so we'd be well-stocked for our time together. Cereal, eggs, bagels, waffles, fresh fruit..."

He just stared at me.

"How about some French toast?" I knew that my husband loved my French toast. He asked for it every weekend.

"Bite me."

"I'll make French toast then." I walked behind him and placed the gag back in place to a slew of curse words. It was nice to have him silent again.

I walked back in front of him. "The next time we talk, I want you to remember that I put ice on your bruises last night." I lifted the ice pack that was no longer frozen. "I gave you a blanket to keep you warm. And I'm about to feed you a delicious breakfast. So there's no need for that foul language or the yelling. Okay?"

I touched the side of his face. I have no idea why I did it. To make sure he understood? Just to touch? *I'm a kidnapper, not a pervert!* I immediately removed my hand like his face had burned me.

He lowered his eyebrows.

Something about the action made my stomach clench. No one had ever looked at me like that. I would have thought it was a murderous glare. Like he was imagining whether to cut my body up in tiny little pieces or put rocks in my pockets and throw me in the lake. But for some reason I was imagining a different thought. That maybe he wished I was the one tied up. It was probably still in a murderous way. Not a sexy way at all. But I felt my cheeks flush regardless, and I quickly looked away.

"I'll be back with French toast." I hurried up the stairs and released a breath I didn't know I had been holding as soon as the deadbolt was back in place.

I tore the mask from my face before my tears had a chance to fall on the thin fabric. My sweater was suddenly too hot. My boots were too uncomfortable. My pants were too tight. My wig was too itchy. I kicked off my boots as I pulled my sweater off over my head.

I felt like I couldn't breathe. I buried my fingers in the fake itchy hair.

There was more to his stare than just the heat I'd imagined. There was an emptiness. He had no idea who I was. I'd feared my husband forgetting about me. Forgetting that at one point I was his whole world. And I knew it had already happened. I'd known it. For months I'd known it. But seeing that emptiness staring back at you? I never expected it to hurt so much.

I swallowed down the sob in my throat. I was nothing to him. And I needed to remember he was nothing to me. I pressed my hands on the cold quartz countertop. The coolness on my palms made it a little easier to breathe.

I'd gotten out of the basement just in time. I couldn't let him see me being weak. The power needed to stay in my hands. And everything was going according to plan. Even though he was a little angry, he hadn't tried to escape. All the ropes were still secure. The next step was a nice, civilized meal.

I took another deep breath and walked over the fridge. This was meant to be an end. And it was a good thing we were both on the same page. I just needed to remember to stop touching him. I pulled the eggs and milk out and looked down at the lace bra I was wearing. What is wrong with me?

Abandoning the ingredients for French toast I went back upstairs to change. Again. I had the right idea last night. I threw my fancy bra on the ground like a barbarian and pulled my comfy pajamas back on. My husband didn't love me. I ran my fingers along the taser in my pocket. And I didn't love him either.

If he wanted to look at me like I was crazy and scream at the top of his lungs with all sorts of profanity? Fine. It was too late for cordiality anyway. Breakfast would be served with a side of tasing.

CHAPTER 5
Saturday

The latest Eminem song faded out on the radio and a Christmas tune started up. I rolled my eyes. Why did radio stations always try to slip in stupid old Christmas carols between real music? I poured the eggs into the hot pan and tried to focus on their sizzling against the oil instead of the familiar song.

I used to love Christmas. Back when I was young and in love and so naïve. So even with the sound of eggs frying, it only took me a second of the intro musical instruments to know it was *Baby It's Cold Outside*. The classic rapey song where the guy singing definitely slips something into the woman's drink and forces her to stay the night even though she keeps trying to get away.

I hummed as I flipped the last two pieces of French toast. Was that how I got the idea for my master plan? Some kind of twisted version of *Baby It's Cold Outside*? My husband and I had danced to this song right here in the kitchen last year. He'd dipped me low with a spatula in my hand and I'd almost slipped because of my socks on the tiled floor. I smiled, remembering how I lightly slapped his ass with the spatula in retaliation and he'd chased me around the kitchen until we were naked on the floor and our dinner was burnt.

Had he known even then that he no longer loved me? Was that moment all an act? I glanced at the basement door. Maybe I was going about this thing all wrong. I could get a tree for the basement and decorate it. We could dance to silly Christmas music. Maybe even watch some of my favorite holiday movies together. I could slowly woo him into a confession. He didn't even know who I was. I could make him fall in love with me all over again.

Stop. My hips stopped swaying to the rapey tune like I was reprimanding myself for my awesome dance moves. *Stop thinking about fixing your relationship.* What the hell was I thinking? Getting a basement Christmas tree was insane. I was done being the perfect housewife, or my holiday decorations would have been up the day after Thanksgiving. And even though I'd slacked the last few weeks by not even changing over my hand towels to the red and green ones, I'd given the whole housewife thing up for good last night. Permanently. By kidnapping.

I turned the radio off. There would be no Christmas for me this year. But I would be getting a wonderful present. Justice. Vengeance? I wasn't sure which yet. I was leaning toward the latter. I slid the eggs and French toast onto two plates and poured us each a cup of orange juice. He'd probably complain that I didn't bring him coffee. But the last thing I needed was a caffeinated captive.

I pulled my mask back on, grabbed the tray of food, and made my way downstairs.

He lifted his head as my footsteps approached, his eyes locking with mine. I was relieved to see that he looked significantly less angry.

I placed the tray down on the small table. I'd thought of everything, even our dining situation. "I'm going to remove the gag, okay? But remember what we talked about earlier? No yelling."

He didn't respond. Well...he couldn't respond verbally. I was hoping for a nod or something encouraging though.

I untied the back of the cloth anyway. He needed to eat. I hadn't pushed his body down the stairs so he'd starve to death. *Dropped. Dropped his body down the stairs by accident.* I was surprised when he didn't start screaming immediately.

"Are you trying to prove to me that this isn't a sex thing?" He nodded toward the pajamas I'd changed into.

I folded my arms across my chest. Maybe I would let him starve after all. "They're comfortable."

"I never said I didn't like them." He flashed me a smile. "You look adorable."

I stared back at him. *Adorable?* Did he actually mean that? Not frumpy? Fat? Ugly? Like I stopped trying?

"You're glaring at me," he said calmly like he had at the bar last night. But he shouldn't have been calm now. He was tied up. We weren't two carefree adults flirting in public. He was my prisoner.

"I'm not glaring." I turned away from him. I was expecting him to still be hostile, not...whatever the hell this was.

"Everything smells wonderful. Do you want to untie my hands so I can eat?"

So that's what this was. He was trying to make me feel comfortable so I would free him. But just because I was adorable didn't mean I wasn't one step ahead of him. "I'll feed you. Do you want syrup or butter on your French toast?" When I first met my husband he preferred butter. But after a few years I'd finally convinced him that syrup was a significantly better choice.

"Syrup."

Interesting. I lifted the bottle, trying my best not to look at him. I would not fall into whatever trap he was trying to put me in. But my hand hesitated before pouring the syrup. "Do you want it on the top or do you like to make a pool on the side that you dip it into?" My husband also swayed between these two options like the syrup newb that he was. There was no method to his madness.

"Which do you prefer?" he asked.

"I'm a dipper." The only reasonable choice.

"Ah. I should have guessed."

What does that mean?

"Whatever's easier for you. You're the one feeding me."

Right. But my hand with the bottle still hesitated. "Do you like a lot or a little?" My husband was also very finicky about his syrup usage depending on how much he'd worked out that day. A longer run meant more syrup. I tried not to sigh as I waited for a response. I would have made something else if I'd thought about how impossible this situation was. Tomorrow I'd serve cereal.

"A normal amount."

Normal was different for everyone, making normalcy a nonsense answer. He was being ridiculous. Or was he being agreeable? He was definitely being confusing. I poured some syrup on the side of his plate that was normal for me and plunged a bite of French toast into it. "Open."

He parted his lips, his eyes trained on mine instead of the fork. Odd choice. What if I was a serial killer? I could just stabbity stab him right in the throat and he never would have seen it coming. Although, I did just use the phrase stabbity stab, so he was probably safe from that ever happening.

His lips closed around the fork and he groaned.

I swallowed hard. He'd made that same noise last night when he kissed me. Like I was the only sustenance he needed to survive.

"Divine," he said. "This is seriously the best French toast I've ever had."

I knew it was divine. I knew it was the best. But hearing it still made me smile. I cut off a piece, twirled it in the syrup, and then took a bite for myself. Before I was done chewing I realized what I had done. I'd eaten off of his plate instead of my own. With his fork. Old habits die hard. "Sorry," I said and swallowed before I finished chewing. Which made me cough. Which for some reason made his smile grow. "I have a clean fork."

"I don't mind sharing," he said.

He was looking at me in that way again. Like when he'd called me beautiful instead of a bitch.

I cleared my throat. "I wasn't sure how you liked your eggs, so I scrambled them." I was the one that needed to keep him unbalanced. Statements like that would help. *Please don't remember me.* I pushed some into his mouth before he had a chance to respond with something disarming.

"You guessed right..."

Of course I guessed right. I shoved more food into his mouth to get him to stop talking. I wasn't sure which was worse...him yelling or him being overly nice. *He's just messing with your head. He wants you to untie him.* But I was smarter than he was giving me credit for. There would be no lulling me into a false sense of security or buying basement Christmas trees for him.

When I forced him to drink orange juice, I poured it into his mouth a little too generously. Some dripped down the side of his chin. I caught the liquid with my thumb at the same time his tongue darted out to stop it. But instead of lapping up the orange juice, his tongue collided with my thumb. We both froze. Well, froze wasn't exactly what I did. I'm pretty sure my temperature skyrocketed.

I was most certainly coming down with a cold. There was no other explanation for why my pajamas were suddenly too warm. I needed to get into bed. Drink hot tea. Guzzle down loads of soup. Maybe add some Nyquil to the mix to make me forget that I had a sexy man in my basement with a very warm and experienced tongue. *Oh my God, stop.* "All done eating? Okay, great." I dropped the fork that I'd stupidly shared with him onto the tray. "I'm just going to..." I pointed over my shoulder. "Later, alligator." *Who says that?* I picked up the tray and started walking toward the stairs.

"Wait! I kind of need to..." his voice trailed off.

I almost forgot to gag him again. I placed the tray back down. But before I could lift the fabric he started talking again.

"Would it be possible to get..."

"No phone calls," I said. "This isn't prison."

He laughed. A genuine belly laugh that for some reason had me smiling.

"I'm not trying to make a phone call. I need to take a piss." He looked down at his pants.

Which made my eyes travel to his pants. *Stop looking at his crotch.* I snapped my attention back to his face. "Right. I prepared for that." I walked over to the corner where I'd stashed some things I might need. I spotted the cleaning wipes first, which were meant to clean up dribbles down his chin. *No more stopping them with fingers.* And then I spotted the pink bucket I used for cleaning. It was a perfect fit for my mop. But I'd definitely need a new bucket after this. I dropped it in front of his chair.

"Um." He looked at the bucket and then back up at me. "What exactly do you expect me to do with that?"

"Pee in it."

"I can't unzip my pants. And I need to...you know...aim."

Right. I shook my head. I knew that. Which was why I'd tied his hands separately. "I'm going to untie one of your hands. But if you try anything...I will tase you." I pulled out the taser I still had in my pajama pocket. "No funny business."

"Yes, ma'am."

I took a deep breath as my fingers landed on the ropes. His other hand and both his feet would still be securely attached to the metal chair. I'd still be in control. I slowly untied my perfect knot. The one I'd studied endlessly on YouTube. "There," I said when the rope slipped from his wrist. I took a quick step back from him and waited.

"I need to stand up," he said.

I kicked the bucket closer to him. "The chair isn't that heavy. You can kind of stand up in a hunched over sort of way." I demonstrated leaning over with a fake chair on my back.

For some reason it made him smile.

I quickly righted myself.

"A little privacy then?" he asked.

"Nothing I haven't seen before."

He lowered his eyebrows at me. The same way he had earlier this morning. But this time I couldn't look away to avoid that feeling his stare gave me in the pit of my stomach. Not because I wanted to see his penis. I didn't. But because if I looked away he might try something. I couldn't let him get away. I hadn't even started questioning him yet. He owed me a confession and access to my money. He owed me at least those two things.

"As you wish." He undid his jeans and then awkwardly stood up over the bucket.

I kept my eyes glued to his face even though my gaze really wanted to wander. If I looked down I might miss something. It would only take him a few seconds to overpower me, even tied to a chair.

I heard the stream of his piss hit the plastic bucket.

"Eyes up here, sweetheart," he said.

I glared at him. My eyes hadn't moved from his face. I was practically a saint. *Not when you touched his abs last night.*

"I actually don't care if you take a peek. I've got nothing to hide." The words fell from his lips so smoothly. Almost seductively. Like a command to my eyeballs.

And I looked down. Not because I wanted to. He was playing voodoo mind tricks on me. And right when I saw it...my phone started to ring.

I don't know if I imagined him taking a step toward me. Or if he was just getting ready to sit back down. But he moved when I went to grab my phone. So I moved faster. I pressed down on the trigger of my taser and made perfect contact with his perfect body.

He started convulsing as he and the chair hit the floor, knocking over the bucket full of pee. The first thing I noticed was that his pants were zipped. He had moved because he was zippering his pants. Not trying to get away.

Oh my God, I tased him for no reason! And oh my God, the only bucket I had to help clean up the mess had pee in it! I stared at the puddle of pee and his writhing body. *Shit.* I really didn't want to have to go to the store today.

CHAPTER 6
Saturday

The hardware store had already been decorated for Christmas last week when I was here buying kidnapping necessities. But now there were Christmas trees for sale in addition to their huge Christmas section to the right when you walked through the sliding glass doors. There were inflatable minions and reindeer lit up with red noses. It was vulgar. For some reason I stopped and stared at the display. Maybe it wasn't vulgar. Everyone looking at the items seemed so happy. That was me once. Hand in hand with my husband. And the reindeer were actually really cute. Maybe putting one of those in the basement would be good. At least it was easier than putting up a tree.

"Back again so soon, Ensley?"

I turned to see a salesman walking over to help me. A very familiar looking salesman with an easy smile and eyes that definitely seemed to recognize me. Had I told him my name last time I was here? There was no way I would have done that. That would have been careless while I had been buying duct tape and rope and...

"Did you get that deadbolt installed okay?"

And that. I'd been buying the deadbolt to put on my basement door. Why the hell had I told him my name? *Probably because you never thought you'd actually go through with it.* But I had gone through with it. And now it felt like this salesman was a loose end. I needed to think of a way to cover my tracks that didn't involve hitting him over the head with a Christmas light-up reindeer. I cleared my throat. "I decided not to use it after all," I said. "I threw it out."

He frowned. "You only bought it a week or so ago. Returns are good for 30 days with a receipt."

"Eh." I waved my hand through the air. "Too late for that. The fewer deadbolts in the world the better anyway, right? More trusting neighbors and all that?"

"I guess?"

I laughed awkwardly. I wish I had my taser with me. I could have lured him out to the Christmas trees and taken him down without anyone noticing.

"So you're not here to buy another one?" he asked.

"No. I'm actually just looking for a bucket. Preferably this big." I held out my hands to show him what size I was looking for. "For mopping," I added before he could come to any wild conclusions about my current bucket being covered in urine. "Several sponges would be good too. For those tiny places I can't reach with the mop." Or so I could toss them after they were soaked with urine. This was going to be the grossest morning of my life. "So if you could just tell me what aisle to head down?"

"I'll show you, Ensley," he said and started walking.

I was definitely going to have to kill this guy. I silently laughed at myself. *I'm not a murderer.* I bit the inside of my lip. I had some hard decisions to make soon. But there was no reason to think about them while I had a puddle of urine to clean up and a waterboarding to perform. Er…interrogation. No torture would be involved. Right?

"Here we are." He turned down aisle 13 and led me straight to the cleaning supplies.

I eyed the rows of options. It really was best to be prepared. If worst came to worst I'd be cleaning up blood instead of urine soon. I needed something to get rid of any DNA. I was no novice to crime scenes. At least the ones on TV. "What's the best to get rid of...germs? Bleach or ammonia?"

"What kind of germs?"

What was the best way to say the germs in blood without sounding like a serial killer? "Like...the AIDS kind of germs?" Oh my God, that was most definitely not the way.

He laughed.

So I laughed.

And then we were both laughing about AIDS in the middle of the hardware store. None of it was funny. Mostly because he knew my name. And he knew I bought a deadbolt, rope, and duct tape. And now he probably thought I had AIDS.

I turned away from him. "So...bleach?"

He was silent for a moment.

I looked over at him. Instead of staring at me like a crazy person, it seemed like he was actually contemplating the correct answer.

"Yeah, I think you're probably right. Bleach would be best. You'll want some gloves though, it's really harsh on your skin." He pointed to some yellow rubber gloves hanging right in front of him.

"Good thinking." I grabbed them more for the lack of fingerprint aspect than skincare, but he didn't have to know that.

"Let me go get you a basket."

"Not necessary." I threw the gloves, a container of bleach, and a few packs of sponges into a bucket and lifted it up. "Basically a basket," I said.

I could have imagined it, but I'm pretty sure he stared down at my hand that had lifted the bucket. My left hand where I'd forgotten again to put my rings on. Did he see the tan lines? Was he just trying to see if I was single? Was he a spy that Detective Torres planted to see if I seemed like a devastated housewife with a missing husband?

I grabbed the bucket with my right hand and shoved my left hand into my jacket pocket. It was tempting to try to explain my lack of rings away. To talk about my husband who was missing. To say I was so spaced out I didn't remember to put them on. That I thought cleaning would keep me distracted while the police tried their hardest to find him. But it all felt forced.

Besides, what were the odds that he was actually working for Detective Torres? There was no reason for anyone to be suspicious of me last week. Unless someone had been monitoring all my recent Google searches about how to tie someone up and gag them. Or all that information I read about date rape drugs. Or the fact that for the first time since I moved into my home, my house wasn't decorated for Christmas at all. My house was pretty much the only one on our street that wasn't lit up at night. I needed to make some changes before I got caught.

"Anything else I can help you with?" he asked with a smile that made it seem like he was on to me.

"I would like to buy one of those light-up reindeer in the display up front. The Rudolph one."

"The one with the red nose?"

What other reindeer has a red nose? "Yup. My husband will love it."

He didn't seem to react at all to the mention of my husband. Which was good. He wasn't interested in me or the case I was accidentally creating against myself.

"Great, I'll go grab you one and I'll meet you at the register."

I breathed a sigh of relief when he disappeared down the aisle. I'd never told him my name. I wasn't completely incompetent. But I had used my credit card when I'd checked out last time. He must have seen my name on my card. So maybe I was a little incompetent as a criminal. But it was my first time. And everyone made mistakes.

Detective Torres would never come here and question the staff. There was no reason for him to. And even if he did? The guy helping me probably wouldn't even be working. I winced when he met me at the register. He was wearing a manager badge. *Crap.* I memorized his name like he'd memorized mine. *Don't mess with me, Jerry.*

Jerry was a situation I might have to rectify at some point. But for now I was in the clear. After all, this guy didn't even seem positive that Rudolph had a red nose. Surely he'd forget about me by next week. I paid in cash this time so I would stop leaving a paper trail. I was getting better at this. Even the best criminals had a learning curve. Take Adeline Bell and Violet Clark. I watched my neighbors' cases like a hawk, but they weren't necessarily role models. They both almost got caught. I wasn't planning on an almost.

I carried my bucket outside, humming *Baby It's Cold Outside* to myself. And I sang along to Christmas music the whole way home. I even hummed as I put on my wig and mask and walked into the basement with my new supplies.

I'd righted him before I left and made sure both his wrists were bound again. He was turned away from the pee on the floor like he was embarrassed, but he looked up at me as I walked toward him.

For a moment I expected a "welcome home." But he was gagged.

"I'm in a Christmassy mood today," I said. "And I got a surprise for you at the store." I put my new purchases, minus the reindeer, in the corner and then placed the soapy bucket down and began sopping up the mess. His urine wasn't very pungent, fortunately for all of us. And he luckily hadn't rolled around in it when I tased him. It was a Christmas miracle.

I looked up at him after a few minutes of silent scrubbing. He was staring at the bleach I'd just placed in the corner.

"That's not your surprise," I said. "It's not for you at all, actually. It's for...dirt."

He didn't respond of course. But he did that thing with his eyebrows again. It seemed like he didn't believe me. I never had been good at lying to my husband. Or reading him.

"It works for other things too, I guess. There's some mold in the master shower grout. Or is it in the caulk? I never remember which goes where. Either way, I might spritz some in there later to get rid of the discoloration and kill all that bacteria. Good idea, don't you think?"

He tried to say something through his gag, but then stopped.

I started to hum again as I finished cleaning, humming louder whenever I had to ring out the sponge.

When his mess was finally cleaned up, I tossed the contaminated sponge into the bucket. "Let me go get that surprise," I said. "But first, close your eyes."

He just stared at me.

"Eyes closed. Don't make me blindfold you too."

This time he shut his eyes.

Good boy. I took the bucket back upstairs and dumped the soapy water out the back door and into the grass. Then I tossed the sponge in the trash and removed my rubber gloves with a snap and tossed them in the laundry room sink.

The reindeer took a little longer to assemble than I thought. But when I finally had it ready, I yelled down the stairs to make sure he still had his eyes closed.

I carried it down gracefully. No accidental slips or pushes. I plugged it in and the white lights lit up all over the reindeer's body and his nose shone red. I smiled. Happy captive, happy wife. Was that how that old saying went? "You can open your eyes," I said.

He looked from the reindeer to me and then back again.

I was expecting a smile or a thank you. But I needed to help him do that. I untied his gag and let it fall to his neck.

No words fell from his mouth though.

"Don't you like it?" I asked. "He glows." I pointed to his surprise.

"Why exactly did you get this for me?"

"I thought you'd be more likely to give me answers if you were happy." I sat down in the chair across from him.

"And you thought a glowing reindeer would make me happy?"

"A glowing *Rudolph*. Yes."

"Ah. Of course."

I leaned forward, placing my elbows on my knees.

His eyes drifted to my breasts and I sat back up straight and cleared my throat.

"So you're happy?" I asked.

"You have me tied up in your basement. You made me pee in a bucket and then tased me while I was zipping my pants. And my whole body hurts, so I'm pretty sure you hit me with a baseball bat or something in order to get me down here in the first place."

"I drugged you actually. And then you fell down the stairs. It was an accident."

"Was it? Or did you push me?"

"What?" I put my hand on my chest. "Why on earth would I push you down the stairs?" *Say it. Tell me why you deserved it.*

"Why on earth would you kidnap me in the first place?" His chair jumped forward slightly as he struggled against his restraints. "You're fucking crazy!"

I sighed. I thought we were getting along so well earlier. And the Rudolph was a peace offering. What had gone wrong?

The doorbell rang and we both looked up at the ceiling.

Shit. Who the hell was at my door? My heart started racing as I stood up. Had Manager Jerry already informed on me? Was Detective Torres just checking in? Was it stupid nosy Sally? Fingers crossed it was the mailman. I ran for the stairs.

"Help!"

My head snapped back toward him.

"Someone help me!"

"Stop it," I said. "Be quiet."

"I've been kidnapped!" he yelled.

"Stop it right now," I said more firmly.

"I'm being held against my will by a psychopath!" he screamed.

I'm not a psychopath. I stared at my prisoner.

He stared back at me.

The doorbell was accompanied by a loud knock this time.

"I'm not a psychopath," I said. "Words hurt."

"You know what else hurts? Having coarse rope tied around your wrists!"

For goodness sakes. "Only because you keep moving," I said. I grabbed the fabric around his neck. It took me longer than usual with his head squirming around, but I successfully gagged him. I grabbed his chin, turning his face to me. "We'll continue this discussion later."

His nostrils flared.

"Be quiet or I'll...hurt you. I mean it." I dropped his chin when there were more knocks in rapid succession.

Whoever it was at my front door wasn't giving up easily. *Please don't be Detective Torres again.* I hadn't gotten a chance to put my rings back on yet because I was scrubbing up piss. And two days in a row was not going to look good.

CHAPTER 7
Saturday

I pulled back the blinds by the door ever so slightly and peeked out. *Son of a bitch.* Detective Torres was standing there holding a stack of papers. He turned his head toward the window as if he sensed my stare. I pushed the blinds back in place and pressed my back against the door. Had he seen me? I touched my forehead and felt the fake bangs of my blonde wig. *Crap.* I threw my wig and mask into the potted plant in the foyer and took a deep breath.

Detective Torres was a terrible detective. He probably didn't even remember what color my hair was last night. And he'd probably been looking at a cat or something outside, not me. I wasn't a suspect. I was an innocent housewife with a missing husband. *Act the part.*

I took one more deep breath and then opened the door just a crack, blocking any view he had of my foyer. Detective Torres was staring back at me with a somber expression.

He knows I kidnapped my husband. I tightened my fingers on the door. My taser was sitting in the pocket of my pajamas upstairs. There was no easy escape this time. "Detective." I shifted so that I could knee him in the crotch if he got any closer. Or at least slam his hand in the door as I made a run for it.

"Good morning, Ensley. The mailman was just dropping off your mail. And your paper from this morning was still on your driveway." He handed me the stack of mail and the paper.

I slid it through the small space between me and the door-jamb. "Oh, thank you." But I didn't mean it. He'd probably been going through my mail without a warrant. I pretended to drop the mail onto a table in the foyer. But there was no table there. So I threw it on the floor instead of abandoning my post.

We were both silent for a moment. Staring at each other.

What was I supposed to say? *Oh, right. Play the concerned wife.* "Is there any news about my husband? Have you found any trace of him? Like through security cameras or anything? Maybe he made some purchases on his credit cards that could pinpoint him at a certain time and location?" *Don't mention credit card statements! They'll find out what I've been buying at the hardware store!* "Not that credit card statements are accurate because of all the crime in this area." There was little to no crime in these suburbs. What was I even saying? But for some reason I kept going because he didn't offer me anything. "Someone could have stolen all his credit cards and fled to California for all we know. Or maybe he was assaulted on his way to work and his credit cards were all stolen! I bet that's it." *For God's sake stop talking.* I pressed my lips together.

"Do you mind if I come in so we can talk in private?"

A few of my neighbors were passing by on their daily walk. I'd never been invited to join their blonde walking party. Instead of waving like I usually would, I kept my hand firmly on the door. Did Detective Torres really want to talk? Or was that just a ruse to get me alone so he could arrest me away from my neigh-bors' prying eyes?

Either way, he absolutely could not come in my house. I had-n't had time to clean up the dishes from earlier. Two plates. Two glasses. Two sets of utensils. All of it was sitting on my kitchen island just waiting to be put into an evidence bag instead of the dishwasher. "I don't mind coming outside. It's hot as balls in here. My husband always controlled the thermostat and I'm lost without him." Before I could slip outside, a loud crash sounded from behind me. I was almost positive I stopped breathing. I waited for another sound. *Please don't scream.* I was pretty sure my heart stopped beating too.

Detective Torres took a step closer. "What was that?" he asked.

For the first time, I realized that his height allowed him to see over my head into my house.

"Huh?" I stepped outside and slammed the door. "Let's go for another walk." I stepped around him and started down the sidewalk.

"What was that crashing noise?" he said without following me.

"Oh." I laughed. "That...that was nothing."

"It's certainly something. Let me take a look for you." He put his hand on the doorknob.

Was he allowed to do that? Just walk in my house without my permission? Wasn't that illegal? Of course it was, but he probably didn't even realize it because he was such a bad detective.

He started to turn the knob.

I ran back up to my front door. "Stop." I put my hand on his. "You'll let him out."

He froze. Or maybe I froze. We both froze.

"Let who out, Ensley?" he said slowly. "Your husband?"

How does he know? I was so careful. Kind of. "My new puppy," I blurted out without thinking.

The tension on Detective Torres' face evaporated. "Ah, puppies can be quite destructive. Can I see him? I love dogs."

That made one of us. I hated dogs. Big dogs, small dogs...I even hated animals that looked liked dogs. Which was all animals.

Because they were all hairy and dirty and gross. So drooly. "He's an ugly little mutt. Not a purebred or anything. You don't want to see him."

He laughed but it quickly died away, probably because he could tell I was serious. "Wait, what?" he said.

"I'm joking. Obviously. He's perfect in every way. I love him more than life itself." *And all that nonsense that pet owners liked to spew.* Now I had to act like a crazy pet owner on top of acting like I thought my husband was missing. "But he's supposed to be sleeping in his crate right now and strangers excite him."

"You're training him to sleep at certain times?" he asked.

Was that not something dogs did? I laughed. "I just want him to be sleeping. I couldn't sleep last night because I was so worried about my husband. And I think it agitated him and he didn't sleep either. And now we're both grumpy and sleep-deprived."

"Dogs are smart animals. They can definitely sense their owners' moods. When did you get him?"

"A few weeks ago."

He nodded. "Puppies need routine. He probably knows your husband is missing too."

"I know. So we're both a mess right now." I pushed my lips to the side and exhaled loudly, trying to look like I was full of despair. If only I could cry on demand. I figured a public break-down would give me brownie points. "How about that walk?" I asked. I didn't want him to hear any more unexplained noises.

"I don't have time for a walk right now, I need to follow through on a few leads."

Leads? Plural? He wasn't supposed to have any leads, let alone more than one. He was supposed to be bad at this.

"I was up late too going through that box of records you gave us on your husband. There was a number he called every week like clockwork. It wasn't someone on the contact list you provided us. And he didn't have the number saved to his phone. So no name or nickname was provided. But I called the number. 555-218-3564. Does that ring any bells?" He stared at me like he was waiting for me to provide the information that my husband had been hiding.

I shook my head. He was lucky I was a good suburban housewife. Flawless in my etiquette. Or else I would have lacked the necessary patience for this conversation with him. I'd handed over a box of records the other night that had information that *I* wanted him to find out for *me. Give me her name.* If I knew it, she'd probably be the one in my basement instead. I hated her almost as much as I hated my stupid husband.

Detective Torres cleared his throat. "That number belongs to a Miss Sophia Tremblay."

I gave him a blank stare. *Sophia.* Of course her name was something sexy like Sophia Tremblay.

"Do you know her?" he asked.

I didn't know her. But I had a feeling I knew what kind of woman she was. I shook my head. "It doesn't sound familiar."

"I'm sorry to be blunt, but I have a flight I have to catch in a few hours, so I really have to cut to the chase. Ensley, is it possible that your husband was having an affair with this woman?"

"Whaaa...." I put my hand over my mouth because my tone seemed more humorous than surprise. "What?" I said more sternly through my fingers.

"She's our number one suspect right now. I was flying out in her direction for some personal business today anyway, so I'm going to stop by her local precinct."

Did my weird credit card story about California actually somehow pan out? "Flying where? California?"

He shook his head. "Ontario, Canada."

Oh that little piece of shit. He'd gone on a business trip to Ontario two years ago. Two. Freaking. Years. Ago. I'd only found out about his affair a few months ago. I hadn't realized it had been going on for so long. My eyes started to water. Not with fake acting tears. These were real ones.

"I'm so sorry, Ensley. I hope to have more answers by tomorrow. It's a very real possibility that your husband will be at her place."

I felt like I was going to be sick.

"Or that Sophia will at least know where he is."

One of the tears escaped, running down my cheek. I quickly brushed it away.

"We'll figure this out." He put his hand on my shoulder. "I promise."

He loved making promises he couldn't keep. I was pretty sure all men did.

Detective Torres let his hand drop from my shoulder. "I do have one more question for you before I head out. What was the last thing you saw your husband wearing?"

I pictured my husband in his work clothes. He looked great in a fitted suit. Handsome. Sophisticated. I swallowed hard when the image shifted and I pictured him in the hotel last night. Sitting at the bar with his leather jacket and jeans. Just as handsome. But in a more rugged way. Is that what he wore around Sophia? The same kind of outfit he role-played in with me? Maybe he didn't even need to role-play with her. Maybe she gave him everything he desired naturally.

"Ensley?"

I looked back up at Detective Torres. He'd asked what my husband had worn to work that morning. Not that night. "A gray suit. Navy tie. White collared shirt." I specifically remembered pressing the shirt right before he got dressed. I'd straightened his tie for him. I touched my own neck. I'd acted as perfect as usual, even though I already knew what I was going to do to him that night. I'd already done all my research. I'd already bought the little white pill. I'd already set up the basement just so.

"Ensley?"

I looked up at Detective Torres. He was staring at my hand that was still pressed against the base of my throat. My left hand. Where my engagement and wedding rings were vacant once again. I quickly lowered my hand. He'd said a *few* leads. Sophia wasn't the only one. And I had a feeling the other one was me.

I lifted my hand and laughed. "Mr. Snuggle Muffins had a little pee accident this morning." *Snuggle Muffins? Where the hell did that stupid name come from?* "I was just scrubbing the floors before you arrived." Technically I had been cleaning a filthy animal's piss. It wasn't even a lie.

"When I'm back tomorrow, you should probably invite me inside," he said slowly. "Don't make me get a warrant. It'll make you look guilty."

I started shaking. I wasn't sure if it was because I was so mad that my husband had a Canadian side piece or because I was actually worried that Detective Torres was on to me. It had taken me a long time to answer the door. Had he already snooped around? Had he looked in the basement window? Had he seen my husband sitting right in the middle of the basement tied up? He'd be fully lit up because of that stupid Rudolph Christmas lawn decoration. *Screw me.*

But then Detective Torres winked. "And I really want to see that cute little puppy of yours. See you tomorrow."

I should have been concerned as he drove off. But I couldn't tell if Detective Torres was kidding or not. It kind of seemed like he was kidding. But even if he was? There was still reason for concern. Because I knew my husband wasn't in Canada with his mistress. He was in my house.

Detective Torres was coming for me. I had one day to get my answers. But the information Detective Torres had given me would make my interrogation today so much easier. Now I knew the name of the whore my husband was cheating with. Well, one of the names. Yes, it stung that my husband had been cheating on me for two years. But I was more interested in his local girl. The one he snuck away to see more frequently than Miss Canada.

He should have been nice after my reindeer peace offering. Because of him I now had to buy a mutt that I didn't want. He knew I hated dogs. I made a mental note to stop by the animal shelter later as I made my way back inside. Being forced to be a dog owner was bad. But that combined with the fact that my husband was a double cheater...now I wasn't in such a forgiving mood.

I walked into the garage to look for the toolkit. It was sitting next to the cart I'd used to wheel his limp body into the house. I lifted up a pair of pliers. *I wonder what would be the best way to remove my husband's balls?*

CHAPTER 8
Saturday

I walked up to the basement door and then back toward the kitchen island again. Back and forth. I knew that I was pacing. Part of me wanted to crucify my husband. But every time I reached the basement door I remembered that I needed answers first. And he didn't remember. He didn't remember me or anything about his life.

But then I'd be back in the kitchen again thinking about Sophia Tremblay. What if he remembered her and not me?

After pacing back and forth for what felt like an eternity, I finally opened the basement door. I didn't deserve to be driven mad when he might have all the answers. Maybe he'd just hit the side of his brain that held all his memories of me.

I stormed down the stairs, the pliers still in my hand.

His eyes grew round when he looked from me to the pliers. He tried to say something, but the words were drowned out by the gag.

I tore it from his face, more harshly than I should have. I was surprised that some of his teeth didn't pop out of his mouth with it.

"What are you doing?" he asked as soon as he was no longer gagged.

He hadn't called me crazy, but I could hear the accusation in his voice. He thought I was nuts. Well...soon I'd have his. Maybe that would make me nuts. But he hadn't seen anything yet. No more reindeer surprises. No more pee breaks. I was done playing nice cop.

I waved the pliers in front of his face. "You asked me what I wanted. I want answers. And you'll give them to me or I'll twist off your balls one by one." I reached for the zipper of his pants.

"What the fuck?" his chair scooted slightly to the left.

"Really? What the fuck? That's all you have to say to me?"

"I'll tell you whatever you want!" His chair slid more to the left as he tried unsuccessfully to get away from me. "Just ask me a question."

"Sophia Tremblay? Are you kidding me?" I could feel the tears burning in my eyes, threatening to escape.

"I have no idea what you're talking about."

My tears started to spill. I could barely even see him in front of me as the basement grew blurry from my tears. But his smug face was ingrained into my brain. "How could you?!" I screamed.

"Saying a name isn't a question. But I don't know her, if that's what you're asking. I have no idea who you're talking about. Or what you're insinuating."

"You cheated on me! With some Canadian girl? *Eh*?" I said, trying to impersonate the accent. "How *a-boot* that for clarification? They don't even know how to say *about* right!" I threw the pliers at his chest.

He made an oomph noise like I'd just knocked the wind out of him. "I would never cheat on you," he said calmly, like I hadn't just assaulted him and threatened to twist his balls off. "Look at you. I'd be crazy to cheat on you."

I wiped the tears from my eyes so I could see him more clearly. "Yeah. You would be." I stared at him staring at me. There was *that* look in his eyes again. The one that transfixed me. I blinked away my remaining tears. "Stop looking at me like that."

"Like what?"

He'd done it at the bar last night too. He was staring at me like he thought I was beautiful. Why did he keep doing that? Why now? I looked up at the ceiling to avoid his gaze. The only reason he was looking at me like that was because he didn't remember me.

"Sophia Tremblay," I said. I wasn't sure how many minutes, hours, or days I had left of him looking at me this way. Because he'd look at Sophia Tremblay this way as soon as his memory returned. "Think about that name. Really think about that name while I'm gone. And maybe I'll let you keep your balls if you tell me everything."

"Where are you going?"

I grabbed the fabric around his neck and pulled it back in place. "I have to get a stupid puppy thanks to you."

***

The pet store had no dogs. What kind of pet store didn't have puppies in the window? I didn't actually know the answer. Ever since I was a kid, I'd avoided pet stores. Maybe they kept dogs in the back because they were smelly.

I ducked down to stare at another empty cage. The store pretty much had no animals at all, except a lizard that was staring at me as I made my way down the aisle. I needed a dog. Any dog. It didn't even really have to be a puppy. I could just say I called him a puppy because he was so freaking cute. *Gross.* I doubted I was that good of a liar.

"Can I help you find something?" asked a young man with an apron and a friendly smile.

"Um...yes. I need to buy a puppy." I know I didn't sound enthusiastic, but his smile didn't falter.

"You're in luck! There's an adoption drive happening by the food court. Right near the fountains where you can get pictures with Santa Claus. We teamed up with the local animal shelter..."

I didn't hear the rest of what he had to say because I was already walking out of the store. I didn't have all day. I'd taken the long way to the pet store to avoid the Santa picture madness. Children crying in line for an hour didn't appeal to me.

The scene by the fountains was more horrifying than I expected. It was loud and hairy and smelled slightly of urine. Cats meowed. Birds squawked. Puppies barked. And the children in line waiting to tell Santa their deepest desires were almost louder than the animals. *Almost.* The combination was already giving me a headache.

I approached one of the makeshift pens filled with dogs. How was I supposed to tell which one would be the least annoying?

"They're so cute, aren't they?" a little girl asked before tossing some dog treats into the pen. It made the dogs behave even worse. They tumbled over each other, yelping.

"Sure are." Was the one in the corner licking another dog's butt?

"I'm hoping Santa will bring me a puppy for Christmas. I already asked him and I've been really good." She pointed over to where Santa was balancing a screaming child on his lap. He looked about at happy as the kid.

I didn't know what to say to the little girl. The thought that she should ask her parents instead of Santa crossed my mind, but I kept my lips sealed.

"Are you looking to adopt?" she asked. "Or just browsing?"

I stared at her. She couldn't be more than 10 years old. I was terrible at guessing children's ages. It was possible she was five. Who knew. Was she one of the salespeople? "Um...adopt I guess. I have to get a puppy."

The girl laughed. "You *have* to?"

Yes, because my husband is an idiot. "Mhm. Because they're so darn cute." I was pretty sure I was grimacing, but the girl laughed again.

"Well, I can help you find one. This is Simon," she said and pointed to a little dog that was running around the pen and barking like he was on acid.

No thank you. "I was hoping for a quieter model."

The girl laughed again. "What about Spot?" She gestured to the one getting his butt licked.

I didn't want such a pushover. Or one that wanted anything near his butt. "No. Not that one."

"Well, what breeds do you like? We have..."

I waved my hand, cutting her off. "It doesn't really matter. I want something that doesn't shed much, is well trained, and is quiet."

"We have some hairless cats."

That sounds so much more appealing. "No, it needs to be a dog."

"Hmm." She folded her arms across her chest. "But all dogs shed. And most of these are puppies so they aren't even potty trained yet. And...they bark. Are you sure you want a dog?"

Of course I don't want a dog! They sounded terrible. What kind of monster wasn't potty trained? "It's a gift for my husband," I said. "He loves them." Maybe I wouldn't even have to torture him if I could teach the dog to bite on command. "Maybe one of the calmer puppies?" I looked around the pen. None of them seemed calm.

A baby crying made me turn back to look at Santa on his throne. He was trying to cheer it up with a candy cane, but the baby threw it back in his face. *Poor guy.* Maybe it was best that I never had children. I wasn't sure I had the patience for it. Or the stamina.

"Oh." The little girl was smiling again now. "How about Blue then." She walked over to another pen and pointed to a puppy that was just lying there. He was a tiny thing, about the size of a cat, with white unruly looking fur and bright blue eyes. All the other dogs were running around playing with children in the pen and trying their best to get adopted. And Blue was just...sitting.

He looked up at me with these big sad eyes. His tail wagged once. Twice. And then he looked back down at his paws. I swore I heard him sigh.

"Is there something wrong with him?" I asked.

"I don't know. He just doesn't seem to get along very well with the other puppies. And he's a little scared of all the people I think."

Huh. "Is he depressed or something?"

"Depressed?" The little girl looked up at me. "What does that mean?"

"Sad."

She nodded and looked back at Blue. "Yes, I believe he's very depressed."

I bit the inside of my lip. Blue sighed again like being here was the most exhausting thing in the world. I'd never felt so connected to an animal before. "I'll take him."

"Don't you want to meet him first?" She stepped over the edge of the pen and lifted Blue up into her arms. Blue looked about as happy to be in her arms as he did to be in the pen. Which was not happy at all. She held him out to me.

What did she want me to do? Touch it?

She held him out even farther.

Fine. I lightly patted his head. He was surprisingly soft. "Yup. He's the one. Can you package him up for me?"

She tilted her head to the side. "I can give you a leash."

I hadn't thought this through. Was he supposed to just sit in my car and ruin the leather seats? "Isn't there something to put him in?"

"Oh." She nodded. "There's a pet store down there to the left." She pointed to the store I'd just been in. "You'll be able to find everything you need. And all the puppies that are adopted here today come with a care package. A little bit of food, a collar, and a coupon for dog school. You just need to come sign a few papers with my mom."

Dog school? They needed an education too? I filled out the necessary forms and was given a small bag and the end of Blue's leash.

I stood there staring at Blue. He looked up at me and sighed.

"It'll be fine," I said. "We can be sad together. Let's go get you whatever else dogs need from the pet store."

Blue looked over his shoulder like he was reluctant to leave the chaos of Santa and an animal adoption going on at the same time. I was doing him a favor, didn't he see that?

"Come on, Blue."

He sighed again and followed me.

The young man that had been helping me earlier set me up with everything I could possibly need. So much stuff that he even offered to carry it out to my car for me, which I accepted. I wasn't sure how else to balance everything in my arms while still holding on to Blue's leash.

As we made our way out of the pet store, I stopped. "Wait, don't I need that?" I asked and pointed to a litter box.

"That's for cats." He started walking again.

"Wait." I had an idea. It would be so much easier to scoop up clumps of cat litter than spilled urine. I shifted the dog bed under my arm as Blue sat there sadly. "How absorbent is your cat litter?"

"Uh..." the guy paused. "Pretty absorbent."

"I have a lot of cats," I lied. "And it seems like they always like to pee at the same time. Like their bladders have all synced up. My current litter box isn't doing the job. At all. I need something that can really take a lot. Like...the biggest load you can think of."

The guy gave me a strange look but then grabbed a brand of cat litter off the shelf. "This should do the trick. How many cats do you have?"

How much did cats pee compared to humans? They were physically probably like a tenth of the size. "Ten." Then I realized how crazy that sounded. I basically just told him I was a crazy cat lady. And I was trying my best to not let anyone think I was crazy. I was about to change it to two cats when he started talking again.

"Then you're going to need more than one thing of litter. And you'll probably want another litter box. I'm going to go ring this up and get a cart to take all this stuff to your car."

"Can you add a new scoop too? My cats like to hide it. They like things dirty I guess," I said with a laugh.

He laughed too, grabbed a scoop, and then headed back toward the cash register.

That was easier than I thought it would be. I'd made up a perfect story about why I needed a litter box. He didn't even ask me about my ten cats. The only bad thing was that I didn't have enough cash left to pay for all this crap. And I couldn't withdraw any from my bank because all my accounts were empty. So I had to leave another credit card trail.

But Detective Torres wouldn't think anything of this charge. He knew I had a puppy in the house. And he was a terrible detective. He was all the way in Canada, far far away from my basement.

Blue sighed. "It's okay, Mr. Snuggle..." What had I told Detective Torres the puppy's name was? *Pancakes? Dumplings?* A woman with a pair of too-tight pants walked past me in the pet store. The pants shoved the fat on her hips up like...*oh, right. Muffin.* "Let's go home, Mr. Snuggle Muffins."

CHAPTER 9
Saturday

I set up all the dog stuff I'd just bought in the garage. A bed, food and water dishes, and tons of toys littered the cement floor. I lifted up one of the toys, squeezed it to make the squawking noise that the pet store employee had shown me, and threw it at Snuggle Muffins.

Instead of trying to catch it, or moving at all for that matter, he let the toy bounce off his body. He sighed.

"Okay," I said. "Well, have fun out here." I started to walk away.

Snuggle Muffins followed me to the door. When I opened it and stepped inside he tried to squeeze past my legs, but I successfully blocked his path.

"No. Stay." I pointed my finger at him.

He looked up at me with his big blue eyes and whimpered in the most pathetic way.

The sound went straight to my heart. I guess it was a little cold out. Even though he was basically wearing a fur coat. "Fine. Just this once." I opened the door farther so he could follow me into the kitchen.

The nails on his paws clattered across the tiled floor. I tried not to cringe thinking about how he'd tear up my hardwood floors throughout the rest of the house.

"Only in this room," I said firmly.

He stopped right by my feet and looked up at me expectantly.

"I don't know what you want."

He sighed and lay down at my feet.

Okay, then. I grabbed a Pop-Tart from the pantry. My husband was always very conscious of his sugar intake. He used to make fun of me for starting my day with worthless calories. The idea of torture by sugar sounded fun to me. Maybe I'd just force him to only eat Pop-Tarts for the next few days. I pulled one Pop-Tart from its silver packaging before putting my wig and mask back on.

Snuggle Muffins blinked up at me.

"What?" I said. "It's hard to pull off being blonde." I tried to ignore his stare as I unlocked the basement door.

Snuggle Muffins stood up and started to follow me.

"You have to stay here. You're a distraction."

He just stared at me.

Now I was the one sighing. "Fine. Just this once." *How many times was he going to make me say that?* I opened the door and we made our way downstairs together.

"Your dog is cute," he said with a smile as soon as I ungagged him. "What's his name?"

"Snuggle Muffins."

His smile grew. "That's adorable."

My puppy was not adorable. He was a menace like all puppies. Snuggle Muffins sat down by my feet instead of exploring the basement. The little girl at the mall was right. He really did seem depressed.

I turned my attention back to what mattered. "Hungry?" I lifted up the Pop-Tart.

"I'll eat anything. I'm starving."

Well, maybe he'd hate it after having it for the next few meals. Death by sugar. I lifted it to his lips and watched him take a bite.

He licked a crumb off his upper lip and my stomach clenched. It was so easy to picture his tongue on my skin instead. *Stop*.

"Have you been thinking about Sophia Tremblay?" I asked and pulled the Pop-Tart back to my side.

"I have."

He didn't offer anything else. And all I could think about was...what exactly he was thinking about her. Was he picturing her naked? Thinking about his tongue on her skin instead of mine? I felt the Pop-Tart snap in my hand. Half of it fell to the floor.

For the first time since I'd met him, Snuggle Muffins seemed energetic. The Pop-Tart was in his mouth before I could even tell him "no."

"Is that bad?" I asked as I crouched down next to him. "Is he allowed to eat processed foods?" I touched the underside of Snuggle Muffins' chin to turn his head up to mine. He looked happier than I'd ever seen him. He didn't even sigh.

"It's fine. He's a dog. Dogs' stomachs aren't as sensitive as you probably think."

"But what about puppies' stomachs?"

I was pretty sure he tried to shrug, but his hands were tied too tightly to the chair. "I don't see how that question has any-thing to do with your dog."

"What?" I dropped Snuggle Muffins' chin. "He's just a puppy. Maybe I should take him to the vet."

"You definitely don't need to go to the vet. And I'm no ex-pert, but that dog seems real old."

"Really?" I turned back to Snuggle Muffins. "But he's so...small."

"Dogs can be small."

Oh. I stared down at Snuggle Muffins. So maybe he wasn't depressed. Maybe he was just old and slow. There was something about a little old man dog that was a lot more appealing to me than a puppy. I patted his head. *Good boy.*

"You were asking about Sophia," he said.

I quickly stood up. What was I doing? I didn't have time for my silly old dog. I had business to attend to. "Right, I..."

"I'd never cheat on you. Ever. You have to realize that." His eyes raked down my body.

My stomach clenched again.

His eyebrows lowered slightly. "It's true, I don't remember. But I don't have to remember to know that I'd never have a side piece. Ever."

I swallowed hard. He didn't actually remember. My husband and I had been through so much together. I thought about the forgotten box in the corner of the basement filled with broken promises and dreams. My husband loved me once. I was his whole world and he was mine. But people changed. We'd changed. He'd gotten new dreams and made promises to women that weren't me.

"You really don't remember?" I asked.

He shook his head.

"You don't remember me at all? Not even a little bit?"

"I'm sorry. You know...you could remind me." His tongue darted out again, licking his upper lip.

I stared for a beat too long.

"Just one kiss," he said.

Was he crazy? Why was he trying to kiss me? He was my hostage, not my house guest. Not that I kissed all my house guests. "That's not a good idea."

"I think it's a great idea. A kiss can be pretty powerful."

I laughed. "Maybe in fairytales."

"Just one kiss. To see if it jogs my memory."

It wouldn't jog anything. I knew that. And yet...I found my-self staring at his lips again. What if he was right? What if one kiss could bring it all back? Like Sleeping Beauty? I shook the thought away. My husband and my story was a lot more like Beauty and the Beast. But it was questionable who was the beast after the last two days. I'd wanted to cut off his balls earlier today. I'd waved around pliers and everything. My eyes darted toward his jeans where I'd tried to unzip him.

Snuggle Muffins sighed. I shook my head, trying to dismiss my wandering thoughts. He was right. I needed to focus.

"There's another woman," I said. "It's not just Sophia. Do you remember someone else?"

"No." He lowered his eyebrows. "I can't remember. But if I did something with someone else...I'm here right now asking for your forgiveness. I'm sorry. There's no way it meant anything. It was just an awful mistake. You have to believe me."

Once was a mistake. Twice...twice was no mistake. It had tak-en me a while to learn the truth about him. And the truth was that it was his job to lie. I couldn't believe anything he said. So I shoved the rest of the Pop-Tart in his mouth so I could have a moment of silence to think. He didn't remember Sophia. Or the local woman. So that left...what? "My bank accounts are all emp-ty. Do you want to tell me about that?" My husband was planning on leaving me. There was no other excuse. I was just lucky I found out soon enough to stop him.

He swallowed down the Pop-Tart and coughed. "Can I have something to drink? That was really dry."

"Answer the question."

"I'm telling you...I don't remember anything. You need to jog my memory somehow."

"Focus."

"I am focused." His gaze drifted to my lips again.

All I could think about was his lips on another woman. I didn't want to play all my cards at once. The Canadian woman was a surprise. I knew more about the other one. I'd even followed her a few times. *Don't do it. Don't tell him everything you know and lose the upper hand.* I squinted at him. "Do you remember Dr. Collins?" I asked. Fuck, why couldn't I keep my mouth shut?

He shook his head. "How about that drink?"

I was almost relieved that he changed the subject. Hopefully he'd forget the name and I could restart my questioning when my old man dog wasn't distracting me by eating too much sugar. And when he wasn't distracting me by staring at me like that. "You know what...I think I will get you a drink." I walked back over to the stairs, Snuggle Muffins on my heels. "Give me a few minutes."

"I'm not going anywhere."

I laughed, even though I wasn't sure if it was a joke.

He smiled his perfect smile. "You can change back into that other outfit if you want. If it makes you more comfortable."

Was he talking about my comfy pajamas? Did he...like them? I looked down at my skintight jeans and sweater. There's no way he liked them more than what I was wearing.

"You just seem tense when you're not in comfortable clothing. Speaking of which...my jacket is getting a little warm."

I stared at his leather jacket. How could I get that off of him without him overpowering me?

"You could also lose the mask," he said. "There's no reason to hide your beautiful face anymore."

My fingers gripped the handrail. *He remembers.*

He stared at me.

I stared back.

He slowly raised his left eyebrow, somehow causing me to blink. He'd won the staring contest. He'd won the game. I gave him all the power. He knew about the missing money. About Sophia. About Dr. Collins. He knew me. He'd even met my dog. *Shit.* "Come on, Snuggle Muffins."

He whimpered as he looked up the stairs.

I followed his gaze. *You're not too depressed to climb up stairs.* "Come."

Snuggle Muffins plopped down on the floor, rolling onto his back. His tongue fell out the side of his mouth.

Was he playing dead? I looked back at the stairs. I guess the distance was a little intimidating for such a small creature. "Just this once," I said under my breath and lifted him up.

"See you in a few minutes, sweetheart!" he called behind me.

I slammed the door closed and secured the deadbolt.

"Shit!" I tore the mask from my face and threw my wig down onto the counter. "What the hell did you do?" I said to Snuggle Muffins.

He sighed and sat down next to my feet.

"This is your fault. You distracted me by eating that Pop-Tart."

I pinched the bridge of my nose, trying to ease a headache coming on. I'd promised to bring down a drink. And I had a clever idea to give him all the alcohol so he'd get loose lips. But now I was more concerned that I'd get the loose lips.

My doorbell rang, causing me and Snuggle Muffins to both jump.

Who could that be? Detective Torres had said he wouldn't be back in town until tomorrow. I shoved my mask and wig into a drawer just in case it was Detective Torres. He'd surely demand to come in my house now. Maybe he set me up this morning with his Canada trip lies to lull me into a false sense of security. That's what a good detective would do.

I went to the front door the long way, through the dining room, so I could peer out the curtains.

My neighbor Charlotte was standing there with a casserole dish and a fake smile. The housewives in my neighborhood all seemed to be friends. Minus me. I'd tried to be part of their inner circle when my husband and I first moved in. But they were catty. I wasn't blonde. I preferred flats over heels. I didn't like to gossip and go on walks, shoving my nose into other peoples' business. And yet...I wanted to be one of them. But today wasn't a good day for it to happen.

I watched Charlotte press the doorbell again.

Under no circumstances could I open the door. So why were my feet inching toward the foyer? Why did I still care about her acceptance? My hand froze on the doorknob. This was a bad idea. She'd ask too many questions. And she might...

A muffled cry for help came from the basement.

No. I'd forgotten to put the gag back in his mouth.

He yelled again.

I had to answer the door now. I had to explain the noise away. But my hand stayed frozen on the doorknob. How? How could I possibly explain a man yelling for help in my basement? *Screw me.*

CHAPTER 10
Saturday

I grabbed Snuggle Muffins, who had followed me out into the foyer. I was glad he'd disobeyed a direct order to stay in the kitchen. I used him like a shield as I opened the door, stepped outside, and closed the door behind me. "Hi, Charlotte!" My voice sounded too cheery. Too high. Too fake. But Charlotte knew all about being fake. Why the hell else was she here?

"Did I just hear..."

"That was my dog," I said, cutting her off. "He's so loud." I turned my attention to him. "Aren't you?" I used that high voice that moms used with children. It sounded even grosser than my greeting to Charlotte.

Snuggle Muffins sighed. I plopped him down, hoping he wouldn't run away. Not that I liked him. I just didn't want to have to go back to that animal drive. But he just sat down at my feet.

"Oh. I didn't realize you had a dog."

"He's new to the family. My husband and I picked him out a few weeks ago. We both love him dearly." *Vom.*

For a second Charlotte and I just stared at each other. It was like she was waiting for me to tell her what was going on. But I wasn't about to tell her that I'd kidnapped my husband. Charlotte and I weren't close like that. Her fault, not mine. I smiled.

"I made you a lasagna," Charlotte said and handed me the casserole dish.

"Thanks." I'm pretty sure it came out more as a question. I took the dish from her and stood there awkwardly. Now was the time when I was supposed to invite her in and let her uncover all my secrets. But that was not happening. The last thing I needed was for her to wander into the basement and see my husband tied to a chair. I placed the casserole dish down on the front step instead, which drew her a little farther away from my house.

"What's up, girl?" I asked. *Girl?* It was time to stop trying to be one of them. Clearly I didn't belong. She was only here because...why? Why the hell was she here?

"I came over to see what was going on. I saw that handsome detective over here late last night. Damien Torres." She fanned herself with her hand. "And then again on my walk this morning."

Ah. Right. Of course that's why she was here. I had been expecting the gossip to start. And honestly, I was a little excited to be the center of it. Maybe I'd be on the news soon. "Yeah." I wasn't in the mood to offer her any information.

"So what are you two doing together?" She raised both her eyebrows up and down. Suggesting...

God no. Why was her first thought that I was sleeping with Detective Torres? Yes, he was good looking, but I was a little busy kidnapping. Planning ball removals. Buying litter to pee in. Leaving a credit card trail. I tried to make myself look sad. I needed to squash any rumors about me having an affair. "My husband didn't come home last night."

Charlotte pressed her lips together. Then put her hand to her chest, right above her fake boobs. "I'm so sorry. I used to know a few people that got divorced. It's an awful thing."

A divorce? Much too simple. Why was that the conclusion she came to? This lady was hella insane. She wanted everyone to be cheating on everyone. Now I was just suspicious of her. Maybe she was sleeping with my husband too. I wouldn't put it past him. "No. He didn't *choose* not to come home. He's missing." It was very important to my narrative that my neighbors thought my husband still loved me. I didn't want to be the jilted murderous wife. I just wanted to be the murderous wife. Charlotte didn't need to know that Detective Torres thought he'd run away with his mistress. That could be my little secret.

Her eyes grew round. "Missing?"

"Yes." I lowered my voice. "I think he may have been kidnapped." Okay, maybe that was a bit much. Especially since I was the only one that knew that for sure. But I was enjoying her fake sympathy.

"Oh, dear." She reached out and touched my arm to continue whatever charade she was playing.

Snuggle Muffins growled.

Charlotte immediately removed her hand from me as we both stared down at my dog.

He could sense that Charlotte was bad news too. *Such a good boy.* "Well, I should probably go keep calling family and friends to see if anyone's heard anything." I did that sniffling thing I was mastering.

"Is there anything I can do to help?" she asked.

Did she not take the hint? She was neither family nor friend. "You've already done too much. The lasagna smells divine." Although, I had no idea why she made me something she'd never eat. Maybe she was just trying to fatten me up with carbs. "Actually, you know what? Could you maybe ask around the neighborhood? See if anyone knows something we could tell Detective Torres."

"I'd be happy to."

Of course you would.

"And you're sure you don't need anything else? If you want to talk...I'm here for you. I could come in and..."

"No." I cleared my throat. "I really just need to be alone." I wiped under my eyes even though there weren't any tears.

"I understand. Stay strong. The cops will find him. This neighborhood's already been through enough."

She was referring to Violet Clark and Adeline Bell. And the funny thing was that she had no idea that I idolized them. They had life right. They took justice into their own hands. I was going to be one of them. The three badass suburban housewives that went down in history. I just needed to get my answers first. A confession that my husband was cheating. And access to my money again. Then I'd be on the run too. "Absolutely," I said. "I'll see you later."

Charlotte was waiting for me to go back into my house.

And I was waiting for her to leave my front porch. If I opened the door she might be able to hear screaming. "Bye," I said, hoping it didn't sound rude.

"Okay. Just call if you need anything. And don't forget that lasagna."

Right. I lifted it up and smiled.

She smiled back. "And if you need any help decorating for the annual Christmas light competition, let me know."

Did she not understand that I'd retired from being a perfect suburban housewife? "Will do." *You're dismissed.*

She finally retreated.

I let out the breath I'd been holding. Soon my whole neighborhood would know my husband was "missing." Everyone would be talking about me. When Charlotte was well out of earshot, I opened the front door. I was expecting to hear yelling, but it was quiet. Snuggle Muffins trotted after me back into the house.

"You know, you were supposed to stay in the kitchen." I looked down at him.

He sighed.

"But you were right to growl. She's a meanie. Don't be fooled by the lasagna." I lifted it up. "Dirty housewife games."

I swore Snuggle Muffins nodded.

"Okay, let's go get wasted. Well, not you. And not me either. Loose lips sink ships. And my ship isn't going down. My husband's is going down. Burn baby burn."

Snuggle Muffins sighed.

Why am I talking to a dog?

***

"Fa la la la la, I have your drink." I set down the tray and lifted up the bottle of champagne my husband and I had been saving for a special occasion. Today felt special to me.

He stayed silent as I poured the champagne into the flutes we'd used on our wedding day. What he didn't know was that the bottle was only half filled with champagne. I was going for drunk. Not a mild buzz. It was half vodka now. And a splash of orange juice to cover the flavor.

I put the flute to his lips and he took a sip. And then coughed. "What the hell is that?"

"You asked for a drink."

He stared at me. "Are you drugging me again?"

"I would never. That was a one-time thing, I swear."

I put the champagne flute back up to his lips but he refused to take another sip.

Damn it. I lifted up my flute and took the tiniest of sips. "See? Not poisoned."

"Drink from my glass."

I rolled my eyes and drank from his glass. "Satisfied?"

"No I'm not satisfied. I'm tied up in your basement."

Your basement. He was still staring at me like he didn't know who I was. I was nervous to come down here because I thought he'd remembered. If he didn't remember, there was no point in getting him drunk. Or did he remember and was just playing games with my head? I stared at him.

"You're glaring at me again," he said.

"I don't glare." I put the glass to his lips but he denied it again.

"Every time you take a sip, I'll take a sip. No more, no less."

He was being impossible. How was I supposed to have the upper hand now? Especially since I hadn't dumped half the champagne down the drain earlier. A lot of it had ended up in my mouth. I took the tiniest sip and then put the glass back up to his lips. He drank willingly.

"Look, I'm going to make this very clear," I said. "I just need to confirm exactly what happened with Sophia Tremblay and for how long. And not just her." Now I was pretty sure I really was glaring. "I want to know about every indiscretion. The length of each. All of it. And I need you to give me the account number that you transferred all our money into. And then you're free."

"I don't know any Sophia's. And I don't know anything about the money."

"Okay." I took a sip. Forced a sip on him. We went back and forth several times. I refilled the glass.

"Just tell me," I said. I was bad at questioning. Maybe if I re-worded the questions? The hit to the head could have made him dumb. I forced more liquor down his throat to stall.

There was a scratching noise at the basement door. I'd some-how slipped away from Snuggle Muffins earlier and he was finally retaliating.

"You should probably let your dog down here."

"He's our dog now." I sighed and stood up. My head was fuzzy. This wasn't good. But if my head was fuzzy so was his. I was close to getting the answers I needed. So close. I wobbled up the stairs and opened the door. My diva of a dog waited for me to lift him up and carry him into the basement.

I placed him down and plopped into my chair. And then I just...waited. For a confession. For all the information to pour out of him willingly.

He licked his lips in that distracting way and stared back.

"Fine," I said. "I don't need a confession." I knew he was a cheat. I didn't need to hear about it. And clearly an "I'm sorry" wasn't coming my way. *Men*. "Just tell me about the money."

"I'm telling you...I don't remember."

Asshole. "Give me my money back or I'll...make Snuggle Muf-fins attack."

He started laughing. Really hard.

Instead of getting mad, I started laughing too. "Snuggle Muf-fins, attack!" The words were barely audible through my laughter.

Snuggle Muffins sighed.

"That was the most unintimidating threat I've ever heard," he said. "Attack dogs can't be named Snuggle Muffins."

"You should have heard him growl at one of the neighbors today. He has some bite to him."

"Which neighbor?"

"Stupid Charlotte. You know...one of the blonde ones."

"Ah. Charlotte."

The laughter died in my throat. "You do remember."

He smiled. Cockily. "I don't remember, sweetheart. I'm just hoping something will ring a bell. And why are you so caught up on Stupid Charlotte having blonde hair? You're a blonde too. A very sexy blonde."

I pressed my lips together. I wasn't a blonde. I took a huge sip from the champagne flute and forced him to do the same. "Do you like blondes?"

"I like you."

"I kidnapped you. I tied you up. I made you pee in a bucket. And I bought cat litter so that the next time you have to go it'll be easier to clean up. You don't like me."

He licked his lips again. "I want to put a pin in that cat litter bit. We need to come back to that. But I do like you. You're spunky. And brave. And maybe a little bit..."

"Crazy?"

"Passionate," I was going to say. "You're exactly my type of girl. I can see why we got married."

I looked down at my ring finger. The rings were still on my bedside table, but there were tan lines. It was easy to tell I was married. I looked back at him. "Where is your ring?" I asked. He had the same tan line on his finger. But his ring wasn't sitting on the bedside table.

"Where are yours?" he asked.

"I have a right not to wear mine. I'll say it again...Sophia Tremblay." I said her name slowly like he was an idiot. "Let's try to refocus here." I wasn't sure it was me or him that needed to focus though. "Does Dr. Collins ring any bells? And what about fucking Charlotte? You seemed to light up to her name."

"Put your rings back on," he said.

"No."

"Sweetheart, I'm asking nicely."

Don't call me that. I took another sip of my monster drink concoction and forced him to do the same. "No."

"I probably just lost my ring," he said. "Or maybe it's in my pocket."

"I already checked your pockets."

"All of them?" He looked down at his pants.

"Yes, all of them. I'm nothing if not thorough."

"You molested me after you threw me down the stairs?" He seemed to find that funny and started laughing again.

"For the record, I checked your pockets before you *slipped* down the stairs. But after this conversation, if we come across another set of stairs together, I will definitely throw you down."

"You molested me."

"I did not molest you! I'm not a pervert. I'm a kidnapper. And clearly you wanted it anyway, so this conversation is pointless."

"You're right." His laughter died away. "I do. You want to molest me again right now? I can't do anything to stop you. I'm all tied up."

Why was that idea so sexy? I hated him. He hated me. But for some reason I found myself getting overheated. He did look good in that leather jacket. And his hair was all mussed up in that way I loved. Who cared if it was because he had been struggling against his gag like a bad prisoner? Hot was hot.

"I'm still waiting for that kiss," he said. "Help me remember."

"I'm still waiting for you to give me my money back." *Good. Stay strong.*

"Okay. I'll tell you everything. *If.*" He stared at me. "If...you kiss me."

Not this again. "You're insane."

"And if you kiss me twice I'll tell you about Sophia. Another kiss and I'll tell you about Dr. Collins. And clearly nothing happened between me and Charlotte. Rumor is she's pretty stupid, and I'm into smart girls. But I'll take as many kisses as you want to give me."

Why was I smiling right now? Stop smiling. "This is my kidnapping," I said. "I'm in charge."

"Of course you are. I'm tied up. Completely at your mercy." His eyes trailed to the V in my sweater.

"But you're trying to make the rules. And I'm the one making the rules." I stood up and the basement seemed to tilt. Which tilted my mind somehow into a great idea. A terrible, awful, perfect idea. "I'll be right back. I'm going to get a confession out of you. It's going to be too hard to resist."

"Oh, I'm definitely hard."

I tried to ignore his dirty words and pulled Snuggle Muffins into my arms. "We'll be back." I practically ran upstairs.

CHAPTER 11
Saturday

He wanted to play a game. So, I'd play a game. But it was going to be my game with my terms. And he was about to get played. I adjusted the straps on my silk lingerie set and stared in the mirror. The red color didn't exactly complement my reindeer masquerade mask, but it worked in a Christmassy kind of way. And the high heels made my legs look amazing. I turned to see more of my reflection. The heels also made my ass look extra perky.

Snuggle Muffins sighed.

I tore my eyes away from my reflection. "Don't judge me."

He just stared at me.

"Why are you even up here? You're supposed to be in the kitchen." *Oh right.* I definitely carried him up here on the pretense that I needed a second opinion. "So, what do you think?" I put my hands on my hips and struck a pose I'd seen twenty-something Instagram models use.

He just stared at me. His eyes said it all. I wasn't instafamous.

"You think this is a bad idea, don't you?"

I swore he shook his head.

He was probably right. But I was having fun. It had been a long time since I'd teased my husband like this. And whenever we used any kind of ropes, usually I was the one tied up. In the middle of our bed. Him being tied to a chair lit a fire in me. I had no idea why. I could do whatever I wanted to him. And I wanted to do something to him. I was pretty sure he wanted it too.

"Stop looking at me like that." I threw my hands in the air and stared down at my defiant dog. "I'm not going to sleep with him." I squinted my eyes. "Of course I swear."

Snuggle Muffins sighed.

"Don't give me that old man sass. This game could help him remember." I gave the lame excuse that he'd given me about the kiss. I shook my head. "I'm not going to kiss him," I said. "I'm just going to tease him a bit. Like...I'll show you my left tit if you tell me about Sophia." I looked back at my reflection. Did I really want to know why he was attracted to her? Would hearing what I didn't have make me feel better? Or a thousand times worse?

God, this was stupid. I pulled my ridiculously short matching satin nightgown over top of my lingerie and then added my baggy flannel pajama top to cover myself even better. At least now I'd have the option to not go through with it. I wasn't exactly in a good state of mind to make a decision like this. I was absolutely drunk. My belly was filled exclusively with vodka, champagne, and orange juice. And I was pretty sure he was drunk too because he hadn't even asked to try Charlotte's horrible lasagna. Fine, not horrible. Average. Mediocre at best.

"Let's go back to our prisoner and take advantage of his loose lips," I said. I was about to lift Snuggle Muffins into my arms when I noticed that he was sniffing a book on the bookshelf. No, not a book. I leaned down and pulled out the white photo album with gold writing on the front. Our wedding album.

Noah and Ensley. I ran the tip of my index finger along the romantic scrawl etched into the fabric. I opened to a random page and saw my husband and I dancing. He looked just as good in a tux as he did in a leather jacket and jeans. And he was smiling. So hard. *What happened to us?*

I turned to another page. He was shoving cake into my mouth and we were both laughing. He'd completely ruined my makeup and I was so happy that I didn't care. *We* were so happy. I swallowed hard and skipped to the last page. All our guests had lit sparklers and formed a line outside the reception hall. I remembered going through that line and then scrambling into the limo, still in my wedding dress. He'd made sure that the whole poofy mess was securely inside the car before shutting the door. And when he'd joined me in the back seat of the limo, his lips were upon me in an instant. I didn't even wave goodbye to the guests because we couldn't wait to be alone. He'd loved me. He was insatiable. He was...a memory.

Snuggle Muffins nudged his head into my shin. I snapped the wedding album shut. What was I doing? Trying to rekindle a flame that had burnt out years ago? Just because he didn't remember...didn't mean it hadn't happened. He'd cheated on me. With at least two women. I hated him. I hated him and I... I still loved him.

"Why do I still love him?"

Snuggle Muffins sighed.

"I know he's a jerk. Obviously he's a jerk. But we had some good years too. So many good years. How did we wind up so far away from this couple?" I lifted the album.

Snuggle Muffins just blinked at me.

"What if I can change his mind? Before you say no...he doesn't remember what we were. And he really seems to like me. He's been begging me for a kiss all day."

Now Snuggle Muffins looked stern.

"What? I know he's my prisoner, but that doesn't mean his feelings aren't real. Prisoners have real genuine feelings too. There's a word for that I think. Stockholm something?"

My silly dog whined.

"Fine. I'll look it up if you're being so whiny about it." I pulled out my cell phone and did a quick Google search for "Stockholm prisoner." The first suggestion that popped up was for Stockholm Syndrome. "Aha. Stockholm syndrome. See." I waved it in Snuggle Muffins' face and then read the definition at the top. Affection felt in a kidnapping by the hostage toward the kidnapper? *Hmm.* That didn't sound like a real thing. Maybe I was thinking of a different term. I read the definition again slowly as the realization hit me. "Oh." I shook my head. "That's not what I was thinking. I just meant that now that he has to listen and actually see me that he realizes he loves me."

Snuggle Muffins sighed.

"I know that that's basically the same thing!" *Damn it.* "He doesn't have Stockholm Syndrome. You're drunk." I laughed at my own joke. Or was it even a joke? I wasn't really sure anymore. "You're a ridiculous dog. Come on. I'm going to go have sex with him."

I threw my hand over my mouth. "That's not what I meant. I promised you I wouldn't. That just slipped out because I was thinking about his perfect abs." I lifted Snuggle Muffins into my arms. "You didn't get to see them the other day, but they were really nice. It's been so long since I've gotten to touch. And he definitely doesn't have that syndrome. You're being ridiculous."

I carried my overly opinionated dog back downstairs and down into the basement. When I set him on the ground, he walked over to the reindeer in the corner and started sniffing it. I was glad he was distracted. Because I was worried I was about to sleep with Noah, and I didn't want Snuggle Muffins to judge me.

"Hey."

I turned around and stared at Noah. He flashed me his perfect grin.

I was wrong. He looked better in this outfit than a tux. "Hey, Noah." I hadn't been using his name. But the jig was up. He'd seen the tan line on my finger. He knew. I knew that he knew. And he was going to tell me everything.

"I like the pajamas better without the matching pants," he said.

The fact that he had no reaction to his name was more proof that he remembered. I was going to get him to tell me everything. "Yeah?" I unbuttoned the top few buttons. "I think you'll like what's underneath even more." I unbuttoned the rest and let it balance precariously on my shoulders. *I guess I'm definitely going through with it. Don't look at me, Snuggle Muffins!*

"We can both agree on that," he said as my satin nightgown came into view.

"So I was thinking. Maybe every time you tell me something I want to know...I'll lose an article of clothing of your choice."

His Adam's apple rose and then fell. "That sounds like a fair arrangement. But first, I'm pretty sure your dog needs to use the bathroom."

"Our dog," I corrected as I looked over Snuggle Muffins. "He's fine. I'm litter training him." I pointed to the litter box I'd set up in the corner of the basement. The two men in my life needed to learn how to share.

"Yeah...that's not a thing."

"Of course it is. He's just as smart as a cat. He'll figure it out."

"Smarter than a cat. Which is why he's never going to use that box. He doesn't want to step around in his own piss."

Huh. I never thought of it like that.

"Yup. He's definitely about to pee on Rudolph."

I watched as Snuggle Muffins started to lift his leg. He was going to perform the perfect fire hydrant arch.

"Bad dog!" I ran over, lifted his furry little body, and got him safely into the litter box before he ruined Rudolph. "There." I sighed when he emptied his bladder in the box. "Good boy." I patted his head. "Now, where were we?" I turned around.

"You're going to make me use that too, aren't you? That's what you were talking about earlier?"

"Let's not talk about your bathroom arrangements right now. You're kind of ruining the mood." I pulled my flannel pajama top closed again.

He raised his left eyebrow. "Then ask me a question. I'll answer it. And you'll lose the flannel top."

"I thought you liked it?"

"I'd like it better pooling around your ankles."

I tried to hide my smile. Which became easier as I thought about my first question. "Do you think maple syrup and hockey are sexy? Like...would you find me more attractive if I guzzled syrup and wore hockey jerseys around the house? Is that what men are into these days?" Just thinking about it made me mad. I'd introduced Noah to syrup. Shouldn't that give me Canadian status in our sex life?

"I don't think maple syrup is sexy unless it's poured all over your naked body. And I'm more of a football fan. But if you wanted to wear a football jersey around the house and nothing else...yeah, I could get down with that. And your French toast is amazing. You can drizzle maple syrup over that whenever you want. Now lose the pajama top."

"What?" I gripped the fabric tighter. "Shit." Why had I asked that question? It didn't get me anything and gave him what he wanted. I was supposed to be playing him, not the other way around. I needed to be smarter about my next question. "Fine." I pulled off the warm fabric and tossed it on the chair in front of him.

"Beautiful," he said.

I swallowed hard. My throat was acting weird. Not having the flannel made me cold. I was probably going to get sick. I swallowed hard again as his eyes trailed down my body. I glanced down at the thin satin fabric. What the hell had I been thinking? I folded my arms across my chest.

He smiled.

I looked back down. Folding my arms had basically shoved my breasts up to my chin. *Damn it.* I dropped my hands to my sides.

"My turn for a question," he said. "How would you feel about tying me to our bed instead of this chair?"

"That's not...that's not how this game works. You don't get to ask questions."

"Why not? You ask one. I ask one. We both slowly get naked. It's a win-win."

"This isn't a win-win scenario, Noah. I'm in charge. Now stop trying to distract me."

"Yes, ma'am."

The way he said it made my stomach clench. God, he was so handsome. *Stop it.* "Tell me about Sophia."

"It was just a kiss. A mistake. A one-time thing. There was too much alcohol flowing in the hotel bar. It meant nothing. Absolutely nothing."

Wait. What? That was not the answer I'd been expecting. Just a kiss? "But the calls. Detective Torres said there were calls to her every week like clockwork."

"To her company, not her. I don't even know if she even works there anymore. I swear. I didn't even know her last name until you told me."

I opened my mouth and then closed it again. Just once? Just a kiss? It felt like a weight had been lifted off my shoulders. Not two years. Just once. He swore it was a mistake.

"Did you say Detective Torres?" He frowned. "Are you talking to a detective about me?"

I stared at his lips as he frowned. "You don't get to ask questions." My eyes locked with his as I tried to remember what I needed to ask. "What can you tell me about Dr. Collins?"

"You had problems getting pregnant."

No shit, Sherlock. I glared at him, trying hard not to focus on the box in the corner. The one with all the unused items for our baby boy that I'd lost.

"Didn't you think there might be a solution? That someone could help? It was just consultations. That's it. I swear. You deserve children if that's what you want. You deserve everything."

He looked so sincere. And his words made my eyes grow slightly watery. I did deserve to have children. Consultations with a doctor? That explained the longer hours at work. Was this really all a misunderstanding?

"Lose the nightgown," he said.

I felt like I was dreaming as I pulled it over my head. Had I misjudged everything? I swayed slightly to the left but caught myself from falling over. My head was spinning. But not enough to ignore the fact that I was wrong. The feeling seeped into me slowly. I was the idiot. Not him. I walked over to the champagne bottle and lifted it ungracefully to my lips. Had I really drugged Noah, tied him up to a chair, and threatened to cut off his balls for no reason? I chugged straight from the bottle. No. *No.* He drained our bank accounts. He was going to leave me. He was a cheat. A master manipulator. An asshole.

"You're lying," I said and pointed the bottle at him.

"I'm not. I swear I'm not. I meant every word. Look at you. No one in their right mind would cheat on you. And that kiss? I swear it meant nothing. It was over before it began. Nothing compares to your lips."

I licked my lips as my eyes fell to his mouth.

"Have I earned that kiss yet?" he asked.

Why did he keep asking questions? "What about the money? Why do our bank accounts have a balance of zero? What the hell?"

"The interest rates on the savings accounts at that bank sucked. I transferred the money to a different bank with better rates. That's it. They're in the process of mailing you a new card. It'll be arriving any day. Now lose the bra."

He transferred it? The money really wasn't gone? He wasn't planning on leaving me? I don't know how it happened, but I somehow wound up on his lap. My fingers were tangled in his hair. And I was kissing him. With relief. With joy. With...shame.

But it was hard to feel that last one. Because the soft look of his lips was deceiving. His kiss was more powerful than I was anticipating. He thrust his tongue into my mouth, tasting me. Savoring me.

I'd made a mistake. I'd made a horrible mistake. This was the only way I could think to fix it. To kiss him back with everything I had. My kiss begged for forgiveness. I was pretty sure his did too. And as far as I was concerned, two wrongs made a right. They had to.

It was like I was back in that limo on our wedding day. He couldn't get enough of me. I couldn't get enough of him. This was a new beginning. A fresh start. Kidnapping him had some-how wiped the slate clean.

He groaned into my mouth.

It was the sexiest sound in the world. Especially when it was-n't surrounded by scheming and lies. My fingers dug into his scalp. I shifted my hips forward, wanting to close the gap be-tween our bodies. And that's when I felt him. He wasn't lying. He was as hard as a rock. And God, I wanted him. I needed him. I could still have everything I wanted. A loving husband. A baby. It wasn't too late. I could fix this. I could still be the perfect subur-ban housewife. With the perfect house. The perfect lawn. The façade I so desperately wanted to uphold. All I had to do was untie him.

I reached behind him and felt the coarse rope around his wrists. What had I been thinking? Kidnapping? Seriously? That wasn't me. I was loving and kind. If anything I loved too hard.

I pulled away from his kiss even though all I wanted to do was stay in the moment the entire night. I needed to say some-thing. To get it off my chest. "I'm sorry." I placed my hands on either side of his face. "I'm so sorry. I thought...I should have just talked to you from the beginning. I shouldn't have jumped to conclusions. Can you forgive me?"

He pressed his forehead against mine. "If you can forgive me?"

"You're already forgiven." I smiled at him. How could I have ever been upset with such a perfect face? I kissed him again, slower this time. Like we had all the time in the world. Because we did. We could grow old and gray together now. I hadn't fucked everything up.

He bit my lower lip and I grinded against him harder.

He groaned.

I needed him. Now. I pulled back again and reached behind him to the ropes. But my fingers paused again. "Do you have Stockholm Syndrome?" I asked.

He laughed. "What? No."

"Are you sure? Because I was reading about it and..."

"We both know this started before you kidnapped me." He smiled. "Speaking of knowing things...you still have to take off your bra."

I stared into his eyes. He remembered me. Why was I questioning this? I doubted he could get Stockholm Syndrome when he knew me. That wasn't how it worked. It was exclusively for strangers. Probably. And this feeling...it was real. I'd recaptured love.

"Can I ask you a question now?" he asked.

"Anything."

"Before we do this." He pulled away so he could stare into my eyes.

It felt like time stopped. If he asked me to put my rings on now, I'd run upstairs and shove them on. I wanted a future with him. I wasn't lost anymore.

"Your name. Tell me your name, beautiful."

My heart stopped beating as my palm connected with his cheek. The slapping sound reverberated around the basement and I was pretty sure Snuggle Muffins yelped from the corner. But I didn't turn. I just stared at Noah. The traitor. The mother fucking liar. "You don't know me?"

"I..."

"Lies," I hissed. "All of that was lies?"

"Probably not. The answers made sense to me."

"But you made them up!"

He laughed.

Oh. Hell. No. I scrambled off his lap. "All of that about So-phia? Dr. Collins? The money? Was any of that true?" My voice cracked.

"What did you expect me to do? You're demanding answers and I don't remember! I told you that. All I know is that I would-n't cheat on you." His chair jumped forward as he struggled against the ropes. "I wouldn't. Not on you. Ever."

"You don't know that."

"You're a fucking goddess. And I'm not an idiot. I'd worship your body. I'd give you everything you ever wanted."

Except a baby. I turned away from him. I felt cheap. And used. I'd believed his lies. Willingly. Just like I'd believed the lies for years. He did love maple syrup and hockey. He liked women who couldn't pronounce "about" correctly. He cheated on me. And I was done listening. "Snuggle Muffins. Come." I walked over to the stairs and my dog came running to join me.

"Obviously I want you. Didn't you feel how much I wanted you?"

I did. In his kiss. I felt him beneath me. But it was all a lie. He didn't know me. He was just manipulating me. *Again.* I was sec-onds away from falling apart. I'd grown accustomed to being used over the past several months. It had somehow become part of our love story. He'd ruined us. But looking him directly in the eyes and hearing the lies? I didn't have to put up with that. I was stronger now. The love story I held on a pedestal had burned to the ground. But Noah had been the one holding the match. He'd ruined us. He'd ruined me.

"Stay," he said. "I'll tell you everything I do know. About my childhood. About college. It's only the last several years that are fuzzy. Please, just stay and talk. Remind me of who you are. What we are. Because I know it's a story for the ages."

My hand paused on the railing. I wanted to stay and talk. When I'd been looking at our wedding album, part of me hated him. But the other part? It felt like I had a second chance to do things right. Who was lucky enough to ever get a second chance?

"Please," he said. "Stay."

But in the past few days I'd had another second chance too. Another chance at living my life. I'd proved to myself that I wasn't nothing without him. I didn't need a him. Not anymore. And besides, I already knew his fucking story.

I walked back over to him. For a second I just stared down at him. But just for a second. I pulled the gag back in place and turned away. "Goodnight, Noah."

CHAPTER 12
Saturday

For the second night in a row, I couldn't fall asleep. I stared at the ceiling instead of trying to count sheep. *I'm single and loving it. I'm single and loving it. I'm single and loving it.* I kept repeating the mantra over and over again in my head. But I couldn't convince my head when I knew it wasn't true. All I wanted to do was run back downstairs to Noah. To straddle him. To untie him and see what sinful things he wanted to do to my body.

I glanced over at the empty spot in the bed beside me. It was still perfectly made. Maybe I wasn't scared of the darkness swallowing me whole. My fingers traced the spot where my husband always slept. Maybe I just didn't know how to sleep without him next to me. Noah's spot felt so cold and empty. Especially since I could so easily fill it back up. He'd asked to be tied to my bed instead of a chair. I could switch things up....*Stop.*

A part of me wanted to go into the basement. I could grab a few pillows and my comforter and make a pretty comfortable nest beside him. Would that help me fall asleep? Just being that close to him? Smelling his cologne? Hearing his light snores? Knowing that I wasn't alone?

I'd walked away from him for a reason tonight. I could have taken things further. But I was trying to get a fresh start. Not stumble right back into his lap. Literally.

But the bed was so cold without him.

Snuggle Muffins whimpered.

I leaned over the edge of the bed and stared down at him.

He was sitting at the base of my bed, staring back.

"Go to your dog bed." I pointed to where I'd put it in the corner.

He didn't move.

"I'm not making you sleep in the garage. I've already given in and let you inside. And up to my room. We're already breaking the rules. What else do you want?"

Snuggle Muffins lifted up his paw and touched the side of my bed.

"No," I said. "Absolutely 100 percent not, Snuggle Muffins. You're a dirty little monster and you can't come up here."

He sighed.

I looked over my shoulder at the empty spot in the bed. Maybe having Snuggle Muffins up here would help prevent me from sneaking down into the basement. Because my body really *really* wanted to be next to Noah. At this rate I'd probably sleep-walk down there if I didn't fill this empty spot. "Fine. Just this once." I leaned down and lifted him up on the bed.

He immediately snuggled into my side. He was really living up to his namesake. Yes, his eyes were blue which made the name Blue suitable. But he was also quite the little snuggler.

Silly dog. "Don't get used to this," I said and patted his head. "I'm serious."

Snuggle Muffins rested his head on my shoulder and closed his blue eyes.

We both knew that I'd said "just this once" about a billion times today. There was no conviction in my words. He knew it and so did I. And we both knew he'd be sleeping beside me from here on out. He easily filled the spot of my dear husband who could die tied to that chair for all I cared. He'd lied just to get in my pants. There was nothing worse than that. *Oh, wait.* There was also the fact that he cheated on me. More than once. And he stole all my money. Those things were worse than the lying to get in my pants. God, I hated him.

I scratched behind Snuggle Muffins' ear. Petting him soothed me for some reason. He was so soft. And warm. *And dirty.* Was I supposed to bathe him or something?

I moved my hand away from him and just stared. The worst part about Snuggle Muffins was that I actually liked him. I liked his stupid little face and his stupid little sighs. And his stupid knowing stare. Even his stupid fuzzy fur. He was crawling under my skin, nestling in right by my heart. The next thing I knew he'd probably be sleeping with my neighbor and stealing all my money. I turned away from him and stared at the wall. I didn't want to be second best anymore. Especially not to the dog that I didn't even want.

***

There was something wet on my hands. Wet and...sticky. And warm. *Ew.* I moved my hand through the thick substance, and my fingers touched something soft. And I had this horrible image of blood. A chill ran down my spine. Blood pouring from Noah's head when he fell down the basement stairs. All I could see was red. Seeping into the wooden steps. Seeping into his hair. Trailing into his lifeless, unblinking eyes. Covering my hands. I stifled a scream.

But that hadn't happened.

Noah was safely in the basement.

There was no blood. *There's no blood, Ensley.* I wasn't a murderer. I wasn't a pervert. I was a kidnapper. Period.

His head was fine, just a little slow in the memory department. Even if he was quick to lie.

So what the hell am I touching? My eyes flew open. My hand was
on Snuggle Muffins' snout and it was covered in...God. I had no
idea what that sticky wet mess was. Saliva? Snot? "Snuggle Muffins, stop being gross."

He sighed.

"I'm only a kidnapper," I said out loud, but the chill didn't go
away.

Snuggle Muffins didn't seem to have a reaction to my statement.

"What's on my hands?"

I swore he smiled. The little demon.

"Bad dog." I climbed out of bed and washed the mess off my
hands. And for just a second, I thought I saw the water run red in
the white ceramic sink. *Stop.* I stared at my reflection in the mirror. I was just agitated. The questioning wasn't supposed to take
this long. Noah was supposed to cave by now. But that didn't
mean there needed to be any blood. I could do this another way.

When I looked back down at the sink, the water was clear
once more. I splashed some water on my face. *Everything's fine. I'll
get my answers today. I'll end this today.* And then I'd still have plenty
of time for the last phase of my plan.

I walked back into the bedroom and Snuggle Muffins was
standing on the corner of my bed, staring at the floor.

"Jump," I said.

Instead of jumping, he lay down on his back and put his
tongue out.

"Come on." I patted my thighs. "Jump. You can do it. Your
little old dog knees can take it, I know it."

He stuck his tongue out farther. He was the smartest dog in the world. I lifted him off the bed and put him down on the floor.

"Do you need to go for a walk?" I knew training him to pee in the litter box was probably a long process. And I didn't have time to be a good dog mom right now. I was in the middle of a felony. Besides, I didn't want to go visit Noah right now. He needed to stew in his lies. I still couldn't believe he lied to me just to see me in my underwear. As far as I was concerned, he could starve to death. I just needed to figure out where to bury his stinky body. *You're a kidnapper, not a murderer.*

Snuggle Muffins whimpered.

"Okay, let me just change real quick. I need to grab something while we're out anyway."

The alcohol I'd forced into Noah's mouth hadn't worked last night. His lips were decidedly unloose. Just soft. And delicious. And masterful in the kissing department. *Stop.*

Alcohol wasn't the only substance I had at my disposal though. The suburbs weren't as straight-laced as everyone thought. The proof? I was a kidnapper. A couple of my neighbors were notorious murderers. The kid down the street stole lawn gnomes. And the teenager across the street from me sold drugs. *Welcome to suburbia.*

***

I knocked on the door and waited. I knew Sylvia Smith was at yoga. And her son who decided not to go to college, to the shock of his parents, would be home. He was always home. I was pretty sure he didn't even have a retail job to cover the trail of his illicit business dealings. *Such a novice.*

I knocked again when he didn't answer. I glanced at my watch. It was almost 10 am. He'd surely gotten his eight hours in. *Come on, Logan. Get up.* I knocked harder. Sometimes a car with tinted windows would pick him up. But they'd always come back in a few minutes. Pretty sure it was his dealer. I knocked again.

Finally Logan answered the door. His eyes were bloodshot and he was wearing a silk robe like he was at the Playboy mansion. He had one arm behind his back, but when he realized it was me, he pulled the joint into view and put it back in his mouth. "'Sup?" The joint hung from the corner of his mouth. If he wasn't careful, he'd burn his mother's oriental rug.

"Hey, Logan..."

"My mom's not home. Can I take a message?"

"What?" Sylvia and I weren't friends who called on each other. We also didn't have parlors or drink afternoon tea. "No. I'm here to see you. I need to buy some of that." I pointed to the joint.

He stared at me as smoke swirled in front of his face. "What? A cigarette?"

Did he seriously think I was as naïve as his mother? I was a freaking criminal now. I was part of his cool club. "Weed. Pot. Whatever you call it. I need some."

He pulled the joint from his mouth. "It's a cigarette."

"It doesn't smell like a cigarette to me."

He smiled.

I didn't smile back. "Fine. Do you have something else that will make someone confess their deepest darkest secrets?"

"Your dog is cute."

He isn't. And what does that have to do with anything? "Sell me what I need right now or I'll tell the cops." I wouldn't. But Logan didn't know that.

"Why do you think I sell drugs?"

"Because you've sold me drugs before." I realized I was rais-
ing my voice and tried to swallow down my impatience. How
high was he the last time I came to see him?

"Nah, I would have remembered that."

God, I was going to kill him. I didn't have time for this. Detective Torres could show up at any time. And the last thing I
needed was for him to see me buying drugs off of this kid. "Even
if you don't remember... I'm...I'm a housewife. I see everything
that goes on in this neighborhood. Including what you do."

"Huh. I'm home a lot too, you know. I see things."

I was pretty sure my heart stopped beating. What did he
mean by that? Did he know that Noah was locked up in my
basement? I'd been so careful when I brought him home. I'd
even closed the curtains on the garage windows. "What kind of
things?"

His eyes trailed down my body.

Well, that wasn't nearly as incriminating. I had a bad habit of
not closing my bedroom curtains because I didn't think there
were any perverts in our neighborhood. "Great, you've seen me
naked. Now sell me something that'll get me really high."

"Really high? Or something for confessing your deepest
darkest secrets?"

"Either one." He was exasperating. "Aren't they the same?"

"Not even close."

"Fine. I need the deepest darkest secret drug then. I'll take
two." Just in case one dose wasn't enough.

He started laughing.

"What?"

"There's no such thing as truth serum. We're not in a spy
movie. Do I look like 007 to you?"

No. He absolutely did not look like James Bond. He looked like an idiot. "Well, pot then. That'll get him to tell the truth, right?" *Oh my God, I just said him.* "I mean me. Or the person. She. Not him." *Shit.* What had I just done?

Logan shrugged. "It will certainly lower someone's inhibitions."

He didn't seem to have any reaction to my mentioning "him." Which was great. But his response was terrible. Noah's inhibitions were clearly already pretty low. Rewarding him with a night of floating on clouds wasn't a good plan. I needed the bank account information. I needed the truth. But I didn't have any other plan. And I was running out of time. "Fine. Get me a lot of that."

"Whatever." He walked back into the house, leaving the front door wide open. Didn't he realize how dangerous this neighborhood was? Anyone could walk in.

Snuggle Muffins sighed.

"What?"

He sighed again.

"It's worth a try," I said. "I don't see you coming up with a better idea."

Another sigh.

"I'm going to bake it into something. He'll never even know he had it." I stared at him. "Stop it. It's a great idea. You'll see. My brownies are fantastic." I tried to ignore Snuggle Muffins' two cents.

"Here you go," Logan said and handed me a brown paper bag.

"Do you take credit cards?" I asked.

"Does it look like I take credit cards?" He gestured to his outfit.

Honestly, it didn't. But I kept a taser in my pocket. He might have a credit card swiper in one of his robe pockets. "Yes?" I said.

"Cash only."

"Okay, great. I'll owe you then." I started to turn around.

"Whoa, what? No. You pay now or you don't get anything." He stepped down onto the front porch and Snuggle Muffins started growling. Logan looked down at the little menace. "I'm not scared of your stupid tiny ass dog. Hand over the cash. Now."

"Here's the thing, Logan. I don't have any cash on me. But now I have evidence that you are in fact a drug dealer." I waved the bag in the air. "You know, I'm friends with a detective and I'm sure he'd be interested in this interaction." Detective Torres wasn't my friend. But Logan didn't know that. When Logan saw him come over today he'd probably shit his pants. "And how do you think your mom will feel about you skipping college and selling?"

He pressed his lips together.

"Don't be sad. I'll pay you soon, I promise. And my dog isn't stupid. You're stupid." It was the lamest comeback ever. But my brain was too preoccupied with recipes for pot brownies to care. I lifted Snuggle Muffins up and walked back toward my house.

CHAPTER 13
Sunday

I wasn't sure exactly what time Detective Torres would be stopping by. Which meant I couldn't make the brownie recipe I'd found on Pinterest yet. If the house smelled like marijuana when he came in, I'd be doubly screwed. Doubly because I had no idea how to ensure that Noah wouldn't scream through his gag.

My fingers drummed on the counter. I could strike a deal with Noah. A "be quiet today and I'll free you later" kinda thing. Would he be so gullible?

Snuggle Muffins rested his chin on my foot.

"How are you tired already? We just woke up."

He sighed.

Snuggle Muffins had been zero help today. And he literally followed me everywhere, which made mopping the floor almost impossible. Despite his best efforts, the kitchen was sparkling clean. At least he could look cute for Detective Torres. I mean...as cute as a dog could look. I glared down at him and resisted the urge to rub behind his ears.

"You know what?" I asked him. "I have a fun idea on how to keep Noah quiet. Starve him."

Snuggle Muffins followed me as I went to the fridge.

I knew exactly how to make someone really freaking hungry. Bacon. "Torture by bacon?"

Snuggle Muffins just stared at me as I proceeded to grab a frying pan. In a few minutes the smell of bacon filled the kitchen.

I slid the deadbolt on the basement door and used the door as a giant fan to push all the greasy, bacony goodness down the stairs. Noah was probably salivating. I left the door completely open as I flipped the bacon. That comforting hiss accompanied the smell to perfection. Poor, sweet Noah. He had no idea that I wasn't going to even give him a bite.

I pulled the frying pan off the stove and slid the bacon onto a paper towel lined plate. "Are you allowed to eat this?" I asked and took a bite.

Snuggle Muffins blinked up at me so innocently.

"Promise you won't be sick?"

He wagged his tail. He hadn't looked this excited since he'd eaten half a Pop-Tart.

"You better be telling the truth." I tossed the bacon down to him and he caught it in his mouth.

I adjusted my wig and mask as he feasted. "This is going to be fun." I lifted Snuggle Muffins and the plate of bacon and made my way down into the basement.

Noah was wide awake, already being annoying and trying to yell even though he must have known I couldn't hear him through the gag. I placed Snuggle Muffins and the plate of bacon down before yanking the gag from his mouth.

"I have to piss! Jesus, you made me drink so much last night and didn't let me pee."

"Oh." *Oopsie.* I'd actually woken up in the middle of the night and had to pee again. Poor guy. "Not a problem. One sec."

"I'm seriously going to piss my pants."

"Calm down." What was he...five? Did five-year-olds pee their pants? I had no idea. I lifted up the litter box and brought it over to him. "Okay, let's get one of your hands untied."

"You seriously want me to go in *that*? I thought you were joking. You used it for the dog."

"His name is Snuggle Muffins. You know that. And what's wrong with sharing? It's fine. I'll scoop it when you're done."

He stared at me like I was insane.

I wasn't. And I didn't appreciate the way he was looking at me. I put my hand on my hip and stared right back.

"Just take me to the toilet," he said. "I won't try to run away, I swear."

"Nope." I untied one of his hands. "Lean over and pee in that like you did the bucket. And if you're lucky I won't tase you this time." I pulled my taser out from my back pocket and pointed it at him.

He closed his eyes and exhaled slowly. "I actually have to take a shit."

"Oh." I wasn't planning on keeping him here this long. And I was really hoping it wouldn't come to this. But I was technically prepared. "Fine." I untied his other hand. "Stand up."

He followed my instructions, his legs still tied tightly to the chair.

I wasn't scared of him trying to run. He'd either fall from the chair or from my taser. And he knew it. I moved the litter box to the seat of his chair and tossed a pack of diaper wipes at him. "Clean yourself up a bit with those while you're at it." The last thing I needed was for him to start smelling down here.

"Are you serious right now?"

"Do I look like I'm joking?" I lifted a piece of bacon and took a bite. "And make sure to use that little shovel thing to cover your business. I don't want to see it. Now strip." I waved my bacon-filled hand at him.

He started to unzip his pants. Instead of staring, I looked away. Last time had been bad. I didn't want him to make a mess again. Besides, I had a watchdog now. I looked over at Snuggle Muffins who was snuggled up to the light-up reindeer, sound asleep. *What the hell, Snuggle Muffins?* "Pst." I snapped my fingers and Snuggle Muffins opened one eye. "You're supposed to be the lookout."

He promptly closed his eyes again.

Son of a bitch. I laughed at my own joke. Snuggle Muffins was literally a son of a bitch. I'd never actually used that term of endearment appropriately before. I snuck one glance at Noah. He was crouched over the litter box with so much shame straining his perfect features.

I'm sorry. I looked down at the cement ground. Would him feeling ashamed make it easier or harder to get the truth out of him? Did any of it matter if he didn't remember me? My cheeks flushed at the thought of last night. He'd wanted me. I'd wanted him too. And I hated myself for it. Snuggle Muffins was right. He didn't remember me. He just had Stockholm Syndrome.

I heard the zipper of Noah's pants and looked up. He wasn't wearing his leather jacket or the t-shirt that had been beneath it anymore. He was just standing there with his perfect six-pack and rock-hard pecks out for everyone to see.

"What are you doing? Put your shirt back on."

He ran a diaper wipe down the front of his chest, making it glisten like his muscles were doused in oil. "I'm cleaning up like you asked."

"I didn't ask you to take your shirt off."

"It was dirty. And you literally told me to strip." He tossed the diaper wipe into the litter box.

"I meant unzip your pants. Not take off your shirt."

He shrugged. "Well, now I'm clean." He removed the litter box from his chair and then sat back down. "Ready to tie me back up?" He innocently held his hands out.

"Not until you put your clothes back on."

"Baby, you're lucky I'm still wearing my pants."

I swallowed hard. *Snuggle Muffins, do something!* I glanced over at him and he was still sleeping. *Damn it.* "Fine. If you want to freeze your ass off, so be it."

Noah ran his fingers through his hair in that way I loved. And then he reached out, grabbed a piece of bacon, and bit into it.

"That's not for you!" I rushed over and quickly tied his hands behind the chair as he swallowed down my torture device.

"It's on my table," he said.

"This isn't your table."

"You always give me everything you put on this table. We've shared silverware. Glasses. The bacon is mine. Can I have another piece? I'm starving." He licked his bottom lip.

And I almost said "yes." Because I was a schmuck. "No." He wasn't supposed to eat it. He was supposed to smell it. All day long he was supposed to just smell it. And get so hungry that he'd tell me the truth. Or at least beg me for it. I'd get at least a little satisfaction out of him begging.

I ate another piece of it as I stared at his abs. *Stop staring at his abs!* I took another bite. *Stop stress eating!* I threw the half-eaten piece of bacon back down on the plate.

"Snuggle Muffins, we're leaving." I snapped my fingers.

"Aren't you going to scoop my shit?" There was a smirk on his face.

He was trying to play this off. Like he wasn't just embarrassed a minute ago when he was crouching over the box leaving a dump in some litter. I'd seen his face. I knew the truth.

"Nope," I said. "I'll scoop it later so you have time to think about what you've done."

I walked over to the boxes along the wall and found the one labeled "Christmas Decorations." It was about time I decorated for the stupid neighborhood lighting contest. And a few decorations would probably help me look innocent. Like I was the perfect housewife who would never kidnap her own husband.

"You're going to leave me down here with no clothes, a pile of shit, and bacon I can't reach?"

"Well when you put it like that..." I let my voice trail off. "Yes." I tried to hide the smile from my face.

I realized I wasn't going to be able to carry both Snuggle Muffins and the box, so I lifted the little dude and tossed him into the box. He yelped.

"Oh, you're fine. I'm giving you a lift." I didn't even bother closing the lid. Snuggle Muffins had given me no indication that he'd be able to jump out of a box.

He sighed from somewhere beneath the tangled Christmas lights.

"You can't just leave me like this," Noah said.

"Of course I can. And if you're a good boy and you're quiet all day long, I might feed you tonight."

"Wait...how long are you going to leave me like this?"

I pulled his gag back in place. "As long as I want." I patted his cheek, my hand hesitating a beat too long on his chiseled jawline.

He tried to say something, but his words were muffled.

"Shhh." I put my finger against his lips.

He kept trying to talk.

This wasn't going to work. I needed him to behave. I needed him to be so freaking quiet all day. I couldn't risk him screaming while Detective Torres was sitting in my kitchen. "Be a good boy and tonight I'll give you whatever you want."

He lowered his eyebrows.

And for some reason I found myself leaning closer. He smelled liked diaper wipes and yet still so much like himself. That alluring scent I couldn't get out of my head. The one that kept me up at night staring at the ceiling. "I promise, Noah," I whispered into his ear. The scruff along his jaw tickled my cheek. "I just need you to be quiet today. Not a peep. And then I'll give you anything you want. Anything." I bit down on his earlobe. *Why am I biting him?*

He groaned.

What the hell am I doing? I took a step back and stared at him like he was the one that had just acted inappropriately. But I was the one with my mouth on him. My lips parted like I was about to apologize, but I pressed my lips back together. We were just going to pretend that didn't happen. I stared at him, willing him to silently agree with me.

Instead...he winked.

My stomach clenched. That wasn't the reaction I wanted. I turned away. "Behave." I wasn't sure Noah knew I was talking to him instead of Snuggle Muffins. I was only having trouble controlling one male in my life. And it was the man, not the dog.

I grabbed my box of decorations and dog and made my way back upstairs. And I was strong enough to only glance back at Noah once. It wasn't fair that he'd taken his shirt off. I silently cursed as I slid the deadbolt back in place. I literally had a hundred shirts upstairs that would fit him beautifully. His stripping was an easy fix. But he'd flustered me yet again. I really needed to make that stop happening.

***

Baby it's Cold Outside was stuck in my head on a loop as I decorated the front bushes. Detective Torres had been by twice already, but he was fairly unobservant. I doubted he'd remember that my house hadn't been decorated yet. And it looked better if I had been prepping for Christmas normally before my husband disappeared, instead of skipping the holiday altogether this year.

Because normally this time of year, my lights would have been up for weeks. I'd actually care about throwing my hat in the ring for the grand prize - a gift card to a local restaurant. It was never about the gift certificate though. It was all about the glory.

I leaned back to get a better view of Charlotte's decorations down the street. She'd won practically every year since I'd moved in. Except for one year when nosy Sally had surprised everyone by hiring an actual actor to play Santa Claus and sit on her chimney. And I don't mean for one day. He was up there for a week. I wasn't sure if she won because her decorations were the best or if people were just worried that giving her the prize was the only thing that would make her let him down. It was probably a neighborhood liability thing.

Charlotte's decorations were as perfect as always. Her lawn was even adorned with beautiful white fake Christmas trees. The whole neighborhood used white lights. It was like an upper-middle-class standard. White lights meant fancy. Colorful lights meant...homey. I looked at the white lights I was currently streaming along my bushes. Every year I used them to fit in, while secretly putting colorful lights on my tree inside. Because wasn't Christmas supposed to be homey? Home for the holidays? All that jazz?

Snuggle Muffins sighed.

I wasn't sure if it was because he agreed with me or because he was still testy about me putting him in a box. I was going to go with the former. "I know, boy. Screw them." I pulled the white lights off the bushes and shoved them back in the box. This year I hadn't decorated a Christmas tree. Which meant I still had the colorful lights to use outside if I wanted. Actually, I had a lot of colorful lights that I hadn't used in years. I used to string them along garland all over my apartment. Because I was just that homey. I grabbed a strand. I was going to peace out from suburbia in style. By ruining the annual Christmas light competition.

"Oh, colorful lights dear?"

I jumped. *Jesus, Sally.* It was like I'd summoned her. She was a sweet old lady combined with Satan. "Hey, *you.*" I always felt weird calling her Sally because she was so much older than me. It felt like she needed to be Mrs. something. But I'd never caught her last name. And as the years ticked by, I couldn't undo not knowing. It was way too late to rectify the situation. I cleared my throat. "Don't you like them?"

Sally smiled. "Actually I do. But I'm not the one judging the contest. Well, I get one vote, but one vote hardly means anything out of 100 votes."

"I'll vote for myself too. Maybe that'll be enough."

She put her hand on the center of her chest. "You're not supposed to vote for yourself."

"It can be our little secret." I turned my attention back to the bushes I was decorating.

"If you say so." There was an awkward pause and I willed her to walk away. She had to see that I was too preoccupied for her nonsense small talk.

I even started humming *Baby it's Cold Outside* again, hoping she'd get the hint that I was a little busy. But I wasn't so lucky.

"I heard about Noah," she said.

I wasn't sure if there was accusation in her tone or if I'd just imagined it. My fingers froze on the strand of lights. My husband was *missing*. I was supposed to be upset. Distraught. Fragile. Why was I humming Christmas tunes and decorating? Yes, it looked good if they were up for Detective Torres. But I couldn't go back in time. And now all my neighbors could just tell him that I'd only decorated this afternoon. This was a terrible idea.

"I'm just trying to distract myself," I said.

"Hmm. It seems like you're in an awfully good mood for someone whose husband is missing."

Well, that was most definitely accusatory. What the heck was her problem? We'd always been civil before this. "Like I said, I'm trying to distract myself." *Now go away, you old croon.*

"I'm not trying to insinuate anything." She took my hand in hers and patted it. "I'm just saying that it doesn't look like you're upset. And there's been a lot of bad things happening in this neighborhood. Housewives...snapping."

I swallowed hard. Did she know? She was staring at me like she knew. *I don't want to have to kill Sally.*

"I know that Noah kept odd hours for work," she said. "I know he came home late. Left early. I know all this. But you need to look upset, dear. Even if you're not. You don't want anyone to jump to some wild conclusion about you being behind his disappearance."

I didn't know what to say. Had all our neighbors realized our relationship was rocky? I'd tried so hard to hide it. I found myself nodding along.

"You don't want anyone suspecting you. That's all I'm saying." She patted my hand again and let go. "Speaking of suspects,

I'm missing another lawn gnome. You wouldn't know anything about that, would you?"

I had my suspicions. But I didn't know for certain. I shook my head.

She sighed. "Oh well. Cute dog, by the way. I saw you pick him up at the holiday adoption drive at the mall yesterday. I didn't realize you even liked dogs."

Crap, crap, crap! I'd told Detective Torres I'd had Snuggle Muffins for a couple weeks. I needed to make sure Sally didn't say anything to make it seem like I was lying. Even if I was. "You're mistaken. I've had him for a few weeks."

She tilted her head to the side. "No. You got him yesterday. I saw you, Ensley. At the mall. At the adoption drive."

You already said all that. "It must have been someone else. I have one of those faces. And one of those dogs."

"Alright, dear. My lips are sealed. Just...don't make a fool of me like Adeline or Violet did."

I'm going to have to kill Sally.

"I know you're one of the good ones."

Maybe I'll have to kill her. "Thanks." I was pretty sure it came out as more of a question.

"And if you want to win the decoration contest, you should hire an actor. Maybe put a sexy elf man in your front lawn?" And with that comment she waved and continued on her merry way.

She knew my husband and I weren't in a good place. She knew I just got Snuggle Muffins. What else did she know?

CHAPTER 14
Sunday

I was crouched in the bushes on the side of Charlotte's house. Eavesdropping. Because apparently I was a stalker now too. I needed to know what Sally knew. I needed to know if I could trust her. But all I could think about were the spiders probably all over me. Every inch of my skin itched.

I leaned forward and strained to hear her conversation with Sally. My name was in both of their vile mouths. And when I concentrated on them talking instead of the spiders, I could just make out their words.

"Do you think that maybe Noah just...left?" Charlotte asked.

"I think it's possible," Sally replied. "But it's also possible that something happened to him. Something...bad."

I leaned through the foliage so I could stare daggers at her. *What the hell, Sally?* I thought she had my back.

Charlotte shook her head. "It's so frightening. What if she...what if she did something sinister to poor Noah?"

Poor Noah? He was a lying, stealing, cheat! What happened to women sticking together and all that bullshit? They should have my back. Not be gossiping behind it.

"We've known Ensley and Noah for a long time. Do you really think she'd be capable of hurting him?"

"I think that I don't trust anyone in this neighborhood anymore." Charlotte sighed. "Except you of course. And Phoenix and Rosie. And the other women in the book club."

That was pretty much every housewife in this neighborhood but me. *Bitch.*

"I've been talking to my husband, and I think we're going to bring up the possibility of a neighborhood watch at the next civic association meeting."

"What a wonderful idea," Sally said. "A proper lookout would certainly make me feel more comfortable."

That was the last thing I needed. A bunch of nosy neighbors snooping around...oh, wait. They already did that! This conversation was pointless. Neither of them knew anything. And honestly it didn't seem like either of them was necessarily out to get me. They just wanted new gossip. And it just so happened I was a hot topic right now.

I sighed and climbed out the back of the bushes, slapping my arms to remove any spiders. And then I started hitting my ass too as I stepped onto the sidewalk. That's when I knew I'd messed up. Not because I was smacking my ass in the middle of my neighborhood. But because Detective Torres was standing there with his arms crossed over his chest and a scowl on his face.

Shit. How long had he been watching me? I glanced behind me at the bush I'd just crawled out of. Was it at all possible he didn't see me come out of there? Based on the expression of his face...negative. I cleared my throat. "Hey, Detective Torres. How are you today?" *Smooth.*

"Ensley, do you want to tell me what you were doing hiding in your neighbor's bushes?"

No, obviously not. "Hiding?" I laughed. "Whaaa..." I shook my head. "Oh, you thought?" I laughed harder. "I wasn't hiding. I'm not a peeping Tom." *Don't give it a label!*

He kept his arms folded across his chest and hardened his stare. "Then what were you doing?"

"Vandalism." *Vandalism? What the ever-living fuck?*

"Excuse me?"

"The annual Christmas light competition is this tomorrow. And I...knew I couldn't win. So I was cutting some of the wires on Charlotte's lights. Snippety snip and victory will be mine."

"With what?"

"What now?"

"What were you cutting Charlotte's lights with? I don't see any scissors. Or wire cutters. Or a chainsaw. Nothing."

I pretended to gnaw through an imaginary wire. And then I laughed. And laughed some more. Trying to buy time. I slapped my leg. "Got you! Do I really look like someone interested in sabotage?" I laughed again. "You should see your face!"

He just stared at me. He did not find this funny. At all.

"Sabotage." I shook my head. "No. No. I...Snuggle Muffins got out!" Now that was a brilliant excuse. Too bad it came to me a few minutes too late. "And I thought I saw him go under these bushes. So I climbed in after him without thinking about the fact that I'm so much bigger. And then I kind of got caught." I twisted my body in the air and froze for effect. "And I couldn't get out. But then I fought through the devil hedge. And Snuggle Muffins wasn't there anymore. I can't lose him too." *Cry. Force yourself to cry right this second.* I wasn't sure if I looked sad or if I was grimacing, but his eyes softened.

"I'm sure he's here somewhere." He whistled. "Here, Snuggle Muffins! Here boy!"

Wow. Detective Torres was a certified idiot. "Snuggle Muffins!" I called.

"Is everything alright?" Charlotte asked as she and Sally hurried toward us on the sidewalk.

"Yes, ma'am." Detective Torres nodded at her. "Ensley's dog got away from her, but we'll find him."

"Oh, he's right there." Sally pointed toward my house.

Sure enough, Snuggle Muffins was sitting on my front porch staring at me.

What a good boy. I'd told him to stay and he had. I knew I should have pushed him back inside when I went to go spy, but he'd made a fuss. So I'd told him to stay and run off into the bushes. And he'd...waited. A smile curled onto my lips.

I ran over to Snuggle Muffins and lifted him in my arms. "You're okay!" I exclaimed for the audience. "Thank goodness!" I kissed the side of his furry little head and tried not to gag. "Thank you for saving me from that sticky situation, mister," I whispered to him. "I really appreciate it." I kissed the side of his face again and this time I didn't even think about gagging.

He just sighed.

"Well, I'm glad we found your dog," Detective Torres said as he joined me in my lawn. "I don't have as good news about your husband."

I tried to ignore the fact that Sally and Charlotte were still staring at me. "He wasn't in Canada?" I asked.

"Do you mind if I come in so we can talk?"

"Of course not." I gave him my brightest smile as I opened the front door. "Come in, come in." Being overly welcoming was on my to-do list today. So was making sure he didn't get a chance to knock or ring the doorbell. Check and check. Hopefully Noah wouldn't even realize I had company. And if he did...hopefully my accidentally illicit promise would keep him quiet.

As soon as I closed the front door behind us I realized just how bad an idea this was. I couldn't trust Noah. I knew better. I wasn't even sure I could trust myself. All I wanted to do was go double-check the deadbolt. I swallowed hard.

"Nice place you have here," Detective Torres said.

"Thanks." I realized I was still holding Snuggle Muffins to my chest. "Go play," I said and set him down. But instead of running off he just plopped down next to me like he always did. "So...um...you said you didn't find Noah?"

Detective Torres shook his head. "Unfortunately not." He shoved his hands into the pockets of his jeans and stared at me. Like he was waiting for something.

I didn't want to invite him further into my house. I wanted him to stay right where he was. "Did you talk to Sophia?"

"The local precinct brought her in for questioning. They let me listen in. I'm really sorry, Ensley. But...your husband wasn't with her."

I nodded. "Okay." My whole body felt cold. But he was having an affair with her, right? I wanted to scream the question at him. But I didn't have to. I knew it. I knew it and yet...ouch. For a second last night I believed that it had only been one kiss. I'd believed what I'd wanted to believe. But Noah was no saint.

"I'm sorry I don't have better news."

"That's fine. Let me show you out." I gestured to the door.

He didn't move. "We have a little more to discuss about Sophia Tremblay. Actually, a lot more."

"We do?"

"Did your husband...did he hurt you?"

Noah never hit me. But the things he said to me? I was reminded of that old lie about "sticks and stones may break my bones but words will never hurt me." That person didn't know my husband. His words were as sharp as knives. "No."

"Never?"

It felt like I was shrinking under his gaze. And I found myself wanting to say…sometimes. *Maybe.* "No. I don't understand what this has to do with him being missing."

"He hurt her."

I shook my head. My husband was a lot of things. But he wouldn't physically hurt someone. He wouldn't. "I don't understand."

"They weren't dating."

"I'm sorry, I really don't understand. Of course they were dating. You just told me that my husband was unfaithful. He..."

"She claims that he was stalking her. That he was obsessed with her." He pulled out his phone and handed it to me.

There was a picture of a brunette woman. Maybe she was beautiful. I couldn't really be sure. Because her face was swollen. A huge bruise encased her eye. Her lip was busted. But despite the injuries, she looked familiar. She looked like me.

"The last time she saw him, he did this to her. You're sure he never laid a hand on you?"

All I could hear was my own breathing. It felt like my throat was constricting. "Never." This didn't make sense. He wouldn't have done this. All I wanted to do was run to the basement and demand answers. But Noah didn't remember. I looked back down at the picture. How could he have done this?

"Are you sure?" he asked. His words hung in the air.

I nodded. I couldn't stop looking at the picture. Detective Torres had to be right. My husband wouldn't cheat on me with a woman who looked so similar to me. But he wouldn't have been stalking her either. What the hell was he doing with Sophia Tremblay? "Do you think...does she look like me?" I finally looked up at him as he pulled his phone out of my hand.

"She was about your height. Same hair color. Same eye color."

"That doesn't make any sense. Why would he be stalking a woman who looks like me?"

Detective Torres slid the phone back into his pocket. "I was hoping you could help me with that question, Ensley."

I shook my head. "I'm as lost as you."

"Are you? Because I took a more thorough look at those documents you gave me. Some of the credit card statements and phone bills only contained half the month. Some months are completely missing. And now that I think about it, you were awfully quick to hand over all that information. Almost like you had it prepared ahead of time. The only suspicious thing at all was that weekly phone call to Canada."

I swallowed hard. I did have it prepared ahead of time. I'd prepped everything perfectly and now it was biting me in the ass. "I'm just organized. And I have a love of shredding unnecessary papers. I don't save everything. I'm not a hoarder."

"I have another theory. I think you knew your husband was up to no good. Maybe you thought he was having an affair instead of stalking Sophia. But either way you knew something was up. So you led me on a wild goose chase to Canada."

"You said you already had personal business in Canada. It wasn't even out of your way. There was no wild goose chase. You were on a trip."

"The reason for my trip isn't the point, Ensley."

I stared at him. He looked...flustered. Maybe his trip wasn't the point he was trying to make, but now I was curious. "Why were you in Canada, Detective Torres?"

"Excuse me?"

"What personal business did you have there?"

He shook his head. "It was *personal*. And this isn't about me. This is about you. I'm doing the questioning here."

I pressed my lips together. The air in the room had shifted. He wasn't just a friendly neighborhood detective stopping by for a chat. He suspected me. He didn't have to say the words, I could see it in his eyes. But there was something else in his eyes too. Guilt maybe? *What are you hiding, Detective Torres?*

"Ensley, do you know where your husband is?"

Tied up right underneath your nose, detective. "No."

"Will you give me the missing records?"

I'd only given him the records because I couldn't trace that damn phone number. But now I knew about Sophia Tremblay. Even if the information didn't make any sense. "I told you. If they weren't in the box, I shredded them a long time ago."

He nodded. "Great. Well, I've requested access to his phone records and bills straight from the source."

Shit. How long will that take? I knew I was running out of time. I knew I was playing with fire. But I couldn't walk away now. I was so close. "That's fine, I have nothing to hide."

"So you don't mind if I take a look around your house?"

I had to hand it to him. That was a perfect freaking trap. "Of course not." I knew he'd eventually ask. I knew it and yet I was still hoping he wouldn't. That maybe, just maybe, chasing Sophia would get him off my back. After all, she had a motive. I thought it would be a classic jealous sidepiece motive, but this was even better. Noah had hurt her. She should have been Detective Torres' top suspect. So why had he come back here sniffing around my house? Had Sophia really seemed that innocent?

I watched as Detective Torres stopped in the hall to look at a framed picture of Noah and me. Could he tell that my smile was fake? Could he really see all the lies that easily? I watched him walk down the hall and into the kitchen.

Snuffle Muffins looked up at me.

It's okay, boy. I'll handle this. I followed Detective Torres into the kitchen. My taser was burning a hole in my back pocket. I had spare rope and an extra chair downstairs just for this occasion. And my litter box was plenty big enough to share. *Sorry not sorry, Detective Torres.*

CHAPTER 15
Sunday

"The last time I saw my husband he was upstairs," I said. "We have this routine where I always straighten his tie before he heads to work." It was a final attempt at stalling him. Because I would tase him. I would. "And he was notoriously bad at matching a tie with his dress shirt. I'm pretty sure he was colorblind. He was always putting tan and gray together."

Detective Torres turned around.

I hadn't left my post in the hallway. I couldn't follow him into the kitchen knowing that there were two doors in there that led to terrible things. One to the garage, which was filled with evidence. And one to the basement, which was filled with Noah. I had to think of a reason, any reason, why Detective Torres should at least avoid the basement. But all I could think about was Noah being incompetent at matching colors. *Oh God.* I also had weed sitting in my utensil drawer. I'd tossed it in there to hide it, but what if he decided he needed a fork for something? Or a knife? "I've already looked everywhere for clues," I said. "But maybe I missed something upstairs?"

"Great," Detective Torres said and walked back toward me. "I'll start my search upstairs then. After you."

If I walked up the stairs ahead of him, he'd notice the taser bulging in my back pocket. "No, after you, good sir." I bowed awkwardly.

He walked past me without reacting.

I ignored Snuggle Muffins' whimpers as I went up the stairs without him. I followed Detective Torres as he made his way from the master bedroom, to the guest room, to an empty room at the end of the hall.

"What used to be in here?" he asked.

I leaned against the doorjamb. "It was going to be a nursery." The walls were still mint green. I'd thought it was so cute. More unique than blue. But the only thing that ended up being unique about the nursery was that it was empty. "I lost the baby."

He turned away from the emptiness. "I'm sorry."

I nodded. I wanted to be able to pretend that I wasn't sorry. That maybe my son would have turned out like his horrible father. But I couldn't pretend. Because what if he hadn't? My son would have been good. I would have raised him right. He would have saved me from all of this.

"Is there a reason why you don't want me in your kitchen?"

I had to hand it to Detective Torres. He kept me off-kilter. "I didn't make any snacks."

He laughed. "I'm not here to eat."

"Then why are you here?"

An awkward silence stretched between us. "Let me ask you a question, Ensley. You knew who I was when I first showed up on your doorstep."

That wasn't a question. "Everyone knows everyone around here."

"No. You were talking about my last case. Did you know either Violet Clark or Adeline Bell?"

I shook my head.

"But you just said it yourself. Everyone knows everyone around here."

I remained perched in the doorway even though every instinct in my body was screaming at me to run. "Right. Of course I've heard of them. I saw them around town on occasion. At the grocery store or at the mall. But they both mostly kept to themselves."

"Do you mostly keep to yourself?"

I'd overheard Charlotte ask Adeline to her book club countless times. Adeline always refused. And Violet lived in the woods, far away from prying eyes. The two of them isolated themselves on purpose. I'd always wanted to fit in. "Not by choice."

"But you do keep mostly to yourself?"

"I'm not like them." The way he was looking at me made my heart race. He thought I was a monster. And he was right. But I wasn't a copy-cat serial killer. I was a kidnapper. That was it.

"Adeline lost a baby. Just like you."

I opened my mouth and then closed it again. What was his point? That didn't make us the same. There was no miscarriage club in town. "I didn't know that."

"Well, did you know that Detective Ben Jones woke up the other day?"

My heart started racing. I knew all about Ben Jones. He was the undercover detective working on Adeline Bell's case. He'd been in a coma for months. I'd followed all of it so closely on the news. What had happened to Ben was a tragedy. The whole town was rallied around him. But in reality? He was a damned fool. "Is he okay?"

"The doctors at the hospital said so. But I never got to see for myself. Because he went missing a few hours after he woke up."

"Missing?"

"Just like your husband, Ensley. Poof. Gone. The same day that your husband went missing. That's quite a coincidence, isn't it?"

My palms were starting to sweat. If I went for my taser now, it might slip. I couldn't risk it. "Yes."

He shook his head and took a few steps closer to me. "I don't believe in coincidences."

Could he see me sweating? Could he tell that I was shaking? Was he trying to make me run? To trick me into making a wrong move? I tried not to flinch when he stepped even closer. "Then what do you believe in?"

"Justice." His eyes bore into mine.

I was wrong before. Detective Torres wasn't a bad detective. Sophia Tremblay should be his number one suspect. Yet...he was here. And I was pretty sure the only thing driving him was his intuition. Which was good. Because I was so freaking guilty. "Aren't there cameras in the hospital? Someone must have seen what happened to Ben. You can rule out coincidence by just looking at the footage."

"They were switched off in that wing of the hospital for maintenance. Can you believe it?"

"Yes."

He shook his head. "But that would be a coincidence. Ensley, we just talked about this. No. No, I think someone switched those cameras off on purpose. Someone planned it perfectly. The only question is...who."

"It wasn't me."

He folded his arms across his chest. "Huh. I never even considered you. But now that you mention it..." He just stared at me.

He absolutely had been implying that it was me. Did he really think I could be part of that disappearance too? That was...ridiculous. I just stared back. "My husband is missing. I haven't been sleeping." At least half of that was true. "I'm a nervous wreck. Are you seriously going to come into my house and imply that I hurt my husband and am somehow involved with some strange guy I don't even know?"

"*Hurt* your husband? I never said anything about hurting anyone."

I was pretty sure he had me right where he wanted me. And I needed him to get the hell out of my house. "If you're here to arrest me, just do it. But I'm not guilty. So you'll never find any evidence to hold me. I'll be out within 24 hours and you'll be 24 hours behind on helping find my husband."

"Would that be 24 hours too late?"

I closed my eyes like his implications physically exhausted me. "I just want to find Noah. I want all of this to be over. I want my life back." All of that was true. But I wanted my old life back. The one I had before I'd ever met Noah. I wanted to be free from him. I just wasn't sure if that was possible.

"Then you won't mind me looking around your kitchen." He brushed past me in the doorway and was already heading down the stairs before I turned.

Shit. I ran after him and tried to get him to go into the dining room. Living room. Family room. Any room. I even tried to force him to go outside and play fetch with Snuggle Muffins, something I was sure Snuggle Muffins would not enjoy. But Detective Torres ignored me and went right back into the kitchen.

He was in the center of the kitchen looking around the island. It was clear to him that I was hiding something. He just had no idea it was connected to the kitchen. Not in it. He opened the drawer next to the one with weed and I swear I stopped breathing. *Crap, the drugs.* If I didn't do something, he'd find my weed stash and he'd have an actual reason to arrest me. Well, another reason. The whole kidnapping my husband thing was a good reason too.

I glanced at the basement door and then back at him. "Are you happy with your search now, detective? Because I think it's time for you to go."

He closed the drawer. "I think only a guilty person would ask a detective to leave her house. I thought you wanted me to look for clues?"

"I would if you didn't think I was somehow mixed up in Noah's disappearance. You're wasting time by being here."

"I'm not so sure about that." His hand landed on the handle of the weed drawer. Like he had a death wish. I could already picture him convulsing on the floor after I tased him. It would be a quick draw, straight from a black and white cowboy film. But I had a feeling he'd be faster. I didn't want a bullet in my chest. This needed to end peacefully even if it meant me begging on my knees.

"Please," I said. I thought of death. Destruction. Natural disasters. Even the horrible image I'd had this morning of Noah dead at the basement stairs. And somehow I mustered the despair to make a single tear fall down my cheek. "I don't know how to live without him."

The accusation in Detective Torres' eyes faded as quickly as my fake tears had formed. His hand fell from the handle. "Then help me understand. Tell me why you don't wear your wedding ring."

Oh. God. I glanced down at my empty ring finger. Why did I keep forgetting to put on my wretched rings? What was wrong with me? "You made it seem like he cheated on me. I thought...I thought you were going to find him with that Sophia woman. Shacking up. I've never felt so broken." I put my hand over my mouth to pretend I was seconds away from breaking down in front of him. There was nothing men hated more than feeling uncomfortable around a sobbing woman.

"It doesn't seem like that was the case, Ensley. It was definitely something more sinister. Do you have any idea why he would be following Sophia Tremblay?"

If I did I wouldn't tell you. "No. I'm sorry. But you have to believe me. I love my husband. I was blindsided by the fact that he might be cheating. But I'd never hurt him." I shook my head. "And Ben? Yes, I like to watch the local news. That doesn't mean I...what...somehow kidnapped him from the hospital? That's crazy." I'd only kidnapped Noah. Geez. "I just like being well informed of local crime." I dropped my voice to a whisper. "Especially since so many of the housewives in the area seem cray cray." I walked around the kitchen island to block his view of the basement door, Snuggle Muffins hot on my trail. I was worried that Detective Torres would see the deadbolt and start asking questions he had no business asking. Luckily Snuggle Muffins looking semi-adorable on the floor right in front of him was a decent distraction.

Detective Torres reached down and scratched behind his ear. "Well, the vultures are starting to swarm the station already. They got a whiff of this case. It will probably be on the nightly news at this rate."

"I never wanted to be on it." But I did. I really really did. It took everything in me not to jump up and down. I was going to be famous. More famous than all the other murderous women in little old Wilmington, Delaware. And I was playing Detective

Torres like a fiddle. I pressed my lips together and shook my head. "I can't believe this is happening. Maybe it's one of those murderous lunatics you mentioned that is doing this. Violet or Adeline?" Throwing my previous neighbors under the bus seemed like a pretty good idea. They were already wanted.

Detective Torres shook his head. "No. I don't think so."

"Maybe Sophia's lying."

Detective Torres shook his head.

"Maybe Noah and she actually got into a lover's quarrel that turned physical...that left him dead."

He sighed and ran his fingers through his hair. "The last thing I need is for this to turn into a homicide. I'm still hoping he turns up." He closed the distance between us. "I'm sorry about earlier. I just...I couldn't get you not wearing your rings out of my head. And the coincidences with Ben disappearing too. I need to figure this out before I..." his voice trailed off.

"Before you what?"

"You saw the news, Ensley. My last partner ran off with a serial killer we were hunting. I let him get away. My job is on the line. I need to find Noah or I'll lose everything. This case is my last chance to prove myself."

I stared at him like I was seeing him for the first time. He looked exhausted, just like a man who was about to lose his job might look. But there was one thing that didn't line up with his story. A man about to lose his job wouldn't have just taken a mini vacation in Canada. It didn't make sense. What the hell was he really doing in Canada?

"You can be honest with me, Ensley," he said. "If your husband did hurt you, I'd believe you." He reached out and lightly touched my elbow. "You can trust me."

Oh my God. Did he seriously think the whole "you can trust me" line would work on me? If he thought my husband hurt me, I'd for sure become his number one suspect if I wasn't already. He'd let Sophia Tremblay off the hook, but I had a feeling he wouldn't let me off so easily. "Noah never hurt me." *He broke me.*

"Okay. Try not to watch the news tonight. At least alone. The vultures are out for blood." Detective Torres' hand slowly fell from my elbow, his fingers trailing down my forearm for a second too long.

I tried not to glare at him. First the whole pretend being worried about me thing. And now the lingering touch? Detective Torres was trying to play me. Could he be any more transparent? It was like he was waiting for me to say, "I wouldn't be alone if you joined me." *How about you just sign me up for an orange jumpsuit and prison cell tonight.* Vomit. I didn't need another stupid guy hitting on me constantly. I already had Noah shirtless and tied to a chair downstairs. That was enough. "Try to find my husband." My tone was icier than I meant for it to be.

He nodded. "Just two more questions for you and I'll be on my way. You have Christmas lights strung outside, but not a single decoration inside. Not even a red and green hand towel. Nothing. Why is that?"

To fool you. "Christmas is the last thing on my mind right now, detective."

"But you still decorated outside?"

"Weeks ago for the silly neighborhood lighting contest." I stared at him for a moment, waiting for him to call me out on my lie. But he didn't. *Such a bad detective.* And I doubted Sally would blab that I was decorating just hours ago. It seemed like she had my back. Kind of. "Noah and I always get a real tree closer to Christmas. We like decorating it kind of last minute to really feel that Christmas spirit, you know? Actually, we probably would have gotten it today if he was here." I sniffled.

He nodded and then stepped around me. "Final question before I head back to the precinct. What do you keep down there?" He nodded at the door behind me. "It's a little unusual to have a deadbolt on your basement door."

Keep breathing. Stay calm. I'd had an answer for this all along. And it wasn't even a complete lie. "Just storage. I've always been scared of basements ever since I was a little girl. I had terrible nightmares. I always made Noah go down there for me. Actually, that's probably one of the reasons I haven't decorated too. All the decorations are down there." The words slipped out of me. And as soon as I said them, I knew it was a mistake. A terrible, horrible mistake.

"Well, let me grab them for you real quick," Detective Torres said. He was already walking around me. "I think a little Christmas magic is just what we need right now."

Why? Why on earth would I tell him my Christmas decorations were down there? That my lovely missing husband couldn't grab them for me? That I was basically a damsel in distress when it came to basements? "That's not necessary."

"It's no problem at all. Your house could use a little Christmas cheer, don't you think?" The deadbolt clicked as he turned it.

"Really, Detective Torres. You're already doing so much for me. You don't have to." *Don't do it. You'll regret it.*

The door squeaked as he opened it. "I don't mind, Ensley." He flicked on the lights.

Fuck. Me. This was it. I was going to have to tase him. But my hand didn't reach for my taser. I remembered the feeling of waking up and believing my hands were covered in blood. The warm sticky feeling on my palms. The way the blood soaked into the wooden steps. The feeling of relief. Maybe it was a premonition. I knew what kind of damage these stairs could do. All I had to do was push him. If I was lucky his skull would crack open. Not only would I get Detective Torres out of my hair, I'd also scare the shit out of Noah. He'd tell me anything I wanted. Kill two birds with one stone. A pretty sick saying for the sick thing I was about to do.

But my body didn't move as Detective Torres took the first step. It was like I was frozen in place. I watched him take another step. And another. My heart was racing too fast. I felt like I was going to faint. And for some reason *Baby it's Cold Outside* started running through my head at a super slow pace. It almost sounded like the song was skipping on an old record player. The eerie scratching echoing around me, like the song was dying slowly. Detective Torres kept descending the stairs as the rendition of *Baby it's Cold Outside* haunted my reality. In a few seconds he was too far away for me to push him to his death.

"Cute reindeer," he called from the bottom of the stairs. "Do you want me to bring him up?"

I waited for his reaction to seeing Noah tied up. A scream. A curse. Anything.

And I waited.

And I waited.

"Ensley?" he said. "Did you hear me? Do you want me to bring the reindeer up? What other decorations are down here?"

Snuggle Muffins barked. An actual bark. Not a whimper or a sigh. It was like he was trying to pull me out of my trance. Like he was trying to save me. I shook my head, trying to get the haunting tune out of my head.

What the hell? Why wasn't Detective Torres talking about the fact that I had Noah tied up shirtless to a chair in the middle of my basement? Next to a litter box and a plate of bacon? For a second I considered slamming the door and locking it. But Detective Torres would find a way out. He wasn't tied up like Noah was.

I'd missed my chance at pushing him down the stairs. I had to suck it up and tase his ass. Before I ran out of time. And I was definitely running out of it. He was probably down there radioing the police station this second. Whispering so I couldn't hear him. I couldn't let him get that call through. I needed to end this. *Now.*

My feet finally started to move. Snuggle Muffins whimpered from behind me when I didn't bring him along for the show. But I didn't want him to see me do this. I didn't want him to look at me like I was a monster too.

I put my hand in my back pocket and gripped the taser. My plan was to tackle him from behind and then tase the side of his neck before he could react. I was ready to jump off the stairs and fly through the air. But when I reached the bottom of the stairs I knew why Detective Torres hadn't said a word about my hostage. It wasn't because he was secretly calling the police station.

No. Detective Torres hadn't said a word because there was nothing to say. The chair that Noah had been tied to was empty.

CHAPTER 16
Sunday

I blinked. Something must have gone wrong with my brain. A faulty wire somewhere. Maybe something had short-circuited. I blinked again, but the chair was still empty. Noah was nowhere in sight. The chair was also pushed against the wall instead of in the middle of the basement. It looked like it hadn't been used in years. I swore it even looked a little dusty. The plate of bacon was missing. It was like it had never even existed. Even the litter box was pushed to the side. Out of sight, out of mind.

I tried to take a deep, steadying breath, but it felt like I was hyperventilating. There was no way I'd imagined kidnapping Noah and trapping him down here. So...where the hell was he? I glanced at the small window above the shelves. Noah's shoulders were so broad. There was no way he could fit through that. Right?

But I wasn't sure. If he twisted just so it was possible that he could get through. All the boxes on the shelves beneath the window looked untouched, though. If he had struggled to fit through a teensy window, he surely would have wreaked havoc on my organization. No. He was still down here. But where?

I glanced toward the crawl space on the other side of the basement. It was pretty much the only place he could be hiding. But if he was down here, why was he hiding? A detective was literally standing here hoping to find him and help him. This was Noah's chance to be saved. It didn't make any sense. The little hairs on the back of my neck rose and I turned behind me toward the stairs. Snuggle Muffins' was sitting at the top of the stairs staring down at me. He whimpered.

"Ensley?" Detective Torres said.

I turned toward him. The lines on his forehead made it seem like he was concerned. Like he'd been trying to get my attention for a while.

I cleared my throat, but it still sounded shaky. "Yes?" Any second now Noah could jump out and yell, "Save me!" My fate was in his hands. I tried to ignore the empty chair. I hadn't imagined it. I...couldn't have. I wasn't crazy. He was down here somewhere. He had to be. And he was just hiding because he didn't want me to get in trouble? That didn't make any sense either. Maybe he was somewhere else in the house? Had the deadbolt been locked? It had. I know it had. *I'd never leave it unlocked.*

"Is this the right one?" Detective Torres lifted a plastic storage container labeled "Christmas Decorations" from the shelf.

I nodded.

"Great. I got this if you want to grab the reindeer." He shifted the container to one side so he could see me. "Are you okay? It looks like you've seen a ghost."

"Not a ghost." But I wasn't sure anymore. I swallowed hard. "I just...it's hard thinking about decorating for Christmas when Noah's out there somewhere." *Somewhere loose in my freaking house!* "Scared." It all came out as more of a question. And I was pretty sure I was the scared one, not Noah. Because I wasn't sure about any of it anymore. What if... I let my thoughts trail off. *I'm not crazy.* "I just love him so much." *Am I crazy?*

"We're going to find him. He'll be home safe before Christmas."

I was going to be long gone before Christmas. And another fruitless promise from Detective Torres wasn't going to change that. But I could feel my own plans crumbling around me. What if I had dreamed of kidnapping him? Just like I imagined his blood covering the steps? The image in my head was so vivid. It felt so real. I picked up the reindeer and hoped Detective Torres wouldn't notice my hands shaking. "I hope you're right."

"What's with the litter box?"

I tried to ignore the fact that it had moved. "I'm litter training Snuggle Muffins."

"Is that even possible?"

"Of course. He's very smart for a dog."

Detective Torres laughed.

I did too. But I didn't know what was funny. I was pretty sure most dogs were idiots. But Snuggle Muffins seemed very intelligent to me. Not that I actually liked him. I looked up the steps again and Snuggle Muffins was still staring at me. He was the reason why I felt like someone was watching me. Which meant...it was very possible that Noah wasn't here. It was possible that he was never here. Noah had called me crazy a few weeks ago when I tried to talk to him about his late nights. He'd said I was "insane." That my "imagination was running wild again."

Detective Torres walked past me and started up the stairs. The odds that Noah was still down here were fairly high. *If* he'd ever been down here.

Stop. There were no ifs. My husband was wrong. I wasn't crazy. He was down here. He was hiding in the crawl space and not getting help from Detective Torres for God knows what reason. And I had to make sure he didn't escape.

I retreated after Detective Torres. When I reached the top of the stairs I wanted to slam the door closed and slide the deadbolt back in place. But Detective Torres was standing there with his back pressed against the open door waiting for me.

"After you," I said.

He smiled. "You have to show me where you want these."

"The family room." I waited for him to leave the door, but he didn't. Because he had no idea where the family room was. I'd tried to get him to search it earlier, but he'd been dead set on searching the kitchen. I started walking toward the family room and the hairs on the back of my neck rose again. But I knew it was only Detective Torres behind me. I placed the reindeer down.

"Don't you want to take that outside?" he asked.

No. I didn't want to leave the house. Because then I'd have to come back in. Noah could move anywhere he pleased if I left the house. But Detective Torres was staring at me expectantly. "Yes."

A floorboard creaked behind me as Detective Torres set down his box. My heartbeat kicked up a notch as I slowly turned around. But it was just Snuggle Muffins walking into the room. He sat down by my feet and almost immediately fell asleep. He was a worthless guard dog. I'd be all on my own when I came back inside.

Detective Torres grabbed the reindeer for me and headed to the front door. It wasn't too late. I could still run back and lock the basement door. But Detective Torres was standing there, waiting patiently for me. *Fuck my life.* I cringed as I closed the front door behind us. Noah had free rein of the house. He could literally go anywhere. Including out the back door. No, he hadn't gotten help from Detective Torres. But that didn't mean he didn't want to be free. Of course he'd escape. It was done. And I'd never get my answers now.

"Is here good?" Detective Torres asked. He plugged the reindeer into a string of lights when I nodded.

"It's perfect." I wanted to cry. All that planning. All those hours perfecting every single detail. It had all gone up in flames. I could picture Noah running out the back door and into the woods. *Gone.*

"Let's see the whole display," he said and rubbed his hands together.

I plugged it in and the strings of connected multi-colored lights came to life. A few of my neighbors had already lit up their displays even though the sun hadn't quite set. The multi-colored lights were already jarring against the other cookie-cutter houses' white lights. "Thank you for your help with these," I said. "With everything really."

He smiled. "Of course. And if you happen upon those missing files..."

"I'll take another look. I promise." He'd fake promised me a lot of things too. Now we were even.

"And if you hear anything about Noah or Ben. You let me know."

Of course. But I had nothing to tell him anymore. Noah was probably already running through the woods out back. And every second I stood here, the farther away he got.

Detective Torres shook my hand before climbing into his car. I watched him drive down the street, past all the perfectly manicured lawns and white lights, until he was out of view.

And then I ran. I knew I should have just gotten into my car and driven away. I had an escape plan and I should have already started the process. But Noah didn't remember me. He didn't remember what he had done. He'd ruined every single one of my plans ever since he'd fallen down the bloody stairs. And I wasn't done with him yet. So I didn't run to the garage to drive away. I ran to the back yard and into the woods.

I pulled out my taser as I ducked under a branch. I wanted to call out Noah's name but I didn't dare, just in case I wasn't alone out here. This was the only way for him to escape. Straight through the woods, past the lake, and out to the main road. He didn't know I was hot on his trail though. I could catch up. *Maybe*.

My feet ached from running in my boots. And my bangs stuck to my forehead with sweat. But I made it to the clearing by the lake in record time. I turned in a circle, staring at the forest all around the lake. But there was nothing out here. Nothing but caution tape, warning you to stay away from the lake.

A snowflake landed on the tip of my nose. I looked up to see the flurries swirling through the air. Snow so close to Christmas always felt special. But today it just felt like a bad omen. Snow meant the temperature was below freezing.

I stared out at the lake as the snow slowly fell. Every inch of that lake had been searched for bodies. A total of three had been pulled out of the cold depths thanks to Detective Torres' failure on his last case. It was the perfect place to hide another one. No one was going to be searching here again anytime soon.

Sinking a dead body into this lake was on my to-do list right after getting my answers. Well, as an option at least. Just in case things went south. It was a great plan. Flawless in every way I thought it through.

There was just one problem. The lake was completely frozen over. I never expected the temperatures to drop so quickly before Christmas. I watched as the snowflakes land on top of the ice in silence.

Actually there were two problems. Not only was the lake frozen, but I'd lost the body that I wanted to hide in the lake. Noah was gone. The snow started to pick up as I stared at the sheet of ice.

Now I'd never get my answers. I'd never figure out if I had what it took to get away with the perfect crime. I thought I'd cry. But instead a scream pierced through the silence. I touched my lips. I wouldn't have even realized it was me screaming if my lips weren't parted. Maybe Noah was right all along. Maybe I was crazy.

CHAPTER 17
Sunday

I opened the front door as quietly as possible. I knew Noah was gone. He'd just run through the woods faster than me so I couldn't catch up. I knew that. It was the only logical conclusion. But a tiny part of me hoped that I was wrong. What if he hadn't left? What if he'd hidden in the crawl space to...protect me?

At the same time though, I hoped he had left. Because I was terrified that he was still inside. I'd drugged him. I'd tied him up. I'd gotten him drunk. I'd tried to starve him. I'd tased him while his pants were around his ankles. I'd made him pee in a litter box. I'd pushed him down the stairs. *Slipped. He slipped down the stairs.*

God, if he was in there, he might try to kill me. If the tables were turned, I'm sure I would try to kill him. I'd think of a million ways to murder him and pick the best one.

Outside was a winter wonderland. Even though the sun had set, there was that strange orange glow in the air that always accompanied snow at night. It was magical. Some of the neighborhood kids were running around their yards catching snowflakes on their tongues. But it wasn't magical for me. Because I was staring into a dark house praying not to be murdered. The children's laughter echoed around me as I pushed the door open farther. Why had I stood at the lake for so long? If I'd hurried back I wouldn't be walking into a dark house.

"Noah?" I whispered.

Silence.

I pulled my taser out and held it in front of me. "Noah?"

Snuggle Muffins barking almost made me scream.

"Jesus, you scared me." I lifted my finger to my lips. "We have to be quiet." I lifted his furry little body and held him in front of me like a shield. I thought his presence might comfort me, but it didn't. Now I was just worried that me and my dog were about to be murdered.

More children's laughter behind me sent a chill down my spine. *Get a grip.* I stepped into the house and quickly flicked on the lights. I breathed a sigh of relief when the foyer was empty.

"See, it's fine," I said more to myself than Snuggle Muffins. "We're fine." I peered into the living room and held my breath as I flipped on those lights too. *Nothing.* The room looked remarkably unremarkable like always. But still I found myself whispering, "Noah?"

There was no answer.

If only I wasn't a criminal, I could have called the cops. Snuggle Muffins whimpered and I realized I was holding him too tightly.

"I'm sorry, boy." I set him down on the oriental rug. "Do you know if Noah's here?" I whispered. "Can you show me where he is?"

Snuggle Muffins just looked up at me.

I pointed back to the foyer. "Go."

And he surprised me by walking away.

Oh my God, he knows where Noah is! I should have been slowly creeping along with my back against the hallway wall, but Snuggle Muffins leading the way somehow felt safe. He was the front line. He'd protect me. But when he led me to the kitchen and started eating from his food bowl, I felt like I was going to throw up. He wasn't protecting me. He was just a tiny mutt.

I turned in a circle, taking in the whole room. I even crouched down and looked under the kitchen table. "Noah?" My voice kept sounding shakier and shakier.

The basement. *I should definitely start in the basement.* Maybe he hadn't moved at all. Maybe he was scared I'd kill him, not the other way around. For the first time in days the basement door was wide open. And I knew that I could be getting myself in a pickle by walking down those stairs. He could easily lock me in if he was up here. But I didn't know what else to do. So I lifted up Snuggle Muffins again and used him as a shield as I walked down the creaky stairs.

"Noah? It's safe to come out. The detective's gone." I stepped down onto the concrete floor and waited a beat for a response.

The only one I got was a grumble from Snuggle Muffins. He was probably annoyed that I'd taken him away from his food and kept using him as a meat shield.

First I checked the window. The lock was still in place. He couldn't have gotten out that way. I glanced over at the crawl space. I really, really didn't want to have to go over there. I didn't want to die today.

I pulled on one of the light cords to illuminate the basement even more. But somehow that just cast shadows and made the crawl space look even darker and more sinister.

"We'll be okay," I said to Snuggle Muffins. Noah wouldn't hurt me when I had a dog in my hands. Yes, he was a monster. But animal abuse? That was a whole other level of evil. My feet shuffled closer to the crawl space. "Noah?" I could barely even hear my own voice. "Please just come out."

No response.

Fuck my life. I tightened my grip on Snuggle Muffins and my taser as I pressed my back against the wall beside the crawl space.

I closed my eyes and took a deep breath. I just needed to get it over with. It was tempting to throw Snuggle Muffins inside the crawl space and wait to see what happened. But I wasn't a monster either. And I liked the little guy more than I wanted to admit.

"Save yourself," I whispered into his ear before setting him down. "And don't eat my body."

He just sighed and sat down next to my feet.

Here goes nothing. Before I could chicken out, I hoisted myself into the crawl space and reached forward to grab the cord. After flailing my arms around for what felt like an eternity, I finally made purchase. I pulled the cord and the crawl space was illuminated. The very empty crawl space. The only thing in it was a pile of rope.

I swallowed hard. It was the rope I'd used to tie Noah up. He had been up here watching me and Detective Torres. So why hadn't he come out? I sat down for a second. What the hell was his game? I was worried I wouldn't live to find out, because my chest felt like it was about to explode. I wasn't sure my heart had ever beat so fast.

All I knew for sure was that Noah had a chance to turn me in. And he hadn't done it. I lifted the rope. He also wasn't in the basement, unless he had dug a hole to China somewhere. I tossed the rope out of the crawl space.

Snuggle Muffins yelped.

I leaned out of the crawlspace to see him maneuvering through the rope.

"You're fine." I jumped down and scooped him up. "And we're not crazy. See, Noah was definitely here. I'm not crazy." I hugged my dog closer to my chest as I made my way back upstairs.

The first thing I noticed in the kitchen was the plate in the sink. The same plate that had once been filled with my torture bacon. Had Noah seriously put the dish in the sink? That hadn't been here a few minutes ago, had it? "Noah, stop it. This isn't funny. Come out."

Silence.

Snuggle Muffins was shaking in my arms again as I walked over to the garage door. That's where I would go if I was planning on murdering my captor. There were so many things in the garage he could use to overpower me. Not that he needed anything other than his muscles. He was freaking ripped. The way his muscles bulged when he was sitting in that chair...*why am I thinking about his muscles right now?*

I opened the garage door, holding out my taser. "Noah?"

Silence.

I flicked on the lights and made my way around the car. I peered in the windows. And when I tried to open one of the doors, it was locked. All the shelves around the garage looked untouched. Even the toolkit was closed and in its usual place. The cart I'd used to transport his body hadn't moved an inch. Everything was in order. I bit the inside of my lip. Where the hell was he?

I closed and locked the door behind me.

"Noah?" I called a little louder this time. "Can you please come to the kitchen for supper?" It was a stupid way to lure him out. And it was weird that I said supper instead of dinner. But it sounded more innocent to say supper than the poisonous dinner I wanted to serve him right this second.

Silence.

Snuggle Muffins whimpered in my arms.

For some reason, instead of trying to console him, I followed his gaze. He was staring at the back door.

"What is it, Snuggle Muffins? Do you see him out there?" There were windows on the top half of the door that looked out into the back yard. I couldn't see out there when it was so dark. But I knew nothing about dog night vision. Could he see Noah out there holding a chainsaw looking like a psychopath?

Snuggle Muffins whimpered again.

I wanted to whimper too and hide. But instead, I forced my feet forward. "Do you see him?" I whispered again.

Snuggle Muffins' tail started wagging against my arm.

I didn't know what that meant. Was he aggravated? Happy? Fucking scared out of his mind like me? I inched closer to the door and he wagged his tail even more. I felt a tear run down my cheek. *God, what is wrong with me? I'm a grown-ass woman. I'm not scared right now.*

But when a snowball hit the window I screamed at the top of my lungs and threw Snuggle Muffins and my taser toward the door.

Luckily we were far enough away and Snuggle Muffins was heavy enough that he landed gracefully on the floor instead of slamming against the door. My taser wasn't as fortunate. It broke in half as it fell to the ground. *Shit.*

Snuggle Muffins started barking at the door. Full, crazy barks that I had never heard him make before.

"Stop it, Snuggle Muffins." I snapped my fingers at him when he didn't quit the noise. It just made him bark louder.

Those stupid little kids having snowball fights on my property were going to get what was coming to them. I was going to kill them. Or at least have a word with their mothers. I grabbed the doorknob and went to yank the door open and almost threw out my shoulder. *Fuck*. But whatever pain in my shoulder I felt quickly disappeared.

Fuck. Me. The deadbolt to the back door was locked. From the inside. Which meant... I turned around and stared through the kitchen and down the hallway. Noah definitely hadn't left.

It didn't make sense. He should have fled. It was the only logical thing to do. He was my prisoner. It was his one chance for freedom. But he hadn't run. He was here. The fucking maniac was somewhere in here.

I pressed my back against the door. My taser was shattered on the floor. Snuggle Muffins was barking so loudly that I couldn't even hear my own breaths. And all I could think about was the fact that Noah was going to make me pee in a litter box when he overpowered me. Or starve me. Or drug me. Or...worse. *I'm going to die.*

CHAPTER 18
Sunday

I couldn't make myself move away from the door. Noah was in here. Somewhere. Why the hell wasn't he coming out? "Noah?" I whispered again.

Silence.

I could run out the back door like I originally thought Noah had. Running away would be a good choice. The safe choice. Really the only sane option. But Noah hadn't run. Why? And why the hell should I run if he hadn't? I couldn't let him win. Again.

Snuggle Muffins nudged a piece of the shattered taser with his nose.

"Don't touch that." The thought of him electrocuting himself made me finally move away from the door. I wasn't sure if the taser would still work, but it was worth a shot. I picked up all the pieces, making sure none of them ended up in Snuggle Muffins' mouth. But after pressing both sides back together, it wasn't looking good. *Shit.*

A floorboard creaked above my head. I swallowed hard. If Noah was right above me, he was in...the empty room. The room meant for our child. Or maybe the house was settling. That was probably it, right? I hugged my arms around myself. As much as I wanted to believe that it was the bones of the house, I didn't believe that excuse for a second. That son of a bitch was up there snooping around. And I needed a new weapon now that my taser was shot. I tossed the pieces on the counter.

Nothing popped into my head that would give me an advantage over his strength. I could get a shovel from the garage, but it would be too heavy. My only advantage was that I was quick. And pissed. I went to grab a knife out of the knife block and realized that one of the knives was already missing. So he hadn't armed himself with rusty tools from the garage. He'd gone straight for a knife. I pulled out a much bigger, sharper chef's knife. If he'd ever spent any time in the kitchen, he'd know that I loved this knife. I sharpened it all the time. And it cut through any kind of meat really, really easily. God, I was going to win this fight. *I really hope it hurts like hell when this goes through his leg.*

I tiptoed out of the kitchen and down the hall. Snuggle Muffins was hot on my trail, but I ignored him as I slowly crept up the stairs. I needed to focus on any little noise, and Snuggle Muffins was a mouth breather. The first thing I thought of was a scene from Home Alone where Kevin McCallister tossed paint cans down the stairs. But there was no banister to hang them from. And Noah wasn't a child rigging our house to kill robbers. Noah was dangerous.

Not that Kevin wasn't dangerous. He was a clever little menace with a penchant for setting people's heads on fire. But Noah? The image of Sophia Tremblay's swollen face flashed in my mind as I stepped up another stair. Noah was Kevin all grown up, with muscles for days. *Stop thinking about his muscles.* Noah also had a fairly sharp knife. And he had so many reasons to want me dead. Or to at least maim me a little. I couldn't even blame him. I'd been torturing him, demanding answers he didn't have because I'd given him a concussion or something. And neither one of us was entirely sure it was an accident.

I gripped the knife tighter. It was bigger and sharper than Noah's. And he was probably still hurt from his fall down the stairs and sore from sitting in a chair for days. Would that be enough to tip the scales in my favor during a knife fight? I knew how to butcher meat, not men.

I stopped when I reached the landing and peered into our bedroom. It was too dark to see anything. But if I switched on the lights, he'd know for sure I was up here. I didn't want to alert him of my presence if he was still in the nursery. The element of surprise was necessary if I was going to overpower him.

I tiptoed down the hall, past the hall bath and the guest room. When I reached the empty room I held my breath. *Now what?* My eyes weren't adjusted to the dark yet. I was surprised I'd made it down the hall without tripping and making a ton of noise. Just thinking about it made my stomach flip over. Going through the darkness with a knife was just as bad as running with scissors. I was lucky to be alive.

Focus. I needed to think of a plan before he came barreling out of the room and threw me down the stairs. I blinked, waiting for my eyes to adjust. But then I realized something... Noah had been up here for a while. He'd probably be blinded by a sudden burst of light and I wouldn't. Trying not to overthink my strategy, I reached my hand inside and flicked on the lights.

No one grabbed my hand to stop me. And no one screamed at the sudden invasion of light. It was eerily quiet upstairs. Too quiet. I peered around the doorjamb. The room was empty. Just polished wooden floors and green walls. I swallowed hard. Had the creaking noise really just been the house settling?

It was possible Noah had left out the front door after I'd run off into the woods. That door was unlocked just like I'd left it. And I'd been gone a while because I'd walked back slowly. I'd thought the game was done. I'd thought I'd failed. But what if I'd given him just enough time to get away?

Snuggle Muffins started barking and I jumped. I walked out of the room, trying not to think about the fact that Noah might be lurking in another room.

"Shh," I called down the stairs.

He started barking louder and I swear he was staring a little to the left. I followed his gaze to our bedroom. Had Snuggle Muffins just seen Noah sneak in there? Was he warning me?

Snuggle Muffins started barking louder as I switched on the bedroom lights. Everything looked in order except for the fact that Noah's dirty shirt was lying in the middle of the floor. *Jesus.*

"Noah?"

No response.

He was messing with my head. It was possible the shirt had been there for a while. But it was equally possible that he'd just put it there. It hadn't been in the basement where he'd originally tossed it. He'd been creeping around my house with it for a while now.

The knife started shaking in my hand as I took a step into the room. "Noah, you can come out," I whispered. "I'm not going to hurt you. I just want to talk. I swear I won't tie you up again." But I was much more worried about the fact that he was going to tie me up and torture me. "Noah, please." I peered behind the door.

Nothing.

I stared at the bed. I lived a clutter-free life. I hadn't been lying to Detective Torres when I told him that, even if I had been lying about the files. My clutter-free life meant that there were no storage containers under my bed. Not even a pair of shoes. Which meant someone could definitely hide under there. The only problem was that there was a bed skirt blocking my view. Instead of inching closer, I took a step back toward the door. There was no fucking way I was about to get down on my hands and knees and look underneath the bed. That was just asking to get stabbed in the face. Besides, I had a perfectly good dog that was probably more than willing to look under the bed for me.

I was done tiptoeing and sneaking around. This was my house. I needed to defend it properly. The thought made me feel like I was back in the plot of Home Alone. I dismissed the thought as I ran down the stairs and grabbed Snuggle Muffins. He immediately stopped barking when I picked him up. Maybe my presence settled him. Or maybe he settled me. Either way, neither of us was shaking when we went back upstairs. I set him down on the bedroom carpet.

"Go," I said and pointed to the bed.

He sat down by my feet.

"Snuggle Muffins, go look under the bed."

He lay down.

"Now." I pointed again.

He rolled over on his back.

Fuck. It looked like he was trying to get me to pet his furry little stomach. *I don't have time for your nonsense.* But Noah didn't know that Snuggle Muffins wasn't behaving. And he might be a monster, but even a monster wouldn't stab a puppy. "Good boy," I said, pretending that Snuggle Muffins was actually a good dog, as I got down on my hands and knees and made my way over to the bed. *I can't believe I'm pretending to be a dog right now.* I started panting loudly, adding to the charade. The little boost of confidence I'd gotten with Snuggle Muffins in my arms disappeared.

Please don't stab me. Please think I'm the dog. When I got to the edge of the bed, I threw up the bed skirt without hesitating. Because a dog wouldn't have hesitated. *I think.* I still didn't know anything about dogs. But it didn't matter because there was nothing under the bed. Not Noah. Not even a single dust bunny because I was a stupidly good housewife. *Damn it.*

I smoothed the bed skirt back in place and accidentally sliced the fabric with the knife. I looked down at the knife in my hand. *Oops.* Normally I would have freaked out and tried to mend it right away. I had a needle threaded just for occasions like this. Well, not *exactly* like this. I rarely knifed my belongings.

But I didn't need to fix it. I was leaving soon anyway. And someone who was skipping town didn't care about the possessions they were leaving behind. I slid the knife down the length of the comforter. The fabric slit beautifully, stuffing pouring out. There was something oddly satisfying about it. Was that how it would feel to slice Noah open? I stabbed Noah's pillow all the way through and the knife only stopped because it hit a spring in the mattress. Would that be what Noah's bones felt like? A little resistance? I twisted the knife.

Snuggle Muffins whimpered.

I stared at the knife in the pillow. What the hell was I doing? I turned back to my dog, ignoring the fact that I'd just been fantasizing about cutting flesh. "I was practicing. Don't look at me like that." I yanked the knife out of the pillow.

He cocked his head to the side, judging me.

I wasn't sure what his problem was. I was protecting him too. It's not like I'd ever use the knife on his cute little body. We were a team. What was I even thinking about? I still needed to finish my search. "Go check the bathroom, boy."

Instead of listening to me, Snuggle Muffins lay back down.

Laziness. That was the only excuse. I made my way over to the bathroom. Snuggle Muffins was in a particularly unhelpful mood tonight. But he'd growled at my drug dealer neighbor earlier. He'd been snippy with Charlotte. He usually had my back. At least as much as a dog could. So I felt fairly safe as I turned on the lights in the master bath. Besides, the bathroom was small for a master and I could tell Noah wasn't in there.

But he had been. I reached down and lifted the damp towel off the floor. Had he taken a freaking shower? There were splashes of water all over the tiled floor. And the rest of his clothes were strewn about. Oh God, was he naked? I should have been terrified that he was definitely somewhere in the house. But I was a little excited at the thought of him running around hiding from me in his birthday suit. His body was more delicious than the candy canes in my Christmas stocking. *Stop it.* I didn't want to see Noah naked. I'd seen it before, but him being gorgeous didn't mean his personality matched. He was hideous on the inside. If his outside matched his inners, he'd be wrinkly with a wonky eye, a crooked nose, and missing front teeth. A monster.

I threw the towel back down on the floor. When I found him, I'd make him hang it up like a normal human instead of the Neanderthal he was. He was so freaking annoying. I was a housewife, not a maid paid to clean up his shit. I shifted the knife in my hand and walked back out into the bedroom. Where the hell could his naked ass be?

Snuggle Muffins started barking again.

"Please stop it." I lifted him into my arms. "You keep freaking me out." He quieted down as soon as he was in my arms. I'd gotten the most needy dog in the world. But I was pretty sure he comforted me as much as I comforted him. And I was never letting him go again.

A siren sounded in the distance. My first thought was that someone had called 9-1-1 when they spotted a butt naked Noah streaking the snowy neighborhood. That would be enough to call the police. It was possible that he was also brandishing one of my knives though. Maybe even yelling things about his crazy wife kidnapping him.

But then the vehicle started honking. By the sound I knew what was actually going on and it had nothing to do with Noah. I threw open the curtains, not caring that my knife sliced through the fabric. The fire truck was still far away. I could just make out its lights a few streets over. But I was positive that Santa Claus would be sitting atop it, waving. The fire department had one of the firefighters dress up like Santa and drive by before Christmas every year. They all tossed candy to the children and spread Christmas cheer. I always loved the spectacle.

A part of me wanted to stay by the window and wait for the truck to reach my street. But I couldn't do that right now. I let the curtains fall back in place. First of all, I didn't have time to wave at Santa when there was a madman loose in my house. And second, if I waved, a knife or a dog would have been in my hand. Neither seemed particularly sane. So now I wasn't just missing out on relaxing during the first snowfall of the year with a cup of hot chocolate. I was also missing Santa gracing my neighborhood. Noah was ruining everything. God, I hated my stupid husband.

"Noah!" I called. This was ridiculous. "I know you're in here! Come out!" I walked back into the hall. My eyes glanced up at the attic for just a second. No way in hell was I going up there. It was the only place in the house that was creepier than the basement. As far as I was concerned, if he was up there, he could stay there. It was his. Squatter's rights galore.

But if he was anywhere else in the house, I was going to find him. Snuggle Muffins and I searched the other upstairs rooms quickly. Noah was nowhere in sight. Then we walked downstairs and proceeded to turn on all the lights in the house. Every single one. We were lit up more than any of the over-decorated houses in our neighborhood. We checked all the rooms we hadn't yet, including the small downstairs bathroom and even the hall closet. Noah wasn't nestled behind the toilet or the winter coats. He was nowhere to be found at all. But when we went back into the kitchen, there was an opened jar of peanut butter on the counter and a piece of bread sitting on a plate. No peanut butter had made its way onto the bread.

I breathed a sigh of relief. All Noah was doing was showering and making sandwiches. He wasn't doing anything menacing. It really didn't seem like he intended to hurt me. At least, I hoped. I'd certainly given him plenty of opportunities to jump out and stab me. Yet, I was still standing. I just had a few things to clean up, thanks to his sloppiness.

I lifted the bread and smiled despite the mess. Noah was hungry. The power was back in my hands. The only food he'd had all day was cold bacon. I knew how to get him out of wherever he was hiding. I pulled the weed out of the utensil drawer. It was time to bake Noah a special treat to lure him out. If there was one thing I was good at, it was baking. All proper housewives were.

CHAPTER 19
Sunday

It was good that I had a recipe or else I would have made the pot brownies all wrong. It seemed logical to just substitute weed in place of some of the flour. But apparently I had to make weed butter to integrate the drug more seamlessly. After a few clicks on Pinterest I came to the best weed butter recipe.

The siren growing louder outside was making it hard to concentrate. Or maybe it was the fact that my phone was shaking in my hands. Or that I kept glancing up every two seconds to see if Noah was about to murder me. It really felt like he was somewhere in the kitchen, even though I'd already double-checked every hiding place, pantry included.

Focus. The article wanted me to make the weed butter in a Crockpot. Were they kidding? There had to be a faster method than this. I didn't want to spend the rest of the night waiting to trap Noah. It was bad enough that it felt like he was watching me right this second.

I turned around, but it was just Snuggle Muffins staring into the hall. For some reason that was even creepier. I knew that Snuggle Muffins knew where Noah was. The staring-into-the-void thing he had going on wasn't fooling anyone. But I didn't know how to make him show me. "Are you excited about seeing Santa on the fire truck, Snuggle Muffins?"

He didn't turn toward my voice.

"Snuggle Muffins?" The little hairs on the back of my neck rose and I glanced out the back door again. God, I was going to have a heart attack and die if I didn't find Noah soon. Screw the Crockpot method. Besides, if I did that, my whole house would smell like a weed factory. The last thing I needed was for Detective Torres to stop by tomorrow and smell pot in the air.

I scrolled through Pinterest and eventually found a faster recipe for the stove, but it still took three hours. Didn't they know I was about to be murdered? *Fuck it.* I'd just do it for less time. I turned on the burner and grabbed a stick of butter from the fridge. Less time meant less potent. So to make up for the weak pot butter, I quadrupled the amount of weed I put into it. I wasn't just trying to give Noah a good trip. I wanted him to freaking go loony for a few minutes before passing out on the kitchen floor butt naked. I paused with my hand on the butter. Why had I gone straight to butt naked Noah? I tried to dismiss the thought as I got to work on my trap.

After a few minutes the smell of weed was already filling the air. *Damn it.* It wasn't just Detective Torres' nose I was worried about. I didn't want Noah to know that I was drugging him either. If this plan was going to work, I had to have the element of surprise on my side. I tried to ignore the fact that it felt like someone was watching me as I hit the fan above the stove. If Noah was lurking in the hallway, none of this would matter. He'd know. I lit a few candles just in case luck was on my side and Noah didn't know I was about to drug him. Again. At least this time I wouldn't push him down the stairs. *Slipped.* He slipped down the stairs.

I looked over at Snuggle Muffins as I went back to the stove. He was still staring into the empty hallway toward the front door. He was being more creepy than comforting. "Here, boy," I called.

"Come hang out with Mommy." I cringed. I was not this old dog's mother. The thought was silly.

His ears perked up, but he didn't move.

"Snuggle Muffins, please stop staring down the hall."

He didn't move.

I abandoned my weed butter and picked up the chef's knife. "Noah?" I whispered as I made my way over to my dog. I peered into the empty hall and swallowed hard. "Noah?" I took a few steps toward the living room. Sometimes I thought the living room was creepier than the basement or attic. I barely ever went in it. For a room with the name "living" in it, you'd think it would be more inviting. *It should be called the dying room instead.*

I peered around the corner but there was nothing out of the ordinary. The knife started to slip out of my hand, but I somehow caught it without cutting myself. How was I supposed to focus on baking when I could barely stop shaking?

Crap. Baking! I ran back over to the pot butter. Luckily the butter hadn't burned. The tedious process of stirring it every few seconds didn't at all distract me from the fact that at any moment Noah could pop out of nowhere and stab me. I pictured the blood from my dream this morning and touched my stomach. It was easy to imagine the sticky redness bleeding through my sweater, oozing between my fingers. I removed my hand and went back to stirring. I hated blood. *If only I could stop thinking about it.*

I tried to hum *Baby It's Cold Outside* to myself to calm down. But I could barely hear my humming over the siren outside. All I could think about was the fact that a siren wouldn't come if Noah killed me. No one would know for weeks because I was all alone. Completely and utterly alone.

Stop. I tried to imagine Noah passing out after taking a bite of my brownies. That didn't comfort me either. I kept glancing over my shoulder, the spoon shaking in my hand.

My eyes were starting to water. I wasn't sure if it was because I was freaking out and getting ready to burst into tears or if it was because of the weed drifting into the air...*no. No, no, no.* I stood back a little farther. Could I get high from breathing this in? That wouldn't give me an advantage. Especially if I stood here for any longer. Enough was enough. I turned off the burner and stared down at the concoction.

Would it even work? I'd barely cooked it for thirty minutes. I bit the inside of my lip. Maybe I could still put a little of the weed into the brownies instead of straining it all out. That would fix it. A true chef knew how to make it work. And this was a make-it-work moment. I put a spoon into the butter and took a tiny little taste. The other part of being a good chef was taste testing. I'm pretty sure I made a face as the weed butter slid down my gullet. It was...not good. But then again, I wasn't a pot buff. I figured it would be fine mixed in with everything else.

I grabbed the rest of the ingredients and got to work at the kitchen island. Now that my back wasn't turned away from the rest of the room, I breathed a little easier. But only the teensiest bit easier. I would have breathed a lot easier if my taser was still working. And if Snuggle Muffins wasn't staring at the basement door now.

"What are you doing? Get away from there. Shoo."

He didn't move.

"Please, you're freaking me out." I started to stir the batter, wishing I could stir it with a knife instead of a spoon. "Snuggle Muffins, get away from there." I lifted the bowl into my arms, preheated the oven as I walked by it, and stopped next to Snuggle

Muffins. The door to the basement was still open. If I locked it and Noah was down there, he'd be trapped. I stared down the dark steps as I stirred. And stirred. And stirred. No, I couldn't close the door even if he was down there. That would defeat the purpose of the weed brownies.

I had to stick to the plan. I added even more of the cooked weed and stirred some more. Would that be enough? I put another spoonful in and then licked the back of the wooden spoon. Salmonella wasn't a huge concern for me when I was waiting to be knifed to death by Noah. I licked my lips. Not half bad. I gave it one more lick and one more stir. There. Done. It was the perfect batter consistency. The perfect chocolaty goodness to get Noah to come out of hiding.

I poured the mixture into the greased pan, pushed it into the oven and then...waited. I heard another creak above my head and my eyes flew to the ceiling. *Son of a bitch.* It was tempting to go up there and look for him again. But it was more tempting to stay alive. So I just stood there in the kitchen, knife in hand, staring into the hall with Snuggle Muffins by my feet.

"Noah?" I whispered into the emptiness.

No response.

This was ridiculous. I wasn't a prisoner in my own house. And Snuggle Muffins and I wanted to see Santa, if we hadn't already missed him driving by our house. I wouldn't let Noah ruin Snuggle Muffins' first Christmas with me. I picked him up and we made our way to the front door. Noah didn't pop out of the living or dining rooms and knife us. I glanced at the staircase before putting my hand on the doorknob. "We're going to see Santa! You're welcome to join us!"

Silence.

Screw you too, Noah. I breathed my first even breath in what felt like hours when I closed the front door behind us. It was snowing harder now and our yard and the street was covered in white. All the white lights up and down the lane looked beautiful under the blanket of snow. But so did my colorful ones. I'd started a war out here and in my own home.

What was I going to do if Noah didn't come out before I was ready for bed? What if he just lurked around our house for the rest of my life? That wasn't an option. Detective Torres was going to find the records I'd omitted. He'd know everything soon enough. I hugged Snuggle Muffins closer to my chest. I wished I'd gotten an attack dog and not my little creeper muffin.

My neighbors started stepping outside too, getting ready for the big man to come.

I quickly hid my knife in the flowerpot by the door so that I'd be able to wave to them and Santa without looking like a lunatic. "He's coming," I said and pointed to the fire truck turning down our street.

Snuggle Muffins barked.

Hopefully once the truck left the neighborhood Snuggle Muffins would stop staring off in the distance. Dogs liked trucks. I was pretty sure that was a thing. Maybe that was what was distracting him, not Noah's whereabouts.

Kids raced onto the sidewalks in front of their houses to catch the candy Santa and the rest of the firemen threw. It was such a peaceful scene. The kids running around in the snow and jumping to catch the candy. But I couldn't make myself smile. Not when it was growing more and more likely that Noah was planning something more sinister than my drugged brownies. *I might die tonight. He's going to try to kill me.* It was the same conclusion I kept coming back to. There was no reason for him to stay and hide unless he was seeking revenge. Which was something I knew my fair share about. Revenge was what had driven me to kidnap him in the first place.

I lifted Snuggle Muffins' paw and we waved together as the fire truck slowly drove by. Santa waved back and rubbed his plump tummy. The driver honked the horn and Snuggle Muffins squirmed in my arms. Yup, he definitely liked trucks. He'd probably be chasing it right now if I wasn't hugging him close.

Sally walked by and waved. I swore she winked at me, but I couldn't be sure. *Sally, Sally, Sally.* Even though her discussion with Charlotte earlier hadn't exactly thrown me under the bus, I didn't trust her. Mostly because it felt like she knew I was up to no good. Normally that wouldn't be a problem. But when you were up to no good and someone suspected you? Yeah, Sally was definitely a problem. I smiled and waved back.

I watched the fire truck make its way to the end of the lane. Our street was one of the last ones in the neighborhood. The sirens would be far away soon enough. The snow danced around us as I waited for all the happy families to retreat back inside. They were probably sitting down to a warm meal, excitement buzzing in the air for the upcoming Christmas break.

That was the dream. Two kids to fill our house. *Us against the world.* Noah had spoken those words to me in his vows. It was him and me now. There was no "us." I'd made damn sure of that.

When the last family disappeared back inside, I pulled my knife out of the flowerpot. Not all dreams came true. I'd never have the family I dreamed of. As far as I was concerned, I no longer even had a husband. Noah had ruined us. He'd ruined my perfect white picket fence life. But I wasn't going to let him end it.

He didn't remember me or our house. I knew every square foot of the space because I was the one on my hands and knees cleaning it every week. He couldn't outmaneuver me in there. I was still in control. And I was done being scared. It was time to have some fun with my lovely husband. Besides, it was the last time I was going to get to play house for a long time. I just hoped it was because I fled safely to Mexico and not because I was behind bars.

CHAPTER 20
Sunday

"Noah!" I called as Snuggle Muffins and I made our way back inside. "You just missed Santa coming by!"

I wasn't surprised by the lack of response. I placed Snuggle Muffins down and he followed me into the kitchen.

"I'm making you brownies! Your favorite!"

Silence.

"They'll be done in ten minutes, so plan accordingly!" I popped open the oven to check on them. They were looking perfect. I'd always been great at winging it with recipes. Baking was a science and not an art and all that jazz? Psh. Call me a scientist then. I started humming again, this time actually feeling it.

I was going to be the opposite of the Grinch. I was going to bring the Christmas spirit back to this dead home. To please Detective Torres. To trick Noah. And maybe a little to go out in style.

"Let's decorate for Christmas!" I yelled. "Come on out and help!"

Noah had never been one to help decorate, so I was extra not surprised when he didn't respond. *More fun for me, grumpy pants McGee.*

"Baby." I lifted up Snuggle Muffins. "It's." I twirled in a circle. "Cold." I shimmied my hips. "Outside."

I was vaguely aware of the fact that I might be high from the weed fumes and the taste testing as I danced us over to the box

Detective Torres had so graciously brought up from the basement. Honestly I wasn't even sure what I was doing drooling over shirtless Noah. Detective Torres was fine with a capital F. Seducing him would put me in a much better position for getting away with kidnapping and holding someone hostage.

I laughed out loud. Getting in bed with a detective was seriously the last thing on my mind. That was almost the downfall of Adeline and Violet's otherwise perfect crimes. Falling in love was so not an option for me. Besides, even though I was trying to be the opposite of the Grinch tonight, I was pretty sure my heart was in fact two sizes too small. There was no use in lusting over Noah or Detective Torres. They were both out of the question. I'd already made my choice. A life of hiding was my future now. I was going to be wanted for...well, I wasn't exactly sure what I'd be wanted for in the end. If Noah kept being a little bitch then murder was still on the table.

"I almost forgot!" I yelled. "We're gonna be on the news, Noah!" Usually I listened to Christmas music while I trimmed the tree. Or if there was an especially exciting Hallmark Christmas movie, I'd turn that on. But watching the story about Noah and me unfold on the nightly news would be a perfect backdrop to decorating for Christmas this year.

I grabbed the remote and turned to ABC. The news was just starting. We were close enough to Philly that the news usually pertained to things in the city. But every now and then someone in little old Wilmington did something naughty enough to be on channel 6. Right now they were just talking about a Toys for Tots donation. Great cause, but nothing to do with me. I lowered the volume and started dancing around again to the Christmas carols in my head.

Detective Torres said the vultures were swarming. I glanced at the screen again but there was no word of Noah's disappearance. I knew it was only a possibility that we'd be on. But I was still smiling for some reason. How many times had I sat on the couch eating dinner alone watching the news about my murderous neighbors? I'd been a little obsessed.

I lifted up a stuffed panda bear with a Santa hat that I'd had since I was a kid. I'd held on to it for all these years, hoping to give it to my kid one day. Detective Torres said that Adeline had lost a child. And I couldn't help but wonder if she'd lost it in a similar way to me. She had killed her husband, after all.

The little hairs on the back of my neck rose and I turned around. But no one was there. "Noah?"

Snuggle Muffins barked.

"Stop it," I whispered. I just wasn't sure if I was scolding Snuggle Muffins or begging Noah to stop creeping around.

Stop it. Maybe I was just saying it to myself. I was done thinking about the past. As soon as I got my money back from Noah I could move on. I could at least move. No more thinking about failed relationships or kids. All this time waiting for answers? Wasted. I knew what Noah had done. At least, I knew enough to be sure that I wanted no part in his life.

I lifted my chef's knife and sliced the Santa hat off the panda bear. The stuffing poured out of the top of his head. For just a second I saw the blood again. Pouring out of his missing scalp. Dripping down into his button eyes. I blinked and the blood was gone. It was just stuffing overflowing from the top of his head.

I didn't need to hold on to stupid stuffed animals anymore. There would be no children in my future to hand them down to. Besides, Snuggle Muffins needed a proper Christmas outfit. I pulled the rest of the stuffing out of the hat and plopped it onto Snuggle Muffins' head.

I swear he frowned at me.

"You look adorable."

He sighed.

"I need a picture of this." I reached into my back pocket, but my cell phone wasn't there. Where had I last put it? I wandered into the kitchen. The smell of brownies was everywhere. But my phone was not. I glanced down the empty hallway. I could have dropped it anywhere while I was searching for Noah. *Shit*. When was the last time I had it? I debated tracing my steps, but quickly decided it wasn't worth it. There'd be plenty of time to do that once Noah was securely tied up again.

I heard a noise behind me and twirled around.

Nothing.

"Noah?" I waited a beat, but of course no response came. "Noah, come out right this second and help me with the Christmas decorations or I'll...punish you!" For some reason I started laughing. Threatening to punish him wasn't exactly the best idea. I'd been punishing him for days. "Just kidding!" I yelled. "If you come out I'll have sex with you!" I slapped my hand over my mouth. Where the hell had that come from?

But instead of correcting my words, I let them hang in the silence. Noah had made it pretty clear that he at least wanted a kiss. Maybe offering the whole package would lure him out. The whole package? *Gross, who refers to themselves like that?* Besides, I wasn't just any package. I was one with that expensive gold shiny paper and a beautiful red ribbon. *Seriously what am I talking about?* I shook my head as I made my way back into the family room.

"Snuggle Muffins, I think I'm high."

He looked up at me. He was still sitting where I left him, the Santa hat sitting askew on his head. I was so upset that I couldn't get a picture of his adorableness.

He sighed.

"I was just kidding about the sex," I whispered. "Obviously. Sleeping with Noah is the last thing on my mind." I ignored the image of his ripped abs as I unwound some of the Christmas garland. "You know I have bigger and better plans than Noah's down under." I started decorating the family room, draping the garland along the TV stand. "Is there a Canadian term for down under? That's probably what he'd prefer. Am I right? Eh?" Stupid Sophia Tremblay and her lies. I knew my husband was sleeping with her.

Snuggled Muffins sat down and his hat fell off.

I started placing my Christmas themed candles around the room. "Yeah, I don't think there is a fun Canadian saying for that either. Not that I'd know. If I knew, maybe Noah would still love me." My hands paused on the candles I was setting on the mantle. *Maybe I'd still love him too.*

"My head hurts." I turned around. "Does your head hurt?"

Snuggle Muffins sighed.

"Oh my God, are you high? Wait, am I high? Did we figure that out yet? You definitely look high, Snuggle Muffins. Your face is all scrunched up." I tilted my head to the side. Or was his face always like that? Had I never noticed his face before? It was rather adorable.

I heard my name being called.

"Noah?" I glanced into the kitchen.

Then his name was being called.

Snuggle Muffins barked.

My head was acting strange. I must have imagined it. But I could have sworn...

My name was being said out loud again. It wasn't Noah's voice though. I turned around. There was a picture of me staring back at me on the screen. *No. Fucking. Way.* I grabbed the remote and turned up the volume.

"Noah! We're on! We're on TV! Hurry!"

I watched our names flash across the screen as the news anchor started talking about Noah's disappearance.

"If you have any news about his whereabouts, please contact the number below."

I'm pretty sure I tuned out the rest because I was seriously in shock.

Snuggle Muffins barked at the screen.

"Oh, it's happening, sweetheart. We're going to be famous!" I started doing what could only be described as a touchdown dance. "High five." I put my hand out for Snuggle Muffins.

And he hit it.

What the what? "High five," I said again and put my hand out.

He proceeded to hit it again.

"Oh my God, Snuggle Muffins! You know how to high five? You're adorable and smart, I knew it."

He sighed.

"Noah, you're missing everything! Half the decorations are already up. We were on the freaking news. And Snuggle Muffins is a dog genius!"

No response.

"Our dog is brilliant! Come see!"

Silence.

Kidnapped men were so lame.

I heard a door close and I screamed at the top of my lungs. I grabbed the scalped stuffed animal and then threw it across the room. That was a terrible weapon. Unless I was trying to scare Noah with baldness. I picked up my knife and tried to steady my breathing.

Kidnapped men were also terribly rude and liked to terrorize me. Had I imagined the door closing? I crept out into the kitchen. My brain was definitely acting up. But I swore the basement door was open before. It was closed now. It could have been a gust of wind. I had a feeling it was my house guest, though.

"Noah?" I whispered.

The timer on the oven started going off and I screamed again. I tried to cover my mouth with my hand and almost stabbed myself in the face with my knife. *Jesus.* I threw the knife across the room, like I just had with my stuffed animal. It made perfect contact with one of the kitchen cabinets and sunk into the wood. *Great.* How was I going to explain that mark to Detective Torres?

I pulled out the knife and then grabbed the brownies out of the oven. Ignoring the fact that the knife had been in a flowerpot earlier, I used it to cut the brownies into perfect squares.

"Noah! Supper is ready!" I giggled and took a bite. It was...a little funky. But actually pretty good. I took another bite. And another. *Oh my God, what am I doing?* I looked down at the half-eaten brownie in my hand. I was already worried about being high. I waited a minute and took a deep breath. But I didn't feel any different. I was fine. Definitely a-okay. I stuffed the rest of the brownie in my mouth. Noah wasn't the only one who was hungry. I'd skipped dinner too because I was too busy trying to find his hidey-hole. Besides, chocolate always soothed me. I was feeling less jumpy already.

I wiped my mouth with the back of my hand. Hopefully Noah was more susceptible to weed than I was. Because I was pretty sure the weed didn't do anything to me. I put the brownies in the middle of the kitchen island, which just so happened to be in perfect view of the kitchen window.

I clapped my hands together. It was time to finish my trap. Abandoning my knife on the counter, I grabbed an axe from the garage. "Noah! I'm going to go get us a Christmas tree!"

No response.

I grabbed the binoculars from the junk drawer. "See you in a bit! It'll probably be a half-hour or so! You know how I am about finding the perfect tree!" He didn't remember. That was why I gave him the fake time frame.

I whistled for Snuggle Muffins and he came running after me. I let us out the back door, but didn't bother locking it. The blanket of snow on the ground would show any footprints to and from the house. I'd know if Noah tried to leave. I'd also know because I'd be watching him the whole time with my binoculars.

The weed brownies were the perfect trap. I made my way into the woods, well out of view in the darkness. Then I peered through my binoculars into the kitchen window. Now all I had to do was wait for Noah to come out of his hiding spot, eat tons of brownies, and fall asleep. I giggled. I'd give it twenty minutes. Those brownies were actually pretty strong. It just took a few minutes for them to kick in. I giggled again and hoped that no one else was out in these woods tonight. Seeing me out here giggling wouldn't exactly make me look innocent. Not that I cared. I was already famous.

CHAPTER 21
Sunday

Snuggle Muffins whimpered at my feet. I lowered the binoculars and looked down at him. He was staring up at me with the biggest puppy dog eyes. His whole body was covered in snow, despite the fact that we were pretty well protected under the trees. Had he rolled around in it?

"What's wrong? Are you cold?" I ran my hands up and down my arms. "Me too." For some reason I hadn't grabbed a winter jacket for me or Snuggle Muffins. As soon as I had my money back, a cute little jacket for my new main man would be the first thing I'd buy.

"You shouldn't have played in it if you were going to be cold. It's called being a grownup."

I wasn't sure how long we'd been out here. I was used to checking my phone for the time, but I'd lost it somewhere in the house. For all I knew we'd been standing out here staring at the back of my house for hours. *Or has it been days?* I touched my forehead. Everything seemed to be moving in slow motion. Or was it moving faster than usual? I ran my hand down my face and realized I hadn't put on gloves. I was the bad grownup. Not Snuggle Muffins.

No, it couldn't have been days. I doubt I would have missed the sun. But would the sun have come out if it was snowing? The sky did look a little orange right now. That was definitely because of the snow though. Or...it could have been a trick. Maybe it was the sunrise. "Did we fall asleep out here?"

Snuggle Muffins whimpered.

"Yeah, I didn't think so either. Let's just...move around for a bit while we wait, okay? Jumping jacks, go!" I started jumped up and down in the woods, small sticks and leaves crunching under my feet. "Jump with me, Snuggle Muffins!"

He just stared.

"Jump with me, Muffins! Oh God." I stopped jumping and put my hands on my knees. "I'm freaking out of shape." I was panting and I was pretty sure I'd only been jumping for...wait...what was time? "Snuggle Muffins, I don't remember what time is. I know there are hands on the clock. But what do they do? And why are they called hands?"

I swore he shook his head.

"Don't look at me like that." I leaned down and brushed some of the snow off his back. "Here, maybe Noah's fallen into my diabolical trap." I lifted my binoculars but couldn't see anything. *What the hell?* I shook them. But that didn't help. How did I always fix those old video games? Right, by blowing on them. I blew on the lenses of the binoculars, but that didn't do anything either. How had they broken? They'd been in my hands the whole time.

Snuggle Muffins barked.

"Oh." I laughed. "You're right. My bad." I'd put them up to my eyes the wrong way. I flipped them around and focused in on the kitchen window.

The brownies were still sitting there. But Noah was nowhere in sight. "Ugh. Why is he being such a turd face tonight? Is it something I did? Don't answer that. I know I kidnapped him and tried to starve him and made him poop in a litter box and all that nonsense. But geez...that was hours ago. You'd think he'd get over it by now. Am I right?"

Snuggle Muffins didn't respond.

"You're in a mood. Do your jumping jacks and stop complaining. We're on a stakeout. Sometimes those take longer than one might think. Can you please be patient for me, little dude?"

This time when he didn't respond, I lowered my binoculars. "Snuggle Muffins?" I turned in a circle. But Snuggle Muffins had disappeared. "Snuggle Muffins!" I screamed. *No.* I turned in another circle. *No.* Where was he? "Snuggle Muffins!" Didn't he know that I needed him? He couldn't leave me too.

I can't breathe. I dropped the binoculars onto the ground and touched my throat. I tried to call for him again, but I couldn't catch my breath.

I started running through the woods, gasping for air that didn't seem to reach my lungs. *Come back to me. Please don't leave.* "I won't make you do any more jumping jacks. And you don't have to pee in a box." I stumbled through the woods, not caring about the small branches scratching against my skin.

I needed him. Why would he leave me? Why did everyone leave me? "Snuggle Muffins," I gasped. I needed to try to calm down. I was vaguely aware of how cold my tears were as they fell down my cheeks. "Snuggle Muffins." I put my hand on a nearby tree and leaned over. *Breathe in. Breathe out.* "Snuggle Muffins!" I called a little louder. *Breathe in. Breathe out.*

I thought about how Noah hadn't come out to get the brownies. What if he wasn't there? What if he was never there? What if I'd made the whole thing up?

I shut my eyes tight. What if Snuggle Muffins didn't exist either? I wiped the tears off my cheeks. I didn't want him to be a dream like the blood. "Snuggle Muffins," I cried. "I'll be a better mommy! I promise. I promise. I'm going to buy you a coat. And I'll let you sleep in bed with me every night, not just once." But he already knew all that.

I opened my eyes. There was no evidence that he'd ever been here. *I'm losing my mind.* Ever since I'd kidnapped Noah, I'd felt it. My sanity slowly slipping away. *I pushed him down those stairs. No. No, no, no.* "I'm not a monster. He slipped! Snuggle Muffins, please. I'm not a monster. I'd never hurt you." He was all I had left.

And then I heard him bark.

I turned around. It sounded like it was coming from the direction of my house. "Snuggle Muffins?" He barked again and I felt a little more certain of his whereabouts as I ran toward the noise. "Snuggle Muffins!"

I ran out of the woods and into my back yard. Snuggle Muffins was jumping around trying to attack the snowflakes falling from the sky.

"Bad dog."

He froze and looked up at me. And then his tongue lolled out of the side of his mouth.

"Did you just stick your tongue out at me? You're a very bad dog." I collapsed into the snow beside him. "You know I don't mean it. But don't scare me like that ever again. Do you hear me?" I squeezed him against my chest. "You can't leave me too. Promise me." I held him closer.

And the little demon licked the side of my face. I almost threw him off me, but as the snow fell around me, I found myself not caring that he was gross. I looked down at his cute little face. *Oh, no. I'm a dog person. Ew.* I cringed. But then I shook my head as I stared at the little bundle of fur in my arms. "I'm not a dog person. But I am a Snuggle Muffins person. So don't leave me."

His face morphed into a distorted smile.

"I'm high."

He barked.

And then I laughed. "We're so high!" I let him go so he could chase snowflakes again. And then I collapsed backward and started making snow angels. I rolled around the back yard making snow angel after snow angel until Snuggle Muffins and I were both equally covered in snow.

"It's beginning to look a lot like Christmas," I sung.

"Is everything okay back there?"

Sally was peering over the fence at me. At least, I think it was Sally. Her face resembled a snake. I squinted at her. Maybe she was just dressed up for fun. Old people were into kinky things too, right? "We're great," I said. I smiled but it felt weird, like my lips were stretched out to my ears. I touched my lips. They went all the way around my whole head. *I'm growing.*

"Oh. I see," Sally said. She turned to look at my house.

My eyes followed her gaze. And I didn't need my binoculars to see clearly into the kitchen window from this distance. Noah was standing at the kitchen island shoving his face with brownies. It looked like he was eating them with a shovel. *Who eats brownie with a shovel?* I needed to give him a fork.

"Hmm," Sally the snake hissed. "Looks like everything is okay here. I'll let you guys be."

I turned back to her. And then back toward the window. If I could see Noah, that meant snake Sally could see Noah too. "Oh fuck."

"Language, dear."

"It's not what it looks like," I said. "That...that's my sidepiece. Noah." *Shit. Why did I just tell her it was Noah?* I was a terrible liar.

"I mean Evergreen. His name is Evergreen. He's a tree. I was just cutting down a Christmas tree."

"What? All I see is two kids playing in the snow." She hissed again and winked one of her big yellow eyes. "See you tomorrow for the Christmas light judging! I have a feeling you and Evergreen are going to win a million dollars. Ciao!"

"Ciao!"

She disappeared behind the fence.

"Snuggle Muffins, I speak Italian!"

"Ciao" he barked.

"We all speak Italian!" I had to enter Snuggle Muffins in all the contests in the world. And speaking of contests, when had the prize for the Christmas lights been upped to a million dollars? I needed to do more decorating! "Snuggle Muffins, we need more lights. Like all the lights. Call that boy from the hardware store. He knows my name, he'll hook us up." I stood up from my latest snow angel and brushed some of the snow off my ass. But it didn't really help. I was completely soaked.

"How long have we been out here?" I turned in a circle and stared down at all the snow angels in the yard. There were at least a thousand. I knew because I counted them real fast. After I was done counting, I spotted Noah through the window, still shoveling brownies into his mouth.

"Forget the lights for now. We'll get them tomorrow. We need to get our tree! We can all decorate together. One big happy family."

Snuggle Muffins barked behind me as I staggered back into the woods. Where had I left my axe? I knew it was around here somewhere...ah. I found it leaning against a tree. "Stand back, good sir. This tree is the one." I swung the axe and it barely made a dent in the trunk. *What in tarnation?* I looked up. "Oh. You're right. It's too big. And I'm pretty sure it's a maple. We need a Christmas tree. Not maple syrup." I pointed to Snuggle Muffins. "No maple syrup ever again, deal?"

He barked.

"Good. Screw maple trees." I yawned. "Do you think we should take a nap first? God, I'm hungry too. Do you think that guy from the hardware store will bring us some takeout? I'm pretty sure that's in his job description. You call him, Snuggles. I'll find us a tree."

But instead of looking for a tree I just sat down in the middle of the woods and started laughing. I pictured Sally slithering by and Noah with shovel hands. And I just laughed and laughed until suddenly it wasn't funny anymore. I blinked. Snuggle Muffins was staring at me, completely drenched. There was water dripping off his little eyelashes.

"How long have we been out here? I'm so sorry. Let's get our tree and go inside." I stood up and my legs felt tired. Probably because I'd made a thousand snow angels. "How does this one look?" The perfect tree was right in front of me. I must have picked it out before nap time. I laughed. This time when I swung the axe, it made perfect contact and a nice cut. I swung it again and again. "Stand back, Snuggle Muffins!" I swung the axe through the air. "Timber!"

The little evergreen fell with a thud in the woods. I grabbed it by its trunk and pulled it slowly toward the house. Again, I was reminded of Kevin McCallister. He'd cut down a tree just like this and decorated it when he was home alone. I was basically doing the same thing. Except I had my dog and hopefully a passed-out Noah inside.

I wasn't sure how long I'd been out here, but the snow was still falling and the neighborhood was silent. It was definitely still nighttime. Hopefully Noah would be sleeping in the middle of the kitchen floor. I couldn't see him at the counter anymore, and I'd lost my binoculars somewhere in the woods so I couldn't get a better view.

I reached the back door and looked behind me. Originally I thought I'd be able to see any footprints leaving the house. But the yard was literally covered in dog paw prints and snow angels. If Noah had left, I wouldn't have been able to tell. What had I been thinking?

At least my brain felt significantly less wonky now. Sally had stopped slithering by a while ago. With her disappearance, all my mistakes became pretty clear. I'd stopped watching Noah through the window. I'd frolicked in the snow. I'd giggled in the forest. And I'd lost my dog for a little bit.

But I'd taste-tested the brownies...hours ago? Minutes ago? I couldn't be sure. Either way, Noah had tried them much more recently than me. And he had shovel hands. So...I was pretty sure he was going to be high off his ass.

I opened the door and peered inside. Noah was indeed in the middle of the kitchen. But he wasn't asleep in the middle of the floor. He was standing there with his arms folded across his chest, staring at me. His naked chest. And instead of raiding the closet like a normal person, he was wearing the same pair of worn jeans that hugged his ass so perfectly. I blinked, trying not to get distracted by all his stupid muscles. That was probably his plan. To distract me with the sexiest outfit in existence.

Snuggle Muffins ran inside and sat down by Noah's feet.

That little traitor. *Get back over here.* But Snuggle Muffins didn't move.

"Having fun?" Noah asked.

I swallowed hard. "Yes?" My voice came out squeaky and high pitched. "What's up?" Maybe he'd forgotten the past few days the same way he'd forgotten about the rest of his life? *Fingers crossed.*

"I think you know what's up...Ensley."

Oh. No. Him knowing my name was not a good indicator of him not remembering. But I had a Christmas tree. I shook my head. More importantly...I had a freaking axe. I brought both inside and then locked the door behind me. It seemed that my plan to drug him had backfired. But Noah had brought shovel hands to an axe fight. *Simpleton.* I just hoped his blood wouldn't splatter on the kitchen stools. Blood was very hard to get out of upholstery.

CHAPTER 22
Sunday

For a few seconds we just stared at each other, waiting for the other person to make the first move. It reminded me of our proposal. We'd been watching the sunset from the boardwalk. I'd felt this nervous energy in the air. I was pretty sure he had been about to break up with me, so I hadn't said I word. I'd just tried to hold on to the moment. But after the most awkward stretch of time, he'd gotten down onto one knee and proposed.

But Noah wasn't about to propose now. He was about to kill me. And I didn't need to pretend that it wasn't about to happen. Because I was going to kill him first. For some reason my eyes were glued to his perfect abs instead of where I needed to slice his throat. *Shake it off. It's go time.* Before I could lift my axe in the air, though, the jerk started talking.

"You're soaking wet."

I swallowed hard. "Excuse me?" There was literally no way for him to know that I was aroused by his stupid body. "It's not my fault that you refuse to put a shirt on."

He smiled out of the corner of his mouth. "Wow. Not at all what I was referring to. You're drenched. Let's get you a hot shower and some dry clothes before you catch a cold."

Oh. I looked down at my clothes. I'd been rolling around in the snow making snow angels. And the snow had inevitably melted. I looked like a drowned cat. I was surprised Snuggle Muffins wasn't chasing me around the house. I shivered. Noah was probably right. I needed to change before I caught a cold.

He took a step toward me.

Not so fast, sweet talker. I knew what he was up to. And it was nothing about being nice. I lifted the axe.

"What the hell are you doing?" he asked, his thick eyebrows drawing together beautifully.

"Doing what I should have done when you were tied up. Unless you want to go back downstairs willingly." I took two steps forward for every one of his steps back.

"You're crazy," Noah said. "You do realize that, right?"

I gripped the axe tighter. "I'm not crazy. I hate when you call me that." I really wanted to chuck it at his perfect face. And it would have made a much bigger dent in his skin than the knife had in the wood. I cringed at the thought of blood dripping down his chiseled abs.

"Babe. You're holding an axe like you're about to chop off my head. That's psychotic. Put it down."

Telling me that I was insane was not working in his favor. "I'm hoping it doesn't have to come to that. How about we go back down to the basement? I'll tie you up to the chair where you belong. And we can go back to normal."

"Normal? Being tied up in the basement isn't normal, Ensley. Nothing about this is normal." He gestured back and forth between us.

Him saying my name was jarring. Him remembering? Horrifying. I held the axe out in front of me. "March." I pointed the axe to the basement door. "Now."

He put his hands up, and for the first time, I realized he was unarmed. His hands didn't look like shovels anymore either. It was like he was transforming in front of me. He didn't even look like he was about to kill me anymore. He looked innocent.

But I knew it was just a ruse. "Where's the knife?" I asked.

He lowered his eyebrows. "What knife?"

"The one you took out of the knife block. The one you're planning on stabbing me with!" I pointed the axe towards the kitchen counter.

"I don't have a knife. I never had a knife. And I swear I'm not planning on hurting you. I'd never hurt you." He licked his lips and dropped his gaze from my eyes to my axe. "I'm not the one threatening bodily harm here, Ensley."

Every time he said my name, my mind scrambled. "But...then where is it?" Noah was a liar. And I knew he was lying right now too. The knife was probably tucked into the back of his jeans. Hidden right above his firm booty. *Stop.*

"I don't know. But I swear I don't have a knife."

I kept my axe lifted in front of me as I made my way over to the counter. Had the knife just fallen or something? I glanced over my shoulder to make sure Noah wasn't moving and then continued my search. It wasn't on the ground or shoved in the wrong drawer. But then I found it on the drying cloth by the sink. *Oh.* I pressed my lips together. Had that been there the whole time and I just hadn't seen it? Or had he just placed it there to trick me? I drummed my fingers on the granite. The answer to that question was very important. Not that I'd ever trust Noah.

But he was looking at me like he was innocent. Like he wasn't dreaming of stabbing me in the chest with a knife. Now that I thought about it, I had used the missing knife recently. And I couldn't remember the last time I'd put the dishes away off the drying cloth. That chore was one of my least favorite things. Like when I did laundry, folded it, and didn't put it away for weeks.

It was possible that Noah was innocent. But if that was true, he wouldn't have been lurking around the house for the past several hours trying to scare me. I pointed my axe at him again. "If you're not planning on hurting me, then what were you doing lurking around the house being all creepy?"

"When you got back from whatever you were doing, I had just gotten out of the shower. You were screaming and acting cra...sorry. You just...you didn't seem quite like yourself, babe. I thought I'd wait it out until you calmed down. I wasn't trying to scare you."

I stared back at him.

"I'm sorry if I scared you."

It was weird getting an apology from him. I didn't know how to respond to that. Had I ever gotten an apology from him before?

"Look, if I was trying to hurt you, would I really spend all this time finishing up with the Christmas decorations?" He waved his arm through the air.

It looked like Christmas had thrown up all over the kitchen. The hand towels were red and green. He'd even changed all the plates over to a Christmas pattern we hadn't used in years because it was such a hassle. I glanced into the family room. It was practically a winter wonderland. "You...decorated while I was out getting the tree?" Not only had he decorated, but he'd done it fast. He was a much better housewife than me.

"Yeah, you were gone for like four hours."

Four hours? *Geez.* It felt more like days. Or minutes. It was hard to know for sure. "Just because you decorated doesn't mean you don't want to hurt me." Hell, I'd started decorating and I was still strongly considering chopping his head off with an axe. Christmas wasn't an all-cure for revenge.

"I hid when that detective came by, remember? I didn't do that for myself. I was trying to protect you." He took a step closer to me. "I know you're in trouble because of what you've done to me. But we can figure this out together. I'll help clear your name."

"Why would you help me after everything I've done to you?"

"Because...you're my girl."

My axe was getting heavy. That was the only reason why I lowered it to my side. It had nothing to do with the fact that the way he said "my girl" made my knees feel weak. "How did you even get untied?" I'd watched countless tutorials on sturdy knots.

"Remember when you were pissed off and threw a pair of pliers at me? You left them." He shrugged. "It took a while but I finally got free."

So much for my perfect plans. I wasn't good at this. I was really really not good at this. I didn't even step away as he drew closer to me, even though I knew I should have. I was supposed to be the one chasing him around with an axe. He wasn't supposed to be stepping even closer. And closer. I could smell his familiar body wash all around me, lulling me into a false sense of security.

"I like you better as a brunette." He reached out and ran his thumb and index finger down a strand of my hair.

I'd forgotten all about my wig. I wasn't even sure where I'd left it. But it didn't matter. He already remembered. I could tell. He was looking at me like he remembered everything. At least, everything before he started adding sidepieces like it was his job.

"And it was sinful to cover this face." He ran his thumb along my cheekbone, sending a shiver down my spine.

I'd also forgotten about my reindeer mask. It was a hindrance anyway. It would have definitely gotten in the way when we kissed. *Kissed? What was I even thinking?*

His thumb traced the freckles under my eyes.

I was broken. He broke me. So I don't know how I felt so whole when he touched me. It didn't make sense. But it was like he was somehow holding together my shattered pieces. I leaned into his touch.

"Ensley." His hand slid to my neck.

Kiss me. Stop. I leaned forward for just a second and then took two steps back. The distance made it easier to breathe. "I made you brownies." I had to get this night back on track, because I was worried I was about to maul him. And not with the axe.

He laughed. "Oh, yeah. I know. I took one bite. They were terrible. You're much better at making French toast and bacon."

I laughed. "They weren't terrible. They just had tons of weed in them." *Oops.* I'd just played all my cards without even hesitating. He was slowly wrapping me around his finger again, just like he used to.

"How many did you eat?" he asked.

"Just one."

He looked over at the pan of brownies. "I'm pretty sure you ate more than one."

I glanced over. A third of the brownies were missing. "No, I'm pretty sure you ate more than a bite."

He laughed.

And then I laughed.

And then Snuggle Muffins started laughing too in his new Italian accent.

"Yeah," Noah said. "Maybe I did eat more than a bite." He nodded. "Right. Yeah, I did. I ate just a little and then started decorating. When I finished I was really freaking hungry. So I ate some more. They didn't taste as weird when I got seconds. And thirds." His eyes grew round. "I only ate them a little before you came in. How much weed did you put in them?" He put his hand up to his mouth.

And I realized I wished I was the one touching his lips. I cleared my throat. "Only a little." *So so much.* Way more than I was supposed to. I'm pretty sure I had eaten more than I was supposed to too. But everything was becoming clearer. His hands barely looked like shovels anymore. And they definitely didn't feel like shovels. They felt warm and rough. And safe. I felt so safe when his hands were on me.

I wasn't sure how it happened, but we were nose-to-nose again. Maybe I had stepped forward. Maybe he had.

He reached out again, letting his fingers trace the neckline of my sweater.

"My hand feels heavy," he said. He looked down at his hand as he pressed it against the side of my neck. "Are you sure it was just a little bit of weed?"

"Mhm. Just a wee little bittle." I laughed. "Bit. A wee little bit."

He nodded like he believed me.

Which was weird because I certainly didn't believe myself. I wasn't even sure if any of this was actually happening. Which meant my plan could still work. I just needed to stall him until the weed got him like it had gotten me outside. He'd be seeing Sally snakes and shovel hands in no time. I just needed to do something, anything, to preoccupy him until that happened. So I did the first thing that popped into my head. I stood on my tiptoes and kissed him.

Well, it was a lot less graceful than all that. I literally attacked him, mauling him like I thought I might. I wasn't sure why I'd decided to go in that direction. Probably because he looked like a million bucks. And smelled like even more. And the way he looked at me when he wasn't accusing me of being crazy? I never felt so wanted in my life.

But he didn't kiss me back. He stood there like he was in shock.

I was about to pull back when his hand slid into my hair.

He groaned into my mouth as he returned my assault.

The sound made my head spin. I needed to hear it again and again.

He pushed me backward until my lower back collided with the kitchen island. The collision sent a jolt of pain through my body. But instead of crying out in pain, I dropped my axe and wrapped my arms around his neck.

His hands slid to my ass as I jumped up and wrapped my legs around his waist. I needed more. Anything. Everything. He was right. I was freezing cold. And his body felt like a furnace. It would be impossible to catch a cold if I stayed glued to him.

I wasn't sure if I was dizzy because I was still high or dizzy because of the way he was touching me. Maybe I was just out of oxygen because I was only breathing him in. But I didn't need air when I had him. I breathed in his exhales as he consumed me. And he was more delicious than any brownies. He was more delicious than life itself.

"I think you promised me something," he whispered as his lips moved to my neck.

"What did I promise you?" I moaned as he lightly bit my neck. God, I knew it was possible he was playing me. But it felt so good to be played that I didn't care. Hell, I was a few seconds away from begging him to tie me up and have his way with me.

"You promised if I came out of hiding..." he nibbled on my skin again. "That I could have all of you."

"I don't remember saying that." Lies fell from my lips so easily these days.

"No?" His lips trailed across my clavicle and down to the V in my sweater. "So you want me to stop?"

I wanted to remember what it was like to be loved one last time. Before the cheating. Before the missing cash. Before he ruined my life.

"Tell me to stop and I will. We can go back to the basement." His index finger tugged the front of my sweater down and he placed a kiss between my breasts.

He was willing to go back to the basement. That was good behavior. And in my book, good behavior was supposed to be rewarded. How else would men ever be trained properly?

"Tell me to stop," he said again. It almost sounded like he was begging. Like he was scared of this being too good to be true.

It was. Of course it was. But when life handed you lemons, you were supposed to make lemonade. Life had handed me a cheating husband, so...I was going to fuck his brains out. It was only fair. "Don't stop."

He lifted me up in his arms. "I'll never stop."

But I wasn't talking about sex. I didn't want him to stop loving me. Why had he stopped loving me? I clung to him like I never wanted to let go.

He'd be tripping longer than I would if I'd really been outside making snow angels for four hours. I could have my way with him and then...what? Tie him to the bed. Get the confession I deserved. And then...

Stop.

I'd made a mistake all those years ago by saying yes to his proposal.

Stop.

He'd robbed so many years from me.

Stop.

Yes, I felt whole with him. Yes, he provided for me and bought my dream house in my dream neighborhood. From the outside looking in, Noah was perfect. But perfect was a façade, just like all the other smiling faces behind white picket fences. Noah was unfaithful. Noah was a thief. Noah was...

Stop.

I thought it was easier to breathe his exhales than oxygen. I thought he was my forever. I thought a lot of things.

But the only thing I was thinking right now? I'd breathe easier when his exhales weren't invading my oxygen supply. And when I cut ties on a forever permanently.

There were no maybes about it. I closed my eyes as he carried me upstairs. I'd have one more fun night. One good memory to hold on to in a sea of terrible ones.

Then in the morning...I was going to get my confession. And then...

Stop.

I closed my eyes tighter.

Stop.

But there was no stopping it. I'd already made up my mind. I was pretty sure I'd known all along I'd go through with it. There was no other way out of this hell.

He kissed me harder when we reached the bedroom. Like he was holding on to as much anger from our past as I was. But that would be crazy. I was the jilted one, not him. I was also the crazy one. He'd said it himself. And I was just crazy enough to kill him.

CHAPTER 23
Monday

For the first time in what felt like weeks, I hadn't stared at the ceiling all night long. I'd actually slept. The combination of pot brownies and a good lay was my new cure for insomnia. Not even the images of blood I'd been seeing bothered me. And that blood had been everywhere in my dreams. Always. Staining the cement at the bottom of the basement stairs. I could easily picture myself scrubbing away the blood on my hands. The water running red. I rubbed them harder and harder until my own hands were pink.

Now that I was awake, that disturbing image came back to me. But I still didn't want to move. I didn't want the warm feeling in the center of my chest to go away. I didn't want to have to go through with my plan. Because today was the day to finally say goodbye.

Goodbye to Noah. Goodbye to this house. Goodbye to Delaware. Hell, I'd even be saying goodbye to the country. And I couldn't delay it any longer. Detective Torres would be getting my missing records soon. He'd be putting all the scattered pieces back together. I'd already made a deposit on an apartment in Mexico. All I had to do was get there and I'd be free. I'd be free of everything. It was go-time.

It almost felt like my eyes were glued shut when I tried to open them. I reached to rid the sleepy from the corners of my eyes, but my hand didn't move. *Ow.* I tried to move my hand again but...I couldn't. I opened my eyes, ignoring the gritty feeling, and looked up.

No.

I pulled on the ropes tying my hands to my bedposts. *How?* I pulled again but they were tied in a knot I hadn't studied on YouTube. *No!* I pulled harder. This couldn't be happening. This was not how last night was supposed to go down. Noah was supposed to be tied up. *Not me.* I tried to wiggle my hands to loosen the grip or the rope, but all that accomplished was giving my wrists a bit of rope burn. *Damn it!*

I pulled my attention away from the perfect knot. The sheets were rumpled around me and I smelled Noah everywhere, but he wasn't there. That was no surprise. But what *was* a surprise was the Mrs. Claus costume I was wearing. Not a real one with a gray wig, round glasses, and long fur coat. But a sexy one that you surprised your husband with as a Christmas present.

What in the ever-living fuck was I doing dressed up like this? I pulled down as hard as I could on the ropes and tried to ignore the tears threatening to escape my eyes. *Ow.* I shook my hands. *No. No, no, no!*

I didn't know where Noah was, but surely he was close. It wasn't like he could just walk outside and....shit! I twisted my body so that I was on my knees facing the headboard. Come on. I pulled even harder, the ropes biting at my skin. If Noah left the house, all our neighbors would swarm him with questions. Detective Torres would show up and start asking questions. I'd be spending the rest of my days in jail instead of in Mexico.

The rope wasn't budging. I looked over my shoulder hoping Snuggle Muffins would come to my rescue. But my silly dog was nowhere in sight. It was tempting to keep trying to get free for as long as I could, but I needed to make sure Noah wasn't going anywhere. Hell, what if he was already with the cops right now?

"Noah!" I yelled and pulled on the ropes. The headboard didn't even shake, but the action made my breasts almost fall out of my flimsy costume. This outfit was only supposed to be worn for good husbands. Not lying cheats. That son of a bitch. "Noah!"

I stopped screaming and stared at my left hand. My engagement ring and wedding band both glistened in the morning sun. And for just a second, I wondered if it was all a dream. Maybe I'd never taken them off. Maybe I never kidnapped my husband. Maybe Noah still loved me.

But that would have been a Christmas miracle. And I knew it wasn't true. Partly because the last few days definitely felt real. And partly because I heard a floorboard squeak.

I turned around as Noah walked in. He was humming *Baby it's Cold Outside* and carrying a tray of breakfast food.

"What the fuck, Noah?" This time when I pulled against the restraint, the bedpost groaned in protest.

"Good morning to you too, Ensley." He placed the tray down on the nightstand. "Toast?" He picked up a piece of toast and put it up to my lips.

"Fuck you."

"Maybe later then." He took a bite of it and then tossed it onto the plate.

I glared at him. He was dressed similarly to me...but the guy version. His outfit was green though, which definitely made him an elf instead of Santa. Mrs. Claus with an elf? What kind of kinky stuff had we gotten into last night? I couldn't remember changing into this. Which meant...*oh my God*. "Why did you put me in this costume?"

He laughed. "It was your idea. I just went along with it." He pulled on one of his green suspenders and let it snap back against his chiseled chest. "You really liked these last night."

"What? I...there is no way in hell this was my idea."

"Do you really not remember last night?" He raised his left eyebrow at me.

I ignored the way the action made my heart race. "I don't remember anything." That wasn't entirely true. I remembered kissing him. I remembered him carrying me upstairs. I remembered straddling him on the bed. His hands. His lips. His tongue. His...I swallowed hard. God, how could I ever forget the things he'd done to my body? But then things got a little foggy. Technically it was possible that after we'd rolled around in the sheets once that I'd wanted to spice things up with the outfits. It could have been my idea. After all, I had bought what I was wearing as a surprise for Noah.

"That's a shame. It was quite memorable for me."

Me too. Until I'd blacked out. I tried to ignore his words and my own traitorous thoughts. "I'm glad it was fun for you. Now untie me or I swear to God I'll..."

"Orange juice?" he asked, cutting me off. He lifted a glass off the tray and took a sip before putting it up to my lips.

I spit in it.

He made a tsking noise and set the glass back down on the tray. "I don't remember being this hostile when you had me tied up, Ensley."

"Then clearly you're not remembering things well either."

He shook his head. "You were the hostile one then too. Starving me. Making me do my business in a litter box. A litter box, babe."

"So this is about revenge?" I knew I shouldn't have trusted him last night. I'd let my guard down for two seconds - fine, two hours - and this is what happened? "So what do you want? You want me to pee in a litter box so that we're even? Great, let's just get this over with then."

He smiled. "This isn't about revenge. I told you I didn't want to hurt you. And I don't."

"Then untie me." *Asshole.* This time when I pulled on the ropes I almost started crying. *Ow.*

"I can't do that."

"Why? We can have a civilized conversation where we're both not tied up. Like two normal adults."

He sat down on the edge of the bed, far enough from me so that I couldn't kick him in the nuts. "Two normal adults. How boring. I think I fell in love with you because you're anything but normal, Ensley."

"Then let me go. Let's be un-normal together." I twisted my body around so that I was sitting on the bed facing him. Then I forced myself to smile. Happy people were trusting people.

"I can't," he said.

"Why do you keep saying that? Of course you can." I slowly inched my foot forward. Maybe I was wrong before. It was possible if I stretched just so that I could kick his balls.

"Technically I can, sure. But after you insisted on the outfit change you started talking about all this crazy stuff. Sorry, I know you don't like the term crazy. But Ensley...the shit you were saying really freaked me out."

I pressed my lips together. He could literally be referring to anything I'd done in the past few weeks. It was better if I stayed silent.

He didn't elaborate either.

If he was hoping for a staring contest, I could definitely win...*crap*. I blinked. "And what do you think I said?"

"You talked about decapitating all the elves in the house. And then drowning them in the lake. Something about a fresh start for Senorita Claus. I was wearing an elf costume." He gestured to his getup. "So naturally you kinda freaked me out, babe."

"I was high." Apparently so high that I'd blabbed my plans to him. Decapitation though? Ouch. I just wanted a clean slice across his throat, not to lob the whole head off. High me was extra crazy. "Clearly I didn't mean any of that, Noah."

"You couldn't have been that high. You were outside for hours after eating those brownies."

"Right. But you had them too. After I did. You probably just imagined me saying all those things."

He shook his head. "I lied."

"How unusual for you." I glared at him. "What did you lie about this time?"

"Well, I tried to tell you the truth last night. Your brownies were terrible. I only had one bite."

"But you said you went back for more. There was at least a third of them missing."

"Yeah, I knew you drugged them. You definitely needed something else in them to hide that taste. I figured you were try-ing to drug me, so I wanted to make it look like I'd eaten a bunch. I tossed several of them in the trash and then warmed up a TV dinner instead. It was sitting on the counter right next to the brownies. You just didn't see it. Probably because you could-n't stop staring at me." He flashed me a smile.

Was that what he'd been eating with his shovel hands? I pressed my lips together. The fact that I thought he had shovel hands last night was probably enough of an answer. "I don't think I was staring at you."

"It's okay." He reached out and grabbed my shin. The rough skin of his palm made me shiver. "I was staring at you too. Kind of like I am now."

I could use this to my advantage. "I have a proposal. Why don't we have a redo of last night?" I bit my bottom lip as I stared into his eyes.

"Maybe later." He reached into his back pocket. "First I have some questions for you." He pulled out a cell phone.

No, not just any cell phone. Mine. The one I'd misplaced last night. *Oh shit.* I cringed as he slid his finger across the screen.

"There was an alarm going off on this at 7 am this morning. A reminder to pack your passport," he said. "That definitely piqued my interest."

I swallowed hard. Why oh why had I not set a password on my phone? More importantly, why did I think it was appropriate to leave reminders about my escape plan on my calendar?

"So I did a little digging," he said.

"Noah, it's not what you think."

He stood up, distancing himself from me. "Really? Because I think it's exactly what I think. You stopped wearing your rings. You have appointment reminders to visit Dr. Collins constantly." He looked down at me. "Is this the same Dr. Collins you were trying to make me think I was having an affair with? It was you, Ensley. *You* were cheating on *me*. And you made me think I was the bad guy because I hit my head and couldn't remember. You made me think I was a monster."

"That's...that's not what I was doing."

"Dr. Collins 3 pm - grocery store. Dr. Collins 1 pm - mall. Dr. Collins 7 pm - office. Dr. Collins noon - Grotto's. You see Dr. Collins almost every day of the week."

I stared at him. "That's not what it looks like."

"Oh, I think it's exactly what it looks like. You're a terrible liar and a terrible criminal. You have 'kidnap husband' on your calendar." He held up my phone. "Did you seriously not think that the detective you're cozying up to would subpoena this for evidence?"

"I'm not getting cozy with Detective Torres."

Noah ran his fingers through his hair. "Right, because detectives usually offer to carry up Christmas decorations for their prime suspects. I heard you flirting with him."

"I wasn't..."

"You called me a liar. You called me a cheat. But it's you, Ensley. It was you all along."

"Noah, please. You don't understand."

"Oh, I found a whole to-do list too." He looked back down at the phone. "Kidnap Noah. Hide him. Notify police. Give police the box of falsified records. Get a confession. Get money back. And then there are a whole bunch of question marks. What the hell are the question marks, Ensley?"

"Untie me and I'll tell you."

"Tell me and I'll untie you," he countered.

I wasn't really in a place to negotiate. My wrists were burning. And I did kind of need to pee, and I wasn't an animal. I'd never actually pop a squat in a litter box like him. "Noah, come on..."

"What are the question marks?!"

He'd been so loving recently. It was strange seeing him mad. Mad enough to hit someone? Like he'd hit Sophia Tremblay? I didn't want to test that theory. "There were several possibilities depending on what was going on. I wanted to leave myself a little wiggle room."

"Tell me some of the possibilities."

He wasn't going to let me go until I told him something. "Burn the house down. With you in it." That had never been the plan. It was always to kill him and hide his body in the lake if it came to that. But I couldn't do that now. The lake was frozen. Although, I was definitely still leaning toward the killing thing. I couldn't let him walk away with everything he'd found on my phone.

"You want me dead that badly? We could have talked about our problems. We could have worked this out. I don't give up that easily, Ensley. I don't want to give up on us."

"There is no us. You made sure of that." I pulled on the ropes.

"Right, when I stole all your money and slept around with Sophia Tremblay and Dr. Collins? Yeah, I heard you the first time. But that's the thing, Ensley. I didn't do any of that. You did."

"I'm not a lesbian." *I love you, you idiot.* I pulled against the ropes again, but it was no use. I needed to get free before I let crazy thoughts of love take over my brain. I didn't love Noah. Not anymore. "I told you it's not what it looks like."

"Then explain it to me."

You're crazy. You're the psychopath. Not me. I wasn't sure he wanted to hear any of that.

He reached out and lightly touched my cheek.

I forced myself not to turn my head and bite him.

"I think you fucked up, babe. All this..." he lifted up the phone. "You left a trail. You're in too deep. But we can fix all this together. I just need you to tell me the truth about everything. Let me help you."

You want to help me kill you?

"I'll call Detective Torres right now. We can clear everything up." His finger hovered over the call icon.

"Noah, don't." It felt like all the air left my lungs. He was going to ruin everything. Months of planning. No, it wasn't the perfect crime, but I could still get away with it.

"Why?"

I struggled against the ropes. "He can't know."

"Why?"

"You don't understand."

"Then help me understand! Why can't Detective Torres know that I'm here safe? That you didn't do anything wrong?"

"Because you're not safe!" I pressed my lips together. For just a second, I thought everything might spill out. I pressed my lips together even tighter.

He lowered the phone. "What did you do, Ensley?"

I tried to think of the best way out of this. Lying, stealing, and cheating were his solutions. Not mine. But I didn't see another way. "Noah. I...you're right to be scared of me. I keep having these dreams..." I let my voice trail off. "After I dropped you down the stairs and you hit your head. I keep seeing these images of blood. It's like I *want* to see the blood. I'm worried I'm going to hurt you."

His eyes softened. Or at least I thought they did. But I guess I was wrong, because he hit Detective Torres' name on my phone to call him.

"Noah, stop!" I reached out with my foot to try to hit the phone out of his hand, but he dodged me.

"It's best if he hears it from you," Noah said. "Tell him I'm home safe."

I tried to kick him in the face but my leg didn't lift high enough.

He grabbed my ankles with one hand and pressed my feet against the mattress. He held me still no matter how much I struggled against his grip. "Behave." He put the phone to my ear. "Tell him to call off the search."

I couldn't do that. I just needed to figure out a way out of these ropes so I could finish my plan. *God, what am I going to do?* "Hang up. Noah, please hang up. Hang up, hang up, hang up!" I tried to squirm out of his grasp, but apparently his biceps were stronger than my hamstrings.

The phone stopped ringing and I had no choice but to stop begging.

"Detective Torres speaking."

"Hi, Detective Torres," I said. "I...I need to tell you something. Important. Could you come by the house sometime today?" *Please be busy. Please be randomly in Canada again.*

"Yeah. I have something important to discuss with you as well."

Oh, fuck. What had he found out?

"Give me a few hours," he said. "I'll be there before noon."

I glanced at the alarm clock on the nightstand. It was a little before 10 am. "Great," I gritted through my teeth. It was anything but great. It wasn't enough time.

The line went dead.

"He'll be here in two hours," I said. "I thought it would be best to tell him in person."

Noah lowered the phone from my ear. "It'll all be over soon, babe."

It would be, whether I was ready or not. I had two hours to get untied. Two hours to get my money back. Two hours to get the hell out of here before I got caught with Noah's blood on my hands.

CHAPTER 24
Monday

"Noah." I tried to keep my voice steady, even though I was freaking out inside. I needed more than two hours to prep everything. Every second I stayed tied up was precious time I was losing. "Can you please untie me now?"

"I will, babe. I promise. As soon as I'm sure you're not planning on hurting me."

Tough luck, ass hat. "I don't think I'm going to hurt you." That was the best I could do.

His hands holding my ankles firmly to the mattress didn't budge. As soon as they did, I was going to kick him right in the throat.

He shook his head as he looked down at me. "I don't believe you. Ensley, you just confessed that you've been wanting to see blood. My blood. I don't believe the sudden change of heart."

I tried to take a deep breath, but it didn't calm me at all. "What if you keep my hands tied together but let me loose from the bedpost? I have to get ready. I'm running out of time."

"Running out of time for what?" He lifted my phone in the air. "Oh, right…the passport thing? You're not going anywhere today, babe." He brushed his thumb over my ankle and I tried to ignore the soothing feeling. "We need to talk this out. And we can't do that until you tell me what's really going on with Sophia Tremblay and Dr. Collins. I need you to tell me everything you know."

I was so upset when I woke up tied to the bed that I hadn't really thought about the questions he was asking. He knew my name. Which meant he remembered. But...if he remembered, why was he asking me questions that I should be asking him. I narrowed my eyes. "I need you to tell me everything you know about Sophia and Dr. Collins."

"What a stalemate. No...wait. You're tied up and I'm not. Which means you have to give me the answers, not the other way around."

"I'm not the one with the answers! You are!"

"Help me help you," he said. "Just tell me what you know."

"About Sophia freaking Tremblay?" I closed my eyes, I couldn't even look at him I was so mad. "You cheated on me with her. I know you did. But Detective Torres said you didn't. That you were stalking her." I shook my head. "But that can't be true. You called her all the time. And talked for hours. And you definitely did something to her. I saw the pictures of her face."

"What did I do to her face?"

"You hurt her. Her eye was purple and blue. Her cheeks were swollen too. There was a gash on her lip. You're a monster."

He didn't reply.

I opened my eyes to see him scowling. "Why does she look like me, Noah? Why did you hurt someone who looked just like me?"

His hands left my ankles so fast I didn't have time to kick him in the throat.

He was staring at me like he was angry with me. But I wasn't the one who beat up women. He was. He should be angry with himself.

"Why did you do it?" I asked again.

He shook his head. "I need to step out for about an hour. I'll be back before Detective Torres stops by, okay?"

"Okay? No, not okay! Noah!" I screamed as he disappeared out the bedroom door. My head throbbed as I thought about him roaming the streets. "You can't leave this house!" I pulled against the ropes. "You can't let anyone see you!"

Silence.

"Noah, I'm serious!" Tears started spilling down my cheeks. He didn't get to ruin my life for a second time. "I swear to God if you leave this house you'll get us both killed! Get back here!"

No response.

"You can't leave!" I was choking on my sobs. "You can't leave me like this!"

The sound of the garage door opening had me pulling on my ropes so hard I thought I'd dislocated my wrists. "Noah!" I screamed as loud as I could. But I knew he couldn't hear me anymore. The garage door closed and I heard the screeching of tires.

I pressed my hands against the headboard. And I let myself cry. *What am I going to do now?* How had I let this happen? *He tricked me. He tricked me.* Of course he tricked me. I'd been duped my whole marriage. I was a sucker. All he had to do was kiss me and I'd let my guard down. I'd let my whole future slip away because of a kiss. *Again.*

I'd had one job, despite all the things on my list. All I really needed to do was keep Noah tied up while I fled town. I could have done without the confession. Hell, I could have done without the money too. I'm sure there were jobs I was qualified for in Mexico. But I'd thrown all my hopes and dreams away for cash and revenge. There were question marks at the end of my to-do list because I wanted the freedom to change course. Yet, I didn't change course when I knocked Noah's memory out of him. And now...I looked up at the ropes. *Now what?*

Snuggle Muffins barked.

Oh, my sweet baby Snuggle Muffins. "Snuggle Muffins!" I called. My puppy could be my savior. "Where are you?"

He barked again. It sounded like he was downstairs. I thought about all the times I carried him up and down the stairs. He acted too feeble to do it on his own. But it didn't mean he couldn't. He was just being lazy. If I was a dog, I'd probably demand my owner to carry me everywhere too.

"Snuggle Muffins, come to Mommy!"

He barked again. It didn't sound like he'd moved at all.

"Sweet baby puppy, I really need you to come upstairs!" I wasn't positive, but I was pretty sure dogs had sharp little razor teeth. At least, they did in my mind. *Huh, maybe that's why I thought I didn't like dogs.* Well, one of the reasons. I also thought they were gross little monsters, but I found my dog to be quite lovely. He was different than the rest. And he would come up here and save me, I knew he would.

He barked again but still didn't sound any closer.

Don't give dogs a bad name again. "Snuggles, you need to go up the stairs!"

He didn't respond.

"Snuggles, I promise if you climb the stairs right now I'll never make you do it ever again!"

Nothing.

"I swear I'll carry your little prince butt everywhere. Even if there's a one-inch step, I'll lift you up!"

Silence.

"Please, Snuggle Muffins. Please, I need you!"

No response.

He probably got distracted by the mailman or something. *Dogs.* I looked back at the ropes. Noah said he'd been able to get out of them with a pair of pliers. I looked at the nightstand. I was on Noah's side of the bed, and I honestly had no idea what he kept in his nightstand drawer. I reached my foot out and somehow wrapped my toes around the little knob. But when I went to slide it open, my foot slipped. God, why didn't I take foot exercises more seriously? This was the kind of shit they should have taught in high school. Valuable life lessons instead of learning U.S. history over and over again for the millionth year in a row.

After several more attempts, I finally got the drawer open.

I wasn't at all surprised to see a few dirty magazines. My husband was the scum of the earth. I picked one up after the other with my toes and threw them on the ground. And then I rummaged around in the drawer. I was hoping to at least find a pen or something to help. Obviously a knife would have been better, and I wouldn't put it past him to have one by our bedside. But there was nothing useful.

Huh. My foot paused on an envelope. It was open. I looked over my shoulder like I was worried he was back and watching me. But I knew I'd hear the garage door when he got back. I lifted the envelope with my foot. After trying to get it to my mouth a few times unsuccessfully, I gave up on that idea. I needed to do more yoga.

Instead of trying to pull out whatever was in the envelope, I stretched my leg over the side of the bed, turned the envelope upside down, and let the contents fall to the floor.

Pictures? Huh. I peered over the bed. No, not just any pictures. Only a handful of them were turned right side up. But all the pictures that I could see were of me.

I was at some sort of café in one. Walking toward an office building in another. There was even one picture of me eating in a dining room. It looked like it had been taken through a window.

There was just one problem. I had no recollection of that café. Or that office building. Or of the dining room. How had Noah gotten so many pictures of me doing things I didn't remember doing?

Wait. I squinted down at the pictures again. There was only one logical conclusion. They weren't of me. At first glance I would have thought they were, but... *Oh my God.* They were of Sophia Tremblay. They had to be. It's not like I went around town not recognizing cafes and buildings I went into.

Was it possible that Noah wasn't having an affair? Sophia Tremblay's testimony was seeming more and more accurate. It really looked like Noah was stalking her. But why? I was still missing something. I looked back at my tied hands. I was running out of time. Honestly, I didn't care what my no-good husband was up to at this point. I just needed to get out of here.

I looked back down at the drawer but there was nothing at all useful. Shit. I looked at the nightstand itself. The bedside lamp was metal, but the light was glass. If I could somehow...

A bark made me turn my head.

"Snuggle Muffins?"

He ran over to the pictures and sat down on top of them.

It felt like I was dreaming. "Snuggle Muffins, you did it! You climbed the stairs. Jump up here."

He looked at me like I was crazy.

"Come on boy, you made it all the way up those stairs. One more little leap."

He lay down on top of the pictures.

"Please, Snuggle Muffins. One last hop. I realize that I promised no more climbing after the stairs, but clearly this was included. You need to use your sharp little teeth to help me get out of these ropes. You're my only hope."

He sighed.

"No more jumping after this. I swear to...whatever god dogs believe in. I'm going to lean down like this." I created a kind of ramp with my back, that led perfectly to the ropes. "And you're going to climb up and bite these ropes, okay?"

No response.

"I'm going to be so good to you. I'm going to buy you a Santa hat. And never make you go up stairs again. And feed you all your favorite foods. You liked bacon. Do you want more bacon?"

I felt the bed sag behind me.

"Snuggle Muffins, you did it!"

He was looking at my back leading up to my tied hands.

"You're such a good boy. Now, free Mommy. You got this."

He started climbing up my back.

If I got my money back and ever figured out who owned Snuggle Muffins before me, I made a silent promise that I'd give them half of it. They had trained this little dude so well and I loved him so freaking much.

He put his dirty little butt on the back of my head as he sniffed the ropes.

Gross, Snuggle Muffins. Maybe I just tolerated him.

He started biting at the ropes.

No, I loved him. I was right before. Screw Noah, this dog was the only man I needed in my life. "Good job, Snuggle Muffins. Just like that. Good boy."

I stayed in that awkward position until my knees started shaking, my back ached, and I'm pretty sure my head smelled like dog ass. But finally I felt my hands fall loose.

"Oh my God, you dog genius!" I collapsed on the bed. I thought Snuggle Muffins would get off the back of my head, but he just kept sitting there.

"I promised you a whole lot, Snuggles, but I did not promise that you could be my permanent crown." I lifted him off the back of my head. "You're amazing. You're wonderful. I love you."

He licked the side of my face and I only kinda grimaced.

"Okay. Now we just need to pack everything really quick." Hopefully I'd remember everything, since stupid Noah had stolen my phone and with it all of my reminder alarms. I jumped off the bed and tried not to cry from how much my back hurt.

I started throwing random clothes into my suitcase. All I could hear was a clock ticking down in my head, slowly counting to zero. I needed to be gone before Detective Torres came. And definitely before Noah came back. I couldn't play that game of high stakes hide-and-go-seek around the house again. I was going to hightail it out of here...

Shit. Shit, shit, shit! I threw the lid down on my suitcase. Noah had my car. That son of a bitch had a way of ruining everything.

I tried to take a deep breath. *Go with the flow. Think of another way.* An Uber to Mexico would literally cost a fortune. A plane or a rental car would require my ID. The last thing I wanted was to be stopped at the border.

I snapped my fingers. I'd hotwire a car. There was a knock on the front door.

I peered out the curtains and stared down at the top of Charlotte's head. Her perfect blonde hair glistened in the blinding light coming off the snow. She was holding another casserole dish. I didn't want her handouts. I let the curtains fall back in place as I lifted Snuggled Muffins into my arms.

I knew exactly where Charlotte was right this second. And it was the middle of the day, so her husband was at work and her kids were in school. It was their last day before Christmas break started. For all I cared, Charlotte could stand at my door all day waiting for news on my husband, gossip that she'd spread like wildfire. Actually I hoped she would stand there for a while. Because in the meantime, I was going to hotwire her car and get the hell out of here.

CHAPTER 25
Monday

I pulled a long wool coat over my ridiculous Mrs. Claus costume, grabbed Snuggle Muffins and my purse, and left out the back door.

Geez that's a lot of snow angels. I touched my forehead. It seemed like Noah was right about last night. I must have been out here for hours making all these.

For a second I just stared at the snow angels and dog paw prints everywhere. Noah knew I was high. And he'd slept with me. I should have felt betrayed. But Noah was an asshole. Taking advantage of women was just part of an endless list of terrible things he'd done.

I bit the inside of my lip. I'd thought he was high, and I'd slept with him. Actually, I'd thought he was way more high than I was. Because most of the weed was out of my system after running around the back yard all night. So actually...didn't that make me the one taking advantage of him? I smiled to myself. But then I immediately frowned. Kidnapper and rapist? *God, what is wrong with me?*

Also, why am I thinking about who raped who last night? I needed to focus.

I trudged through the snow toward Sally's fence. All I needed to do was get through Sally's yard undetected to get to Charlotte's. But if I wanted to go unnoticed, it would be best if I didn't go through her back yard. I made my way into the woods, being careful not to slip on any of the ice or trip on any of the snapped branches.

"Ensley? Is that you?"

God, Sally, give me a break! I turned to see Sally peering over the back of her fence at me. "Hey," I said and smiled. I would have waved but Snuggle Muffins was in my arms. I'd made him a promise about walking, and I was a woman of my word.

"Ensley, what on earth are you doing back there?"

"Just taking my dog on a walk." I was getting used to having a go-to excuse. Who knew that having a pet was so useful at getting away with weird things?

"Oh, well, let me join you."

What? No, you crazy bat. "I'm actually not feeling very well. I don't want you to catch whatever I have."

"Ah, probably because you were outside without a coat last night."

Oh, no. The image of her with a snake face came back to me. Had that actually happened? If it had...that meant she'd seen Noah through my kitchen window. *Fuck me.*

She opened the back gate and joined me in the woods. "Don't worry, it would be hard to catch anything from you with all this fresh air." She took a deep breath. "I love the smell of freshly fallen snow."

I wasn't worried about her catching a fake cold. I was worried about her catching *me*. If she told Detective Torres that she'd seen Noah, my whole plan would be ruined.

"Are you excited for the Christmas light contest tonight?" she asked. My fingers are crossed that you'll win it this year."

I nodded, but I barely heard her words. For a few seconds we walked in silence, the only sound the snow crunching under our feet. I needed to say something. Anything that would make her keep her mouth shut. I was considering threatening the wellbeing of her lawn gnomes when she broke the awkward silence.

"As a good neighbor, I should have seen it." She stopped at the end of her property line.

"Seen what?" I didn't want the answer to my question. I was worried I had to end this right here. I glanced behind me. We were all alone in the woods. Snuggle Muffins had bitten through a rope for me. If I told him to bite off her head, would he do it? Sally was a terribly nosy neighbor, but I wasn't sure I had it in me to kill her myself.

"Our two neighbors." She sighed. "Violet and Adeline. They were in bad situations with bad men. I should have seen it."

"No one saw it. You can't beat yourself up." I didn't have time for a therapy session right now.

Sally smiled, but it looked forced. "I made a promise to my-self to notice the important things. And I noticed you and Noah. It helps that I'm right next door. I know he hurts you, Ensley."

"He...he doesn't hurt me." I pictured Sophia's face. He hurt her. Badly. That so easily could have been me. It had been me.

"I hear the yelling."

"He doesn't hurt me." My voice was quieter now. Noah promised he'd never hurt me. He promised.

"Emotional abuse can be just as painful as physical abuse. I was trying to talk to you about this the other day...but now I'm afraid I'm running out of time."

I pressed my lips together.

"You know, I remember how happy you looked when you were pregnant." She shook her head. "I'd never seen you so hap-py."

"I was happy." Honestly, I was pretty sure it was the last time I was happy. I was so excited to meet my baby boy. I held Snuggle Muffins a little closer to my chest.

"I heard the yelling that night," Sally said. "Something happened, didn't it?"

I swallowed hard. "I slipped." I remembered all the blood at the bottom of the stairs. I remembered trying to wash the blood off my hands in the sink. I couldn't stop picturing it. The life seeping out of me. The water in the sink running red.

Sally reached out and grabbed my hand. "Did you slip? Or did he push you?"

I blinked when I noticed there were tears in my eyes. "I don't remember." I dreamed of that night all the time. In my dreams, I always felt the slap of his palm on my face. I saw his smile when I tried to dodge him and I lost my balance. I don't think he pushed me. But he certainly hadn't tried to catch me when I fell. He wanted me to lose the baby.

At least, Noah wanted me to think that was how I'd lost the baby. But my baby was already slowly dying when I fell. I found the abortion pills later. Along with all the depression and sleep medication. Back then my mind was foggy all the time. It was one of the reasons I couldn't remember my fall. I'd lost years of my life in a miserable blur. Because I was getting close to his secrets. He didn't want me to know the answers to my questions. He wouldn't even tell me when I kidnapped him. I just wanted the truth. I needed the truth.

Noah preferred me doped up on drugs. And I didn't know how he got them in my system. So I stopped drinking any beverages he handed me. I'd killed a lot of plants by pouring tea, wine, and juice in their soil. I also stopped eating any food he prepared, TV dinners becoming my choice of nourishment. When he questioned me, I'd down the food he made and immediately throw it back up afterward while the shower was running.

He didn't know that I knew. And I could see his frustration with my questions. I knew he'd never give me a real answer. And when I saw our bank accounts close? I knew I was running out of time to find out. Two could play the game of slipping pills. So I dressed up and drugged him back.

The baby was our tipping point. But not just because I lost him. It was because I finally got a glimpse of the truth. My husband was a monster.

"It's okay if you don't want to tell me," Sally said. "But you're allowed to be happy again. Let me help you."

It's too late.

"Just let me know what you need. We can get you out of this mess."

I didn't think I had anyone to reach out to. I didn't think anyone cared about me in this stupid neighborhood. But Sally was standing here caring. A few days too late. I shook my head. When I was doing all my research about knot tying on YouTube, I'd entered a rabbit hole on criminal activity. Lock-picking tutorials. Car hot wiring tutorials. But all I knew about stealing cars was from a video. And Charlotte might not even still be banging on my door.

"Can I borrow your car?" I asked.

Sally nodded. "Okay."

Really? That was easy. I didn't even need to fake cry. I blinked. Maybe because there were real tears on my cheeks.

"Come with me." She tucked her arm through mine. "My car is parked at the end of my driveway so that I wouldn't have to shovel very much."

That was smart thinking. So was four-wheel-drive, which was what I'd opted for.

We walked out of the woods and through Charlotte's yard.

"Wait here and let me go get the keys." She left me by her car. But really she left me to the wolves.

"Ensley! I was just looking for you," Charlotte said as she appeared by the car like the witch she was. "I brought you a chicken pot pie." She thrust the pan into my arms, despite the fact that Snuggle Muffins was there.

He sighed but didn't seem to mind as he sniffed the container.

"Um. Thanks," I said.

"I hope you enjoyed the lasagna?"

"Oh it was delicious."

"You ate the whole thing already? Oh my." She looked me up and down.

See. She was a bitch hiding behind nice actions like homemade pot pies. And I had nothing to say to her. Little did she know that I was dressed in a sexy Mrs. Claus outfit underneath my coat. And I looked damn fine, thank you very much.

"If you've finished it, do you mind giving me the dish back?" She smiled at me like she wasn't acting obnoxious.

"Of course. I'll drop it by tomorrow." *Psych.* I'd be long gone.

"Great. Oh, I almost forgot. I got a very interesting text about half an hour ago. Phoenix swore she saw Noah in town this morning. You know Phoenix. She lives down the street."

"Yup."

"Well, this is good news. I thought you'd be a little...happier."

Bite me. I smiled but I was pretty sure it looked more like I was grimacing.

She reached out and squeezed my arm. "This means he's safe. Just...not here with you."

Why were pretty girls so horrid? I wasn't surprised that Noah had been spotted. But I was surprised how stupid all these women were.

Snuggle Muffins growled at her and she dropped her hand.

"You might want to look into training your dog."

"Actually, he's already trained. He's perfect. Aren't you, Snuggle Muffins?" I hugged him a little tighter and resisted punching Charlotte in the face.

"Cute name. Sounds like something my five-year-old daughter would choose."

Bitch.

"Is everything okay out here?" Sally asked, her car keys jingling in her hand.

"Just great, Sally," Charlotte said. "I was just letting our dear Ensley know that Noah was spotted in town. Oh, wait, I almost forgot." She turned back to me. "Noah was talking to some woman. Phoenix didn't recognize her. But apparently they seemed pretty cozy, if you know what I mean." She gave me a sympathetic smile.

How I wished I had kidnapped her instead and made her poop in a litter box. That would have been so satisfying. There was still time. I could shove her ass in Sally's car and take her to Mexico. I was pretty sure the laws there were more lax. Maybe I'd even be able to get away with murder.

A car pulled up behind Sally's on the street and Detective Torres popped his head out. "Ensley. Do you have a minute?"

What is my luck? I never would have guessed that Charlotte would be the one to ruin everything at the last minute. All my planning never accounted for her blabbering. I should have just

stolen her car. It didn't help that Detective Torres was unfashion-
ably early either.

This was bad. Really bad. Noah could come back at any moment. *What am I going to do?* I cleared my throat. "Of course,
Detective Torres."

"Call me after, dear," Sally said and patted my shoulder. "I'll
be waiting." She waved at Detective Torres and made her way
back toward her house.

"Hi, Detective Torres," Charlotte said and ducked down so
she'd be eye to eye with him in the car. "How are you this afternoon?"

I swore she batted her fake eyelashes at him. *You're married.
Stop flirting with the law.*

"Great." He peered around her. "Ensley? I'll meet you at the
house."

I nodded.

"It's good you have company, Ensley. Now you won't eat that
whole pot pie yourself," Charlotte said before Detective Torres
pulled away.

I felt my cheeks turning red. I knew he'd heard that. It was
one thing to be mean to me. It was another to make fun of me in
front of other people. "I don't want your disgusting chicken pot
pie." I shoved it back in her arms. "You're rude. And cruel. And
unbearably awful. Go poison someone else with your over-salted
casseroles."

She gasped.

I'd finally told Charlotte off. And I'd slapped her with the
sickest burn a housewife could give another housewife - a jab at
her cooking. If that was the last thing I did before being hauled
off to prison, I could live with that.

The shocked expression on her face was more satisfying than shoving Noah down the stairs. I didn't even bother scolding myself and pretending that he slipped. I'd shoved him and I'd do it again. After all, he did it to me first.

Detective Torres was parked out front of my house. He was leaning against his car with his arms folded across his chest and his sunglasses covering his eyes. I figured there was a 90 percent chance I was about to be arrested.

CHAPTER 26
Monday

"Nice snow angels," Detective Torres said.

I looked at my front yard. Just like out back, the ground was covered in snow angels. I didn't even remember coming out front. God, when had I had time to do all this? "Thank you." I hated that it came out as more of a question than a statement.

"It seems like you had some fun last night."

I couldn't read him when he was hiding his eyes behind his sunglasses. It felt like a tactic. I didn't like being played. "Mhm," I said, offering him just as little in return.

"Did you have something to celebrate, perhaps?"

I shook my head. He wasn't as good at this game as I thought. He'd pretty much just showed all his cards. If he was waiting for a confession, it wasn't coming. "I drank too much wine and wanted to play outside with Snuggle Muffins. We got a little carried away it seems." I looked down at my dog. Growling at Charlotte must have worn him out. He was sleeping peacefully in my arms.

"I see. So it was more of a drowning your sorrows kind of thing?"

That sounded better than accidentally getting high. "Exactly."

"Do you mind if I come in? It's pretty cold out today."

I knew it wasn't really a choice. "I don't mind at all." I didn't know what kind of disarray my house was in. Noah had been loose all morning while I was tied up. All I knew was that there were definitely shredded ropes in our bedroom. Hopefully Detective Torres wouldn't come up there.

I plugged in my Christmas lights to buy time. They always looked extra magical under a blanket of snow, even in the daylight. A chill ran down my back like someone was watching me. I looked over my shoulder, but it was only Detective Torres standing there.

He smiled, but the sunglasses hid whether the smile reached his eyes.

I held Snuggle Muffins closer to my chest. The chill was replaced with an unsettled feeling in the pit of my stomach. As soon as Detective Torres came inside, I was basically begging to be caught. Noah would show up. He'd ruin everything. And I'd be the one that ended up behind bars, even though he was the monster. At least Snuggle Muffins' furry little body was a little comforting.

I glanced once more at the Christmas lights as I unlocked the door. Maybe the chill I'd felt was just the Christmas season finally getting to me. And the pit in my stomach was just a desire for gingerbread cookies. There was magic in the air today. Christmas was only a few days away now. It would be the first Christmas since I'd met Noah that I'd be spending it alone. I could already feel myself falling in love with the holiday again. Snuggle Muffins stirred in my arms. And now I had my own little family to celebrate with. I tried to hide my smile as I stepped inside the house.

Oh no. Screw me. One glance in the living room and I saw end table drawers hanging off their hinges. The dining room was no better. There was even broken China on the floor that Noah must have shoved off shelves while he was searching for...*what?* What the hell had he turned the house upside down in search of?

"What happened in here?" Detective Torres asked.

"Just...reorganizing some things."

"Huh." He took off his sunglasses and peered around me into the dining room. "Not a fan of those plates anymore?"

I didn't bother to look at the glass shards all over the floor again. "I hate family heirlooms." At least, I hated those. They were Noah's grandmother's or something and they were hideous. *Good riddance.*

He nodded.

I was right before. There were definitely no smiles reaching his eyes today. He looked...pissed off about something. I just wasn't sure what exactly he was upset about. He pulled off his coat, like he was planning on staying a while.

If only he was as easy to get rid of as bad china. "So..." I let my voice trail off. I knew I'd asked him to come here today. He was probably waiting for me to tell him my important news. But Noah wasn't here right now. So I didn't have to do anything I didn't want to. Besides, Detective Torres said he had news for me too.

He looked back in the dining room as he hung his sunglasses on the neckline of his shirt. "Were you looking for something?" he asked.

"Hm?" I tried to keep my voice even, but I knew I sounded guilty.

"It looks like you were searching for something..." He started to walk into the living room.

"Do you want a drink? I'm parched from my walk. All that fresh air and exercise always makes me uncomfortably warm. Let's get some water."

He hesitated in the entrance of the living room, a frown on his face. "Yeah. Sure. That would be great." He followed me down the hall toward the kitchen. "But if you're overheated, you should probably start by taking off your winter coat. It's pretty hot in here."

I swallowed hard. I was wearing a Mrs. Claus outfit under my coat. A sexy Mrs. Claus outfit. There wasn't a chance in hell that I was taking off my jacket in front of Detective Torres. "I'm not hot actually. I lied." *Don't admit to being a liar.* "I'm just...parched. Exclusively parched."

"Gotcha." He looked at the Christmas tree that was lying forgotten in the middle of the kitchen floor.

For the love of Christmas. No, it wasn't even a Christmas tree. It was some kind of ugly bush. A shrub maybe? *God, I was so high last night.* The hack job on the trunk was as hideous as the bush. It looked like the wood had been eaten by rabid raccoons. *How could you let me bring that in the house, Snuggle Muffins?* For all I knew it was actually filled with rabid raccoons. I placed Snuggle Muffins on the ground, hoping that he'd attack anything that jumped out of it.

Snuggle Muffins just blinked, annoyed that he'd been awakened from his nap, and went back to sleep.

"Um. What is that?" Detective Torres asked.

"That?" I pointed to the shrub, stalling. "Well, *that* is a...Christmas bush."

"What the hell is a Christmas bush?"

I laughed. And then laughed some more, shaking my head like Detective Torres was an idiot. "I'm an environmentalist," I said. *Oh, nice one.* Being a hippy was basically an excuse to do weird stuff. "Christmas trees are bad for the environment. So Noah and I always decorate a Christmas bush."

"I thought you said you and Noah always pick out a Christmas tree together every year?"

I shook my head. "God, Detective Torres. If I had a nickel for every time I had to explain this to someone...I'd have several dollars. I just didn't want to have this conversation explaining the pros and cons of real Christmas trees for the umpteenth time. You wouldn't understand."

He nodded, but it didn't look like he believed me. "Right. Because you know me so well?" He smiled at me.

How flirtatious, Detective Torres. I smiled back and shrugged my shoulders.

"Did you get this Christmas bush before or after you drank too much wine and made all those snow angels?"

So maybe not flirting. "Fair enough. It was after. Usually I'd make a much cleaner cut through the trunk." *Oh, no. Don't say that either.* I didn't want him to know I was experienced with an axe. "Well, Noah does. Speaking of Noah...you said you had some news?"

He ignored me as he looked over at the kitchen sink. "It looks like you were feeding a whole army this morning."

God, Noah. He was such a slob. There were dishes everywhere. Hadn't he just tried to force-feed me toast and orange juice? There was no excuse for this much of a mess. "I'm still trying to figure out the perfect blend of nutrients for Snuggle Muffins."

"You make homemade dog food?" He nodded like he was impressed.

"Yup. Of course. Let me get you that water." I knew that every second I didn't hear the garage door was a blessing. Noah could show up at any moment. There wasn't time to have casual conversations and beverages with Detective Torres. But the house was warm and I was starting to sweat in my winter jacket. I poured us each a glass and guzzled down half of mine before I handed his to him.

"Mmm, those brownies sure look good."

I turned in horror to see the dish of weed brownies still sitting on the counter. "Those are dog biscuits," I blurted out. "And they're gross. A total failure."

"He's eaten quite a few. Must not be so bad."

"He's a dog. He doesn't know what he likes."

Snuggle Muffins sighed.

Sorry, boy. I didn't mean it. I'm just trying to keep us out of jail. Was there a prison for dogs? If so, Snuggle Muffins was quite the accomplice, which made him just as guilty as me. I was trying to save his ass too.

Detective Torres leaned against the kitchen island. "So what was so important that you wanted to discuss?"

"Did I say important?" I shook my head. "I don't remember saying that."

He raised both his eyebrows. "What, you just wanted me to stop by?"

There it was again. It really seemed like he was flirting with me. That would have made Noah really mad. I tried to hide my smile. If Detective Torres really was flirting with me, it opened up a few more options on how to get out of this. Maybe he'd actually offer to be tied up...

"You definitely said you had something important to tell me." His gaze locked with mine and I felt frozen in place.

"Or did you say that?" I asked.

He shrugged his shoulder. "We both did. But I'd rather hear your news first."

I gestured to all the Christmas decorations. "I just wanted to show you that I was able to decorate. Thanks to you bringing up that box. I can't believe you were able to lift it all by yourself. It was so heavy." I leaned against the opposite side of the kitchen island. Normally when I leaned this far over, my breasts would be on full display. But I was still wearing the stupid freaking winter coat.

"Yeah, I can see that. Christmas bush and all. Tell me, Ensley, why were you really drinking last night? Sure you didn't have anything to celebrate?"

I flipped my hair over my shoulder. "My husband is missing. Of course I didn't have anything to celebrate." I ran my finger down the condensation on my glass. "Just me all alone in this big empty house."

He lowered his eyebrows. "Ensley, are you feeling alright? You're looking a little...sweaty."

I was hoping the jacket was making my skin flushed and sexy. I wiped a bead of sweat off my forehead. But Detective Torres was correct, I was sweating bullets. "Yeah, I'm fine." This time when I flipped my hair off my shoulder it was because it was unbearably hot against my neck. Some of the strands stuck to the sweat.

"I need to discuss something with you," he said. "And I need you to be completely honest with me."

Nothing I ever said to him was honest. I needed to get closer to him if I was going to woo him out of questioning. "Of course, detective. How about we go get more comfortable in the other room." I walked away before he had a chance to respond.

It was a bad idea to come into the family room. Last night it looked like a Christmas wonderland. Today it looked like a tornado had swept through. I ignored the wreckage and gestured to the couch.

"I'm good," he said and leaned against the doorjamb.

Apparently my sweatiness was a huge turnoff. I collapsed on the couch, breathing hard. I needed to figure out a way to get him out of my house before I internally combusted. And before Noah got back. I was two seconds away from taking off my jacket and doing a seductive dance for him. I wasn't even sure how that would help, but my brain was becoming mush from the heat.

"So you called the police station Friday about your husband being missing, correct?" he asked.

"That is correct." I unbuttoned my jacket but kept it firmly wrapped around me. It let a tiny amount of cool air hit my chest.

"You said you saw him that morning?"

"Mhm." The small amount of air wasn't helping. It was too freaking hot. Had Noah turned up the thermostat?

"I went down to his office to ask his staff some questions."

That wasn't good. Neither was the fact that I was pretty sure I was about to faint from heatstroke.

"No one there has seen him since Tuesday."

"Tuesday? Oh, that's weird. I wonder where he was going instead of work?" It came out more sarcastic than I'd intended.

Detective Torres just stared at me. "That's what I was hoping you could help me with."

Was he really that dense? "Let's see...my husband skipped work for a few days to..." I snapped my fingers but it made a sad noise because my hands were sweaty. "Oh right. He's a dirty cheat. He probably went to Canada to sleep with Sophia Tremblay. Or stalk her. Or whatever she claimed."

"We already confirmed that he wasn't sleeping with Sophia," he said. "Which means that Noah has been missing since Tuesday. Wednesday morning at the latest. Yet you claim you saw him on Friday morning. Did you see him Wednesday and Thursday morning too?"

"Yes." I didn't even have to lie about that.

"So your Canada trip theory doesn't exactly pan out there, Ensley. Leaving for Canada in the morning and coming back each night? A little hard to pull off."

I opened my coat and closed it again, creating a breeze. I didn't even care if Detective Torres saw my costume at this point. If I didn't cool off I was seriously going to pass out. "Right, and you're the expert on how long it takes to get back and forth to Canada. What were you doing there again?"

"Visiting...family." He cleared his throat. "I have family up there. Lots of them. I try to visit a few times a month."

Wow, Detective Torres was a terrible liar. If he had family up there he'd be guzzling maple syrup and saying 'eh' all the time. He was definitely about to say something else. What? Did he actually have business up there? It was out of his jurisdiction. Originally he'd told me it was personal business. Personal business did have to do with family. So why did it seem like he was lying?

"What did you do on your personal trip to Canada?"

"Caught a hockey game."

Damn it, that actually checked out. Canadians loved hockey. But I was pretty sure Detective Torres was sweating more than me now. I was about to ask him another question, but he beat me to it.

"Ensley, this isn't about my business in Canada. I'm here about Noah. And despite the fact that flying back and forth to Canada in that time frame each day would be difficult...I know for a fact that he didn't do it. I ran it through the system. He hasn't checked in to any international flights for weeks."

"Maybe he took a private jet."

"Does he do that often?"

How should I know? I'd made it pretty clear that I wasn't my husband's keeper. "He doesn't exactly keep my up to date on his business. And even if he didn't go to Canada, it doesn't mean he wasn't seeing a mistress instead of going to work. He's been seeing someone in town too. I know he has."

"And you didn't think it was important to tell me that information a few days ago?"

"It's a little embarrassing telling a complete stranger that you're not even good enough for your own husband!" I pressed my lips together. The heat was making me have loose lips. God, I really was about to faint. I flapped my coat collar to create a lackluster breeze.

"You know, I heard what Charlotte said. About not eating the whole pot pie yourself. Ensley, you must see that she only said that because she's jealous of you."

"Jealous? Of me?"

He nodded. "If anything, I'm certain you're too good for your husband. So how about you tell me when the last time you actually saw him was. Let's get him back safe and sound and then I can help set you up with a great divorce lawyer. I'll help you figure it out, okay? I promise."

I promise? Why did he keep saying shit like that to me? He wasn't flirting with me. He was just trying to mess with my head. "I told you everything I know."

"Ensley, no one at the office got a phone call from you once Noah went missing. You said you checked with everyone you know. Yet you didn't check with the people he works with every day? That's suspicious."

"I don't like his co-workers. Speaking of which, they're a bunch of liars. Noah probably was at work and they're just being stupid. Or covering for his cheating ass." I couldn't even think about what I was saying anymore. I was literally turning into a puddle. I stood up so I wouldn't melt into the couch.

He took a step back like he thought I was about to attack him.

"Are you seriously scared of me?" I asked.

"Should I be?"

I swallowed hard. *Maybe.* If he stayed there much longer...yeah, maybe. I wasn't going to let a bad detective be the one to bring me down.

"Ensley, your husband has been missing since Tuesday night. Not Friday. Why didn't you notify us right away?"

"Because he wasn't missing. I just told you...I saw him Wednesday, Thursday, and Friday morning."

Detective Torres shook his head. "See...I don't think you're being completely honest with me. And I also think you know where he is."

"Well, that's your opinion. And your opinion is wrong."

"You need to tell me where Noah is right now. Before something happens that you'll regret."

"I don't regret anything I've done." There was a lump in my throat that wouldn't go away. It felt like I was choking. God, I'd basically just confessed. I needed to backtrack. I needed to say anything.

"Ensley, what have you done?"

"He killed my baby." Tears started to pool in the corners of my eyes. "Detective Torres, I lied. He did hurt me. Emotionally. Physically." God, all I could ever see was the blood at the bottom of the steps. "He drugged me. For years I was just...nothing. He made me think I was crazy. But he's a monster. You have to believe me."

"I believe you, Ensley. Let's go down to the station and I can get your full statement. And you can tell me exactly what you did."

I shook my head.

"Okay. Then tell me here. What did you do?"

I tore my jacket off because it was like I was standing in Satan's fire.

"Ensley, it's against the law to try to bribe a detective." His eyes stayed firmly on my face instead of wandering down to my revealing Mrs. Claus costume.

Yeah, he hadn't been flirting. He was using me. Tricking me. His promises meant nothing. No one ever kept their promises to me. "I'm not bribing you! It's freaking a thousand degrees in here and you're pointing a finger at me for murdering my husband." I threw my jacket at him.

He dodged it like it contained a bomb.

It didn't. But God, I wish it had. I could just picture stupid Detective Torres exploding into a million colorful pieces.

He shook his head. "I didn't say anything about homicide."

Oh no. Had I said that? My brain was rapidly becoming less mushy now that I could breathe again. "We both know what you were thinking." It was a lame excuse. I needed to do better.

"Ensley, did you murder your husband?"

"No. Of course not. I'm not a lunatic! But he was an asshole. I'm sure a lot of people would be happy if he was dead." *Stop talking about Noah being dead.*

He was staring at me like I was indeed a crazy woman. "You said he *was* an asshole. Past tense."

"I meant *is*. He *is* an asshole. I went to public school. I never properly learned my tenses."

"Noah was cheating on you. He abused you emotionally and physically. He drugged you. You had every reason to want to kill him."

Fuck yeah I did. I pressed my lips together, not willing to risk saying anything else damning.

"Ensley, I'm placing you under arrest for the murder of your husband. Obstruction of justice. And bribing an officer."

"Silence isn't consent! I didn't murder Noah. I told you everything I know. And I was wearing this outfit before you showed up. You can't arrest me. Detective Torres, you said you believed me..."

"Place your hands on the back of your head. Turn around. Kneel."

"But I..."

He drew out his gun and aimed it at my scantily clad chest.

Shitballs! "Okay." I held my hands up. "Okay. But I didn't murder my husband. You're going to look like such an idiot when you bring me in. Kind of like last time when you let your prime suspect escape. Do you really want that?"

"Now, Ensley."

I gave him my most innocent smile. "Damien, come on." I thought using his first name would help, but if anything he looked angrier. "I'll give you whatever you want. Just lower your gun and we can talk about this." I bit my bottom lip, wishing that I wasn't a sweaty mess right now.

For just a second, his eyes dropped to my breasts.

Oh thank God. It was a Christmas miracle.

But then he pulled out his handcuffs with his free hand as he shifted the aim of his gun to my forehead. He wasn't trying to injure me. He was going for the kill shot. I wasn't the one that deserved to die. My husband was. But life wasn't fair. I knew that better than anyone.

"I'm giving you to the count of three, Ensley."

That wasn't enough time to think of an escape.

"Three," he said.

There was a small glass Christmas tree decoration on the mantle. I could stab it into the side of Detective Torres' throat. But I'd never be able to grab it in time.

"Two."

Where was Snuggle Muffins when I needed him? If I whistled would he come to my rescue? Or would trying just make Detective Torres shoot a bullet into my skull?

"One."

I put my hands on the back of my head. There was no way out. I turned around. My detailed to-do list never planned for this. Tears ran down my cheeks as I knelt. *Game over.* I felt the cool metal of the handcuffs click around my wrists.

CHAPTER 27
Monday

"Detective Torres, you don't have to do this."

He yanked me to my feet. "You have the right to remain silent."

"But I didn't kill my husband. It was just a figure of speech."

"Anything you say can and will be held against you in a court of law."

"Like...when you say Santa Claus' belly shakes like a bowlful of jelly. He hasn't actually raided the pantry for all the jam and binge-eaten all of it. His stomach just kind of looks like jelly jiggling."

"You have the right to an attorney."

"I'm not a murderer! I swear to God. You have to believe me." I tried to shove my heels into the carpet to make him stop moving me, but it was no use. He was too strong. "Detective Torres! This is ridiculous. You know I didn't kill anyone."

He kept his hand on my bicep as he led me out of the family room and past Snuggle Muffins. "If you cannot afford an attorney, one will be provided for you."

Do something, Snuggle Muffins. Attack! Anything. Help me.

For a second, Snuggle Muffins stood up. But thinking better of it, he sat back down like his mom wasn't being carted off to jail.

I narrowed my eyes at him, hoping he could sense that I was serious.

I could have sworn he narrowed his eyes back. Then he yawned and lay down.

No one's going to feed you while I'm gone. I tried to stop Detective Torres in his tracks, but he kept pulling me. "I need to make a phone call."

"Ensley, what didn't you understand about anything you say can and will be held against you in a court of law?"

"All I've said is that I'm innocent. You're not listening to me."

He pulled me forward.

"Please, I just need one phone call."

"You'll be given a phone call when we reach the station."

"But I need to call Sally. She'll take care of Snuggle Muffins for me while I'm being wrongfully held. Please. I can't leave him here all alone. He needs someone." He needed me. But Detective Torres had made it pretty clear that he wasn't planning on letting me go.

"And like I said, you can call her from the station." He pushed me down the hall.

"At least let me change out of this outfit. Or put on a coat. It's freezing outside." *And if I wear this to a holding cell, I'll surely end up being someone's bitch.*

"You should have thought about that before you tried to seduce an officer."

"I wasn't trying to seduce you. I was already wearing this."

"And you knew I was coming over." His rebuttal was flimsy at best.

"You were early. Besides, you're not an officer. You're a detective. You're better than this."

He stopped in front of the door. "Then tell me, Ensley. Who were you wearing it for? Your husband? If he's alive and you know where he is...tell me now."

I couldn't do that. "*You* were supposed to figure out what he's been up to." That was the only reason I'd involved the police in the first place. And maybe a little for the notoriety. "You weren't supposed to arrest me. He's the guilty one."

"And if he's alive when we find him, we'll talk to him about what he did to Sophia."

"Sophia?" I tried to keep my voice even. "What about everything he did to me?"

"There's no proof that he was drugging you. There's no proof that he hurt you. It would be your word against his. But if you tell me where he is, maybe we can work something out. Maybe you can be home in time for Christmas."

I didn't care about Christmas. And I certainly didn't care about this home. All I cared about was Snuggle Muffins and Noah. I swallowed hard. Noah? I didn't care about Noah. I hated Noah. He was an asshole. And he left me tied up upstairs. Me being in handcuffs was his fault. All of this was his fault. So why the hell did I still care about him?

"He hurt me," I said.

Detective Torres pulled me closer to the front door. "And when I told you about Sophia, you looked me in the eye and swore that he never hurt you. So, I don't believe you."

"Why? Because I don't have my face beaten like Sophia? Are you seriously telling me I waited too long to come forward? What kind of fucked up policy is that? Time doesn't erase the fact that he hurt me."

"Time erases the proof."

"Bullshit. Time doesn't erase anything. My memories are proof. The fact that I can't sleep at night is proof. All the drugs in my system are proof. And I'm telling you that he…"

"Ensley, just tell me where he is. Either we go to the station and we talk about it there or you just tell me here. Where is your husband? Final chance to tell me the truth."

I pressed my lips together.

"If he's alive, why won't you tell me where he is?"

"Because I did something bad." *Really, really bad.* I swallowed hard. I'd already said too much.

"What did you do?"

I shook my head. The only way out of this was Noah walking through the front door and helping me. I couldn't go to jail. I wouldn't be able to explain my way out of this. But Noah loved me. He swore he did. He'd help me out of this mess that he'd created. Or it would be the proof Detective Torres needed to send me away for a long time. It came down to how well he'd studied my case. How thoroughly he knew both me and my dear husband.

I was pretty sure I knew Detective Torres better than he knew me. I'd watched all the interviews. I'd studied him when he should have been studying me. He'd let one guilty housewife get away. And I was banking on the fact that he'd let another one go too.

"Okay," I said. "I'll tell you everything."

He let me turn away from the front door to face him. And it was lucky that I did, or else I would have made a terrible mistake. I would have jeopardized everything when I didn't have to.

Because Noah was standing behind him. And that alone was enough to have my brain forming a whole new plan. One that involved absolutely no chance of me winding up behind bars. I just needed a second to think, but Noah's stupid elf costume was distracting me from focusing.

Detective Torres must have seen the glee on my face, because he turned to see what I was looking at. "Noah?" he asked and then laughed. "Jesus, man. Your wife made it seem like you were dead." He thrust his hand out for him to shake. "Nice to finally see you in the flesh. I was worried there for a second."

The plans in my head stopped formulating. I blinked. Detective Torres called him Noah. Detective Torres saw it too? I wasn't crazy. I touched the side of my forehead as I stared at Noah. Really stared. The laugh lines around his eyes. His dark hair. His slightly lighter stubble. The freckles that were scattered right beneath his eyes. They were all familiar. I'd woken up to him thousands of mornings. He was my husband.

But when I looked harder? Really looked? My eyes narrowed in on him. The stubble was actually a lot lighter than his hair. His hair was really, really dark. Unnaturally so. Like it had been dyed. Like he'd been trying to hide his true identity.

It came back in a rush. A piece clicking back together in my brain. My husband had told me that I was crazy. That I was seeing things. That there was no possible way that there were two of him. But he kept appearing somewhere that he wasn't. I'd kept it all written down. Every time I spotted him somewhere, he claimed he hadn't been there. He'd found my calendar tracking him. He'd given me more medicine, trying to erase my memories. He'd whispered lies into my ear. And I'd eaten it up. For a short time. While I was still being drugged.

But they were all lies. And his plan hadn't worked. There were two of him. This was one of him. And the other one of him...

No. I'd been fighting with myself. Half the time I thought it was really Noah. Half the time I knew it wasn't. But I was never sure. Never really sure. Because it was easy to doubt yourself when you were belittled for years. And I wanted this to be my actual husband. Because if it wasn't...

Noah stuck out his hand to shake Detective Torres'. "Nice to finally meet you too." He flashed me a smile.

No. No, no, no. I blinked again. The Noah standing there shaking Detective Torres' hand wasn't the real Noah. He looked like my husband. He even sounded like my husband. Because he was supposed to. But this Noah was not my husband. Because the real Dr. Noah Collins?

I held my breath. I wanted Detective Torres to be right. That this imposter was Noah. I wanted it to be true. Because if it wasn't...I was pretty sure the nightmares I had been having were true. I was almost positive that the real Dr. Noah Collins was dead. And if he was dead...I was worried I knew where he was. Detective Torres couldn't know. He wouldn't believe me. Just like my husband claimed he didn't believe me. They'd lock me up. They'd think I was crazy. *I'm not fucking crazy.*

Detective Torres looked between us, eyeing our strange Christmas getups. "So...what the hell is happening?" he asked. "Please tell me this whole thing wasn't a ruse so you can win that stupid neighborhood Christmas light contest? Some kind of grand entrance to shock your neighbors?"

Noah laughed. "Well, we will be wearing these costumes to that. As for the whole me being missing thing? This has all just been a huge misunderstanding. Actually, I have some files here that I think will clear everything up." He held up the files that were in his hand. "Ensley, I want you to see these too. Come here, baby."

I felt like I was going to throw up. I had no idea what was in those files. But I knew it was most likely damning. And even if it wasn't? A dead body surely would be.

I needed to get Detective Torres out of the equation so I could have a second to think. My hands were still cuffed behind me, so I did the first thing I thought of. I kicked the back of Detective Torres' knees so he buckled forward.

"What the f…" he started.

But he didn't finish his statement. Because I kneed him right in the side of his head. He crumpled to the floor with a thud.

"What the hell did you do that for?" Noah said. "I was going to smooth everything over! I had a plan. You just assaulted a detective. You could go to jail, Ensley." He raked his fingers through his dyed hair. "What were you thinking?"

I took a step away from him.

"Baby, it's okay we can figure it out." He closed the distance between us, probably assuming my sudden movement was fueled by regret over kicking Detective Torres in the head. And not out of fear of the man still standing in front of me. "I won't let anything bad happen to you. I'll keep you safe."

Safe? I wasn't the crazy one. He was. *Think of a way out of this.*

He touched the side of my face and I tried not to hurl. He'd sat in the basement saying he loved me. That he'd never cheat on me. He'd pressured me into believing. He'd said it all with my husband's face.

But this man was not my husband. And I had no idea who the hell he was or what he wanted with me.

"It's okay," he whispered. "We'll figure it out together." When he leaned down for a kiss, I let instinct take over again. I bit his lip so hard I could taste blood, and then I kneed him right in the junk.

He groaned and leaned forward, grasping at the front of his tiny elf shorts.

And then I ran as fast as I could.

CHAPTER 28
Monday

"Ensley, stop!" Noah screamed through a slur of curses.

I ran faster, which wasn't that fast when my hands were still cuffed behind me and I didn't want to topple straight onto my face.

I reached the back door in the kitchen and turned around to work on the lock with my hands.

Snuggle Muffins was still sleeping in the middle of the kitchen floor, as if my assaulting a detective and kneeing Noah in the crotch was uneventful.

My hand paused on the knob. I couldn't leave Snuggle Muffins behind. He was more than just my accomplice. He was...all I had left. "Come, Snuggle Muffins. Now." I couldn't lift him up with my hands behind my back. He needed to get up and run to me. *Run to Mommy.*

His ears twitched up but he stayed exactly where he was. Eyes closed and all.

Noah came barreling into the kitchen with a terrifying scowl on his face that didn't match the joy of his costume in the slightest.

I opened the door behind me successfully, but I couldn't leave without Snuggle Muffins. I refused to.

Noah reached me and slammed the door closed. "Where the hell do you think you're going?" He kept his hands on either side of me, caging me in.

And in a flash I saw my husband again. Angry and cruel. I cowered beneath him. Waiting for the sharp pain of his palm hitting my skin. But it didn't come in.

Because he wasn't my husband. He was… I looked back up at him. "Who are you?" He was too close to me. He looked too similar. And my mind loved to play tricks on me when it came to my husband.

"Are you kidding me? You knew I wasn't Noah this whole freaking time?" He took a step back and ran his fingers through his dyed hair. "You've been calling me Noah for days. You had me believing I was your husband after you knocked me unconscious. All of this could have been cleared up a lot earlier if you didn't keep acting like I was your husband. Messing with my head. You had me believing everything."

And I just stood there staring at him. "You know you're not Noah?" Part of me had been playing along with him being my husband. It had been so easy to get lost in that fantasy. To hope. To believe I hadn't done something terrible.

"I didn't realize the truth until this morning. I was looking all over the place trying to piece together what happened. Trying to figure out why the hell I couldn't remember my own family."

Family. He thought we were a family. Wasn't that all I'd ever wanted to be? Part of a family?

I looked past him into the ransacked family room. I knew he had been searching for something. But I had no idea he was trying to piece together his past. Or that I'd confused him into thinking he was actually my husband. When he was confusing me back by acting like my husband. And having my husband's face. We'd done the ultimate role-play, all completely by accident.

"And when I found your phone, with all those appointments with Dr. Collins, I lost it. You'd been saying I was cheating on you. When really it seemed like you were the one cheating on me."

I nodded. All the Dr. Collins notes in my calendar were just me tailing my husband. Trying to figure out where he was going. Where he was at all times. "But then I mentioned Sophia. And her face looking like mine." I remembered his hands falling from my skin. The angry look on his face. I thought he was angry with me. But...that must have been when he remembered the truth. That he wasn't Noah.

He nodded.

"You remember now?" I asked.

"I remember everything," he said.

I swallowed hard. I didn't. I knew most of it, but there were still blurry parts. It had been so long since I'd been able to think clearly. "If you're not my husband, then who are you?"

"I work for him." That was all he offered.

I'd been to his office before. No one there had his face. I shook my head. "I know all of his employees."

"His other business. Ensley, your husband was doing illegal procedures." He grabbed the files he'd tried to show Detective Torres. "Like this."

I opened the first file. It was medical records for a man named Aiden Brown. The man looked a little like my husband. I turned the page. There were sketches outlining a reconstruction procedure. The shaving down of his jaw. Tweaks to his nose. Even changes to his ears. The final effect was a picture of a man that almost looked identical to my husband. I looked up. "You're Aiden?"

He nodded and handed me another file. This one was for a woman who looked a little like me.

The sketches of the procedures were on the next page. And on the next...a woman that looked so eerily like me that you could easily mistake us as the same person. Or was it me? I touched my cheek. Was I this woman? I wanted to claw my skin off. "Is this me?"

He grabbed my hand, his touch comforting. "No. That's Sophia Tremblay. Your replacement."

"My what?"

"It all came back to me this morning. When you said Sophia looked like you. That she had been beaten up. This woman." He stabbed a finger at Sophia's face. "She's your replacement."

I shook my head. *Replacement?*

"You knew that, Ensley. You knew your husband was cheating on you. It's why you kidnapped *me*."

I shook my head. I did know that. But this? The files felt heavy in my hand. He put my face on another woman. To steal my money. To leave me. That was insane. But I also believed it. Because for months I'd been suspicious that my husband had a doppelgänger. He'd tried to erase the memories. Swearing he was just cheating and that he'd stop. Promising it wasn't true. But this was what he'd been doing behind closed doors. Creating monsters.

"I was supposed to keep you...preoccupied until he came back from Canada. But whenever I came around, you just peered at me through the dining room window like you were seeing a ghost. You wouldn't let me inside." He shook his head. "You finally answered one of my calls, agreeing to meet me at that bar on Friday night. I figured you knew I wasn't your husband. But you didn't even flinch when I said my name was Noah."

I touched the side of my head. I remembered him coming around the house the past week. I'd thought I was staring through the glass at my husband's ghost. And then I'd gone to the bar that night, wanting to believe he was real. I wanted to believe I hadn't done something terrible. Because I never got my answers. I needed the fucking answers. "And what about my money?"

"He had this whole plan to use Sophia to steal all your money. That's why he changed her face. To get access to your accounts through her. And I guess they covered their tracks afterwards by hurting her. To make her look less like you again in case they were contacted by the police."

I shook my head. "He'd need my license. They wouldn't just trust that she was just me without identification."

"He took your license."

I walked past him into the family room where I'd left my coat and purse. I rummaged through my purse and grabbed my wallet. The clear sleeve that always held my license was empty. I frantically pulled all my credit cards out. But my license wasn't there. *Son of a bitch.* "Is the money with her?"

"Or him." He shrugged. "I know you probably still have a million questions, but we need to get out of here. Before Dr. Collins comes back. If he finds out I told you the truth, he'll kill both of us."

I just stared at him. "Why did you agree to it?" I touched my own face to show him what I meant. I couldn't say the words.

"I wanted an out. When he first started this, he was doing good. He was helping people without insurance. But it turned into something ugly. I owed a debt to your husband. But I never agreed to this crazy shit. I didn't know he was drugging you. I didn't know he hurt you. He said if I did this, he'd let me leave. Alive. Which was something that had become rare in the past year. All I had to do was run some errands pretending to be him.

That was the deal. His face for freedom in a few months. You were supposed to be my last assignment."

He changed his face for freedom? I didn't blame him for that. I'd get plastic surgery on my whole body if it meant I could leave my husband.

"Like I said, we can talk about this in the car. But we really have to get going."

"You still want to come with me?" I asked. "Even though you have your memories back?" For some reason, the face alterations made sense. But him wanting to escape with me? That was impossible.

"I meant every word I said the past few days."

"You don't even know me."

"That's not exactly true. Part of this assignment was to know everything about you. Yeah, I forgot when I fell down the stairs." He said it like it was a question, probably still suspicious that I'd pushed him. "But I remember now. Your favorite color is green. Like the nursery color upstairs."

Something in my throat constricted. My husband didn't understand why I chose green. But Aiden had put the pieces together pretty easily.

"You fell in love with this neighborhood and the white picket fences. You inherited a hell of a lot of money when your grandparents passed away." He shook his head. "You're smart. And stubborn as hell. And so beautiful it hurts."

I felt my cheeks heating.

"And you taste like cinnamon. The curve of your body fits perfectly against mine. You have a birthmark on the inside of you right thigh that looks like a heart. And I'm pretty sure I fell in love with you before we ever even met."

I didn't know whether he meant a word of it. Or if Snuggle Muffins was right and he had Stockholm syndrome. But it felt like my Grinch heart grew a few sizes. I barely knew a thing about this man. But God, how many years had I been hoping for a knight in shining armor to come save me from this hell.

I stepped forward and leaned my head against his chest.

He wrapped his strong arms around me.

I breathed in his familiar, yet different scent. He wasn't scary like my husband. He wasn't threatening my life. He was trying to save it. I'd been slowly slipping the past few days. Wanting to believe in a second chance. That I could still have a life that wasn't in shambles. *I love you too.* I didn't know if it was true, but I was pretty sure I loved him more than I had ever loved my husband.

"Now let's get the hell out of here before your crazy ass husband comes home. I checked in with some of our colleagues and he hasn't gotten back from Canada yet. But he could arrive any minute. And I'd feel a hell of a lot better if we could get a few states between us and him. Maybe we can clear up what happened to him too." He gestured to the hall behind him where Detective Torres was still passed out. "Figure out a way to make Detective Torres understand that none of this was your fault. But the distance will make me feel better, just in case he doesn't understand."

I took a deep breath. Aiden wasn't my husband. And I wasn't insane. It should have been a relief. But with a clear head came the most terrible realization of all. After what I'd done, I didn't have a choice.

As Aiden grabbed the keys off Detective Torres' belt and uncuffed me, all I wanted to do was run away from this mess. I ran my thumb along my wrist. For some reason, it still felt like the cuffs were on me. Shackling me to this house. Keeping me locked up in this nightmare.

"Come on, we have to go," he said.

I didn't move. "He already came back."

"What?"

"My husband came back Tuesday." I wrung my hands together. "I knew he was seeing someone behind my back. I knew he was up to something shady. And I was so freaking mad."

"What are you talking about?"

"I did something bad. And putting a few states between us and this house isn't going to solve our problems." Aiden wasn't the first person that I drugged and tried to bring to the basement for questioning. But when I shoved my husband down the stairs…he didn't just lose his memory. He lost his life. The blood seeped into the wooden steps. It had taken hours to scrub away all the stains. I didn't know how I'd forgotten about it. Joyful moments were always easy to remember. And God, I'd never felt more joy than when I saw all that blood drain from my husband's head.

He waited. I was pretty sure he wasn't breathing.

"I killed him. Don't look at me like that. He deserved it, and we both know it."

CHAPTER 29
Monday

Aiden stared at me in a way that my husband never had. Almost as if he was frightened of me. It was weird being on the other side of someone's fear. I was usually the one trembling. Until I realized I didn't have to anymore. Until I took things into my own hands.

But I hated the way he was looking at me. I liked when there were stars in his eyes. When he was whispering sinful things against my skin. What if that was gone? What if I'd killed my future and my past?

"Maybe I killed him," I added. I didn't want Aiden to look at me like that anymore. My husband was the monster, not me. He knew that. He'd worked with the lunatic. "I mean...I don't know." Everything felt upside down and turned around. Hell, for all I knew, I was still staring at my husband right now. Which meant the body rotting away in my house actually didn't exist. *Maybe.*

No, not maybe. I'd done it. Detective Torres was right. My husband did technically disappear on Tuesday night. But I hadn't lied about seeing him the rest of the week. I saw him Tuesday. Wednesday. Thursday. That was the truth. But he'd been dead, in various states of decay the whole time. I'd kept checking on his body because I kept seeing his ghost outside my window, trying to get inside. And I stopped checking on his body on Friday when I got a phone call from him, asking me to meet up at that bar.

I hadn't realized that the ghost and the phone call were actually Aiden. I'd thought I was losing my mind. I was more than a little confused. Maybe a little regretful. Trying to hold on to anything I could to prove to myself I wasn't a murderer. But I knew Aiden wasn't Noah. Well, I knew that for sure *now*. I'd had glimpses of that over the last few days, going in and out of denial. For a few moments there, I thought he was my husband. The other moments? I thought he was…an imposter. One that might have the answers to what my husband was up to. One that might know where my money was. Because a man with my husband's face should have the answers.

And Aiden did have them. He knew everything I wanted. My husband was having an affair. I wasn't crazy. "My husband didn't have the money with him on Tuesday. So it's safe to assume that it's with Sophia right?" I asked. I wondered how many Sophia Tremblay's there were in Canada and how hard it would be to track her down.

He shook his head, like he couldn't believe I'd changed the topic from murder to money. But a girl had to ask. The money was mine, after all. And my husband was already dead, so he didn't need it anymore. I wasn't going to let some chick with my face take my inheritance.

"You killed him," Aiden said slowly. "You pushed him down the stairs…on purpose?"

Yes. "I think it might have been an accident. I don't know. I've been on a lot of medication."

"Jesus, Ensley. You *think* it was an accident? Either it was or it wasn't." He shook his head. "Maybe it doesn't even matter at this point. You've been lying to Detective Torres about it for almost a week."

"Yeah, I don't think it matters. So, can we go back to the money thing real quick?"

He started pacing back and forth, ignoring my very important question.

"Please." All of this had to be worth something.

"The money wasn't at Noah's office, I checked this morning. No one even knew he was back in town. So yeah, it's probably with Sophia." He kept pacing.

"So…what's the plan?" I asked. I had a few ideas, but I was curious to see if Aiden could come up with anything better. Because I really, really, really didn't want to go through with my original plan anymore. Not now that I knew him.

He continued to pace, back and forth, back and forth.

I cleared my throat. I only had one back up idea. "I was thinking we could set the house on fire…"

"And torch Detective Torres along with everything else? Ensley, that would just make everything worse. We need to get the hell out of here before he wakes up."

"What about Noah's body? I really feel like we should get rid of that. I looked up all sorts of stuff about lye, but I already went to the hardware store a couple times and thought buying the ingredients would look a little suspicious. And the lake out back is frozen, so we can't sink him. I really think a fire is the best bet."

"Show it to me."

"The kerosene for the fire?"

"No. The body." He finally stopped pacing. "Where have you been keeping it? I don't smell anything. Has he been on ice or something?"

"Well, kind of. I haven't checked on him in the last few days because…well…because of you. But his body is in the little attic above the garage. It's really cold out there." *I think. I think he's there.* "You should probably just see for yourself." Mostly I wanted him to see because having the two of them next to each other would finally put my mind at ease. I'd finally know the truth for sure.

Snuggle Muffins woke up when I opened the door to the garage. He came running over. Part of me didn't want him to see what I had done. But holding him brought me comfort. And he was my main accomplice. We were in this together. I lifted Snuggle Muffins into my arms as we all made our way out into the garage. He sighed when my arms started shaking.

Please let it have all been a nightmare. Please don't let this be real.

Aiden stopped and stared at me, waiting for me to point him in the right direction.

"You have to get a ladder in order to reach it. The entrance is right there," I said and looked up.

Aiden grabbed the ladder, climbed up, and pushed the trap door open. I took a deep breath and followed him into the garage attic.

"Fuck." Aiden covered his mouth. It looked like he was going to hurl.

I stepped around him to see what he was looking at. There was a clear Sterilite storage container in the center of the attic. It was the same kind I stored my Christmas decorations in. But this one wasn't filled with lights and wreaths. It was filled with Dr. Noah Collins. My dearly departed husband. Well, it was filled with pieces of him. I remembered he didn't quite fit. I had no choice but to remove some of his limbs to try to wedge him inside properly. There were a pair of bloody hedge shears lying next to the container.

And the blood. It was everywhere. Seeping into the wooden floor beams. I'd been too tired to clean it after scrubbing the basement so thoroughly. I'd always meant to come back and clean up the stains. But then...Aiden fell into my lap, along with a new plan to get out of this. The blood didn't matter for that. Actually, it kind of helped. I hugged Snuggle Muffins tighter. But now I kind of wished I'd cleaned it up. Because I didn't want to follow through with my plan. I didn't want to frame Aiden. I wanted us to be able to run away together.

My eyes lifted from the blood stains to the plastic container. Even after removing my husband's arms, hands, a few fingers...he still hadn't quite fit. I was usually so good at packing things. It was quite a failure on the part of a housewife.

"You cut him up?" Aiden turned away and started gagging. This time he did throw up, heaving in the corner.

And all I could think about was how perfect that was. Now his DNA was up here. And mine wasn't, because even though I hadn't cleaned up the blood, I had wiped my prints off the hedge shears. *Stop.*

I kneeled down to let Snuggle Muffins out of my arms so he could explore the new space. "He wouldn't fit," I said. I studied the decapitated head resting on top of the container. And then looked back at Aiden. The resemblance was uncanny. But it was definitely my husband that was dead. I waited for that guilt to set in like it had right after I'd done it. The shock. The repulsion. But I didn't feel anything but relief. Even though I'd assaulted a detective and was going to be wanted for murder, my life seemed a lot less hellish now than it had while Noah was still alive. And I didn't think that made me a monster. The world was a better place without Noah in it. I knew that. *I'm not a monster.*

I took a deep breath and was glad I didn't smell anything too repulsive. "He's not really rotting that much," I said.

Aiden nodded, but he didn't turn back. "I think we have to take him with us," he said. "We'll find somewhere to drop the body. Maybe we can bury it somewhere." He finally turned back around to look at me.

"*We?*" I asked. "You still want to run away with me? I…I murdered my husband." I gestured to the container of body parts.

"You said it was an accident. Like when I slipped down the stairs?"

"Yeah. He just…slipped." But I knew that wasn't true. I remembered it, just like I remembered how I'd "slipped" down the stairs a few months ago. My husband had wanted me to fall. He'd smiled. And on Tuesday, I'd wanted to make sure that he knew that I knew the truth. I wanted to get even. I pushed Noah down the stairs on purpose. Shoved him really hard, actually. But I didn't think he'd die. So in that sense, it kind of was an accident.

With Aiden's fall though? I thought it was an accident. He was my last chance at answers. All his sexy muscles made him extra heavy. I hadn't wanted to hurt him. I knew it in my gut. I bit the inside of my lip as I stared at him. He could be my future. All I had to do was think of a better plan then the one rolling around in my head. The only problem was that it was a really solid plan. It had been my plan since the beginning. All the question marks at the end of my list were just for show. I'd always planned on framing Aiden for the murder of my husband. I'd just gotten a little lost along the way.

Aiden nodded slowly. "Okay. You grab one end, I'll grab the other." He started to pick up the container.

I touched his arm, trying not to smile at the warmth our connection always gave me. The last thing I needed was to scare Aiden off by smiling at my husband's dead body. "It doesn't matter if we take him," I said. "His blood is everywhere. We just have to go. Put as much distance between this and us as possible. I have a place already set up in Mexico. We can leave now. We can go together."

He looked down at the blood on the floor and shook his head. "Okay. But we have to hurry. Detective Torres is going to wake up. We have to get out of here now."

I nodded. We were still a we. He still wanted to come.

"I'll go pull the car into the garage," he said. "Let's get the hell out of here." He started down the ladder while I hung back to grab Snuggle Muffins.

I almost screamed when I saw blood dripping from Snuggle Muffins' chin. But after pulling him into my arms and inspecting him, I realized it was just one of Noah's fingers in his mouth. "Where'd you get that?" I grabbed the finger out of Snuggle Muffins' mouth.

He blinked up at me.

"No, I don't want to frame Aiden anymore."

He sighed.

"I know you're right, boy. I know it. But I really like him."

Snuggle Muffins sighed again.

"He didn't look at me like I was crazy when I told him." *Maybe he looked a little scared.* "Yes, he was surprised. But…he got over it. He just said he wanted us to get out of here together."

I swore he shook his head.

I looked down at the finger in my hand. "Framing Aiden won't necessarily get me out of this mess."

Snuggle Muffins eyes gravitated back to the finger.

"Okay, fine. I'll prepare a few things just in case. We have a long ride ahead of us to think everything through. We shouldn't make any rash decisions." I kissed the top of his head and then shoved Noah's finger down the front of my Mrs. Claus costume. *Just in case.* Just to make Snuggle Muffins happy.

CHAPTER 30
Monday

Aiden rolled down the window. "Get in."

"I need to grab a few things…"

"Ensley, time isn't on our side here. We need to leave. Now."

"My whole life is in that house. I just…give me five minutes to grab a few things. Five minutes and I'll be ready, I swear."

He shook his head, but said, "Go."

I threw Snuggle Muffins through the car window and sprinted inside. There was nothing in here that I wanted. The house filled with memories of a man who terrorized me. For all I cared, the whole thing could burn.

But there were a few things I might need. I grabbed a backpack from the hall closet and then opened the medicine cabinet, not surprised at all when bottle after bottle fell into the sink. It was stuffed so full of drugs to keep me numb. I grabbed the bottle I was looking for and shoved it into a backpack. *Just in case.*

I put a bunch of Snuggle Muffins' toys into the backpack too. He'd need to be preoccupied during the drive. An idle mind was a bad mind, especially in the case of me and Snuggle Muffins.

I grabbed a knife from the knife block, just as a precaution, and put that into my backpack too. Who knew what kind of people we'd run into in Mexico. I also packed us some granola bars, drinks, and a whole bag of dog food for Snuggle Muffins in case any of us were feeling snackish. I doubted we'd be stopping anywhere for a while. And Snuggle Muffins and I both got whiny when we were hungry. Like Momma like dog baby.

The only other thing I needed was Detective Torres' phone. I couldn't rely on chance to find Sophia Tremblay, whenever that time came. I needed her address. He might have it. I knew he'd looked her up. It was possible it was on his work computer, but didn't everyone use their phones for everything these days?

Detective Torres was still lying unconscious in the middle of the hallway. I crouched down in front of him. Before I reached into his front pocket, I saw his gun. A gun was better than a knife. And it definitely wouldn't hurt to have both. *Just in case.* I pulled the gun from his belt and put it into my backpack. It squeaked against one of Snuggle Muffins' toys.

His phone was easy to find. It was in the second pocket I checked. But when I slid my finger across the screen, it requested a fingerprint in order to unlock. I grabbed Detective Torres' limp hand and pressed one of his fingers to the screen. It immediately unlocked. There was just one problem. I wasn't super familiar with iPhones. I was a Samsung kinda girl. And I had no idea where to look to fix the settings so that I wouldn't need his fingerprint over and over again. *Shit.*

I bit the inside of my lip as I looked down at Detective Torres. I already had one of Noah's fingers shoved down my shirt. What difference would two fingers make? But Noah deserved it. Detective Torres was an innocent bystander. He didn't deserve to lose his thumb.

I heard the clock ticking down in my head. The last thing I needed was for Aiden to storm in demanding it was time to leave, catching me red handed with Detective Torres' phone. Aiden didn't understand my need to track down my money. He didn't understand what I'd been through. I had my whole life to catch

Aiden up. But I only had this one chance at getting the upper hand on my doppelgänger.

Yes, Detective Torres was innocent. But Sophia Tremblay wasn't. And he'd believed her word over mine. He said I didn't have evidence. That time had erased it. *Fuck him.* Time didn't erase my pain. And Sophia was the liar, not me. My husband was stalking her? *Yeah right.* He was replacing me with a younger model.

I took a deep and pulled the knife out of my backpack. I didn't have a choice here. I spread Detective Torres' fingers wide on the wooden floor. He'd be fine without all five fingers on one hand. And really, this was his fault. If he'd believed me...or at least validated me? Maybe we'd be in a different position.

Thinking better of it, I grabbed his left hand instead of his right. The odds were that he wasn't left-handed. He'd miss this thumb less. *Hopefully.*

I cringed when the knife went through bone. I was getting used to the crunch of metal on bone. But I wasn't used to the person I was cutting waking up. Luckily Detective Torres was more focused on his hand being mutilated than on who was doing it. He opened his mouth to scream, but I slammed the handle of the knife against his head, again and again, until his body stopped moving.

God, double assault on a detective? And cutting off his thumb. I lifted the bloody digit. And then there was the bit about murdering my husband. If Detective Torres ever caught me, I'd go to prison for life. And I couldn't let that happen. I liked fresh air too much.

I grabbed a few tissues and wrapped them around the bloody stump on his hand. He wouldn't bleed out. He'd wake up soon and get the best medical attention in the city. Detective Torres would be fine. I pressed my hand to the side of his throat, waiting to feel a pulse. For a second, I felt nothing. My heart started racing. I'd just wanted his finger, I hadn't meant to kill him.

But then I felt the light thumping of his pulse. It was slow, but it was there. *I'm so sorry.* I leaned down and lightly kissed the top of his head. *But you should have believed me.*

I wrapped his finger in some tissues too, and then shoved it and his phone into my coat pocket. I grabbed a coat for Aiden too, lifted my backpack over my shoulder, and ran out into the garage.

I climbed into the car and Aiden tore out of the garage before I was even safely strapped in. There were already families outside drinking hot chocolate and cider, Christmas music blaring. It wasn't dark yet, but the Christmas light competition festivities had already begun. The whole neighborhood would be filled with lights, costumes, and tons of drunk parents until well past midnight. It was the biggest neighborhood party of the year. A tradition I used to love. One that I'd actually miss.

I watched my house disappear in the rearview mirror. And for just a second, I wondered if maybe this year I would have won. Aiden turned left out of the neighborhood. I thought I'd feel better when we got out. But my heart was still racing.

I glanced at Aiden out of the corner of my eye. Maybe my heart was racing because I still had no idea who he was. I pulled Snuggle Muffins onto my lap. *We'll be okay, boy. No matter what happens, I promise we'll be okay.*

He sniffed my coat pocket and I moved him away from it. The last thing I needed was for Snuggle Muffins to eat Detective Torres' thumb. It was the key to getting my money back. I pulled out some dog food to preoccupy him.

"Do you still have my phone?" I asked Aiden. I had my whole life to question him. Right now I needed to figure out if my mutilating Detective Torres' body was all for nothing.

He kept his foot on the gas as he shifted to pull it out of his pocket. I grabbed it and stealthily switched it with the one in my pocket. And I even more stealthily put Detective Torres' dead thumb to it. The screen unlocked.

"I'm going to bring up some directions," I said as I opened up Detective Torres' emails.

"Sound good," he said.

I held the screen away from him and searched. "Turn right up here to get onto I-95." I'd already memorized the route to Mexico. I didn't need directions. I continued to scroll through Detective Torres' emails.

There was only one email starred on the whole page. That seemed like a good place to start, so I clicked on it.

"We're running low on supplies again."
-T

T? *Who the hell is T? T.* The letter rolled around in my head. *T.* My mind stopped spinning when I remembered why I wanted Detective Torres' phone in the first place. T for...Tremblay? It was definitely possible. Detective Torres had acted so weird whenever I brought up Canada. Like he was hiding something. I copied the email address into the search bar but no other emails from that address appeared. Why would Sophia Tremblay be emailing Detective Torres?

"You look pale," Aiden said. "Is everything okay?"

"Yeah, I'm okay." I thought about Noah's finger shoved down my bra. And Detective Torres' finger hidden in my coat pocket. No, I wasn't okay. I wanted Sophia's address, not…this. I had a sinking feeling in my stomach. What if Detective Torres was in on it?

My fingers shook as I continued scrolling through the phone. But there were no more starred emails. So I started at the beginning, opening and closing each one, searching for any more mention of T.

Aiden sped up as we merged onto I-95. We were getting farther and farther away, but I didn't feel like I was any closer to the truth. And then I found an email worse than the one mentioning T.

"We got A now. The plan's a go. It's time."
-T

T for Tremblay. And A for…what? I glanced at the man beside me, who claimed to love me. The man who knew my favorite color. The man who had studied a file on me. A man that had changed his face for my husband. But…what if he hadn't changed it for my husband? What if there was some other plan behind his copied face? *A* could easily stand for…Aiden.

My head spun and so did my stomach. I felt like I was going to be sick.

We got A now. The plan's a go. It's time. Did that mean that they had Aiden on board with the plan? But what plan?

I looked at the time stamp on the email. It was sent on Friday morning. Aiden had called me Friday afternoon for our bar date. *The plan.*

I tried to duck my head so Aiden couldn't examine me. Aiden knew he wasn't Noah. He knew that Noah had been MIA for days. So why hadn't he knocked Detective Torres out when I was being arrested? Unless... I stole another sideways glance at Aiden. Unless he was in on it too.

Snuggle Muffins sighed.

I know, boy. He didn't have to spell it out for me. Aiden was leading me into a trap. I could feel it in my bones.

CHAPTER 31
Monday

Aiden turned on the radio, blasting cheery Christmas music through the car.

The music was too loud when my mind was already screaming. All I could feel was Noah's severed finger pressed against my chest. I needed to make up my mind about what to do before we made it any closer to Mexico.

Aiden swore he knew me, but I didn't know him. All I really knew was that he worked for my husband. And that he might be plotting something with Detective Torres. Neither one of those were good things. Neither proved that he loved me. Neither proved that I could trust him even a little bit.

I should have been celebrating my escape. Instead, I was worried that I was just bringing my problems with me. I slammed the volume button, turning the radio back off. *Stupid Christmas music.*

Aiden's knuckles turned white on the steering wheel. "Not a fan of Christmas music?" he asked. "Good to know."

"What kind of debt did you owe my husband?"

He licked his bottom lip.

Stop looking at his lips.

"My father was on the wrong side of the law. He needed to disappear. And not just with a sketchy fake ID. He paid half up front, but then skipped town when the other half was due."

"He left you with his debt?" I thought Aiden must be a criminal. I hadn't considered that he might have inherited his father's debt.

"I didn't have a choice," he said. "Noah threatened to take my mom and sisters if I didn't work for him."

"What do you mean *take* them?"

"Take them to use their identities for his clients." He pulled his eyes away from the road for just a second. "It's cleaner to take a real identity when you change your face. He usually killed the originals."

Jesus. That's probably what my husband was going to do to me. If I hadn't killed him first, it would have been me dead. It didn't sound like reasonable self-defense in the eyes of the law, but it felt right to me. "How much was the debt?"

"Two million."

"So changing your face to look like my husband...that was worth 2 million dollars to you?" He would have had to pay me 100 million to make me change my face into a monster's.

"He would have killed my family."

"But surely you could have figured out another way to get the money rather than doing something so extreme."

"I didn't exactly have an inheritance to fall back on, Ensley."

Ouch. I let the awkward silence fill the car as I looked back out the windshield. A light snow was starting to fall. Normally I would have been thrilled for a snowfall so close to Christmas. But if I was going to head north instead of south, it just made things trickier. I wasn't fooled by Aiden's sob story. I believed it, but that didn't suddenly erase the fact that he'd worked for my husband, doing God knows what else. I couldn't trust him.

"I'm sorry," he said. "I didn't mean anything by that. I just...I wish I hadn't had to go through with it. I can't even look in the mirror without cringing."

It was really hard to be mad at him. "You don't look *just* like him. You have laugh lines around your eyes. My husband didn't laugh enough to have those."

That earned me a small smile from Aiden.

"You knew about Sophia withdrawing the money. And my husband's plan to leave me. Was he...was he planning on killing me?"

"Yes."

I couldn't actually imagine my husband killing me. Hurting me? Sure. But why get his hands bloody if he didn't have to? Why be plagued with nightmares if you could avoid it? "You said you ran errands for him that he didn't want to run. Was that going to be one of them? Killing me?"

His Adam's apple rose and then fell. "I would never hurt you."

"That doesn't really answer my question. Did he or did he not ask you to kill me?"

He pulled his eyes from the road. "He did. But I wasn't going to go through with it."

"You changed your face to protect your family. I'm a stranger. I know you would have killed me in order to protect them."

"You're not a stranger."

Snuggle Muffins stirred in my lap. He could feel my agitation. He was the only one in this car that really knew me. No, Snuggle Muffins didn't know what my favorite color was. Or why I fell in love with the white picket fence neighborhood. But he knew me better than the man beside me swearing he loved me. The one saying he was helping me escape. The one saying he never would have killed me.

"Were you in contact with Sophia Tremblay?" *We got A now. The plan's a go. It's time.*

"I have her address, if that's what you mean. I'm not sure if she'll still be there or not." He told me the address from memory.

Either he had a really good memory, or he was in cahoots with her. I tried to study the side of his face to see if he was lying. But I didn't know his tells. I didn't know him. I felt more uneasy the farther we drove. Maybe just a little of the unease came from the fact that I hadn't needed to cut Detective Torres' finger off after all. Aiden had known Sophia's address the whole time. But at least I'd seen those emails. At least I knew something was up. The loss of a thumb was worth that.

"So what was the plan exactly?" I asked. "Trick me into opening the front door for you because you had my husband's face? Then you were going to kill me?"

"I never got the final instructions."

Because I killed him. I ran my hand down Snuggle Muffins' back to calm him. I knew he was growing agitated from Aiden's answers too. He had been planning on killing us. What was to say he still wasn't? I needed to just ask him about the emails directly. I was never one to beat around the bush when it came to life or death.

"I took Detective Torres' phone."

He turned to look at me again. "Why would you do that? Lying to him and kicking him in the back of the head wasn't enough for you? Now add theft to the list." He sped up.

Also cutting off his finger and knocking him out again. But Aiden didn't need to know about those things. "There were a few weird emails." I discreetly used Detective Torres' thumb to unlock his phone. "We're running low on supplies again," I read. "It was signed T." I waited to see if he had a reaction. He didn't. "I think T is for Tremblay. I think Detective Torres was working with my husband."

"Why would you assume that? T could stand for anything."

Or it could stand for Tremblay. "It would make sense that she was hiding out until after I was dead. Someone could have recognized me."

"Do you know a lot of people in Canada?"

I glared at him. "Other than my husband and his mistress? No, not many."

He licked his lips again.

Maybe I did know one of his tells. It seemed like he licked his lips when he was nervous. Which meant…he was hiding something. Why else be nervous? "Here's another fun email," I said. "We got A now. The plan's a go. It's time. Signed by T again."

Aiden shook his head. "These are so vague."

"Not that vague. I really think T stands for Tremblay. And I'm thinking the A stands for Aiden."

"What? I'm not working with Sophia or Detective Torres. Ensley, I'm literally driving you to safety right now."

"That last email was time stamped before you called me on Friday. Your whole plan to make me think you were my husband? I think the e-mail refers to that plan."

"I swear to God, if Sophia and Detective Torres were talking, I had nothing to do with it."

"Are you a believer in God, Aiden?"

His jaw clenched. "It was a figure of speech. But I swear to you all I care about right now is getting you to Mexico."

"Why? Do the police already know I'm going there?"

"No." He looked over at me. "I mean…hell, maybe. I have no idea. But if they do, I certainly didn't tell them. What do I have to say to prove to you I'm on your side?"

"You have to tell me Detective Torres' first name." I was hoping I could catch him off guard with my lack of segue.

"Damien, I think?"

Traitor. There was no way for him to know that. "You only just met him. He never said his name. How do you know that?"

Aiden shrugged. "It's a small town. He's been all over the news because of that serial killer case."

"I need to look in your eyes so I can see if you're telling the truth. Stop the car."

"We can't stop right now. We're barely thirty minutes out. We need…"

"Stop the car, Aiden."

"We're in the middle of the highway. I can't stop."

"Then take the next exit. We just passed a sign saying it would be in one mile."

"If we stop now…"

I pulled out Detective Torres' gun and held it up to his head. "Stop the fucking car."

He looked more shocked now than he had when I'd confessed that I'd killed my husband. "Where the hell did you get a gun?"

Snuggle Muffins started growling at him. My beautiful little menace was just like his mother.

"Stop the car," I said, ignoring Aiden's stupid question. "Or I'll blow your brains out all over I-95."

CHAPTER 32
Monday

Aiden took the exit right away. But he didn't follow the signs for the local diner or gas station. He just pulled over to the side of the road as fast as he could, cut the engine, and lifted his hands into the air.

I ignored the dusty town in the middle of nowhere Delaware and lifted the gun a little higher. "Tell me the truth. Are you working with Sophia and Detective Torres to take me down?"

"No. No," he said a little more firmly when I didn't lower the gun. "I had no contact with Detective Torres before this afternoon. And I wasn't on security detail for Noah. I didn't communicate with any of his mistresses."

Mistresses. I knew it. That son of a bitch. There was a sinking feeling in my stomach, and it was growing by the second. "Are there any more women with my face running around?"

He shook his head. "Not that I know of."

"Are there more men with Noah's face running around? Your face?"

"It's just me," Aiden said. "Please lower the gun. You can trust me."

Snuggle Muffins started growling again, tapping his little feet on my thigh like he was considering pouncing.

"I can't trust you," I said. "You agreed to kill me."

"And I never would have gone through with it. Hell, if you hadn't drugged me on Friday night, we would already be in Mexico. I swear, Ensley. I'd never hurt you. Ever."

I stared into his eyes. I believed him. I did. My hands started trembling. I believed him, but I knew I shouldn't. Trusting him would be stupid. And I wasn't stupid. "You swear you only knew Detective Torres' first name from the news?"

"Yes. Everyone's heard about that serial killer case with Violet. He's a local celebrity."

A bad one. "Then who are T and A? If it isn't you and Sophia, who is it?"

"I don't know. Maybe the T stands for Tremblay. Maybe it doesn't. But I know for sure that I'm not A."

No, I wasn't stupid. But his face reminded me of the man I'd married. His eyes held grief that matched my own. But they also held warmth, and hope, and a future. And his lips...*stop*. I wasn't stupid. But I was a little worried that I might in fact be falling in love with him. Even if it was crazy.

I shouldn't be falling for a man that looked like a monster. But he wasn't my husband. He wasn't. "If A isn't you, who else could it be?"

"It could be anyone," Aiden said. "I'm sure Detective Torres was working on more than one case. It might not even have anything to do with you."

That was such a guy thing to say. What, did he think I loved being the center of attention? I was trying to get away with murder here. The only attention I wanted was his. "I don't think everything has to do with me."

"That's not..." he sighed. "That's not what I meant. Ensley, all I know for sure is that I'm the only one that has your back here. It's just me." He flashed me a perfect smile. "Well, me and maybe Snuggle Muffins."

Definitely Snuggle Muffins, thank you very much. I looked down at my wonderful dog. As soon as I moved my gaze, I realized my mistake. But I was a second too late.

Aiden knocked the gun out of my hand so fast that I didn't even get a chance to fire. And then he lunged at me. The car horn beeped as his hip slammed against it.

I screamed at the top of my lungs, but there was no one around. We were in the middle of nowhere and Snuggle Muffins chose now to jump to the back seat and explore the car. *Traitor!*

Aiden's fingers dug into my wrist, reminding me why I hated men with his face. My knee hit the gear shift as I struggled to push him off.

"Get off of me!" I yelled. But it was no use. He was too strong. I felt behind me, trying to grab the door handle.

"Jesus, Ensley, stop!" He pushed both my hands down as he straddled me on my seat. "Stop!"

I couldn't move my legs. Or my arms.

"What the hell is wrong with you?" Any warmth I had seen in his eyes was gone. "Threatening to shoot me in the fucking head on the middle of the highway? You would have killed us both."

I tried to move my arms, but they were pinned. God, why was he so big and strong? *Stop.*

"I'm trying to help you here," he said. "And you're...what? Giving up on life so easily?"

"I'm not giving up on life. I'm giving up on you."

His eyebrows lowered as he stared back at me. "I'm not Noah. I'll never hurt you."

"You're hurting me right now!"

"Only to prevent you from killing me." His grip on my wrists lessened. "I'll say it again, Ensley. I'm not Noah. I'll never hurt you. And you'll never cut me up into little pieces and try to fit me in a storage container. Deal?"

I stopped struggling beneath him, the air suddenly felt different in the car. The windows were fogging up. And I could feel him. His length hardening, pressing into my thigh. This was turning him on? That was crazy. He was the crazy one, not me. I shifted slightly, trying to move him closer to where I was craving him. Fine, maybe I was a little crazy too. Just a little. "No deal," I said. "Stop acting like you know me."

"I know you." He lowered his head closer to mine. "You won't."

"Bite me." It was an invitation. And we both knew it.

He let go of my hands and buried his fingers in my hair, his teeth lightly nipping at my bottom lip.

Screw everything else. My hands pushed underneath his coat. I hated his face. I hated the fact that he thought he knew me. And I hated that he used to work for my husband.

But I loved his mouth. His lips. His biceps. My fingers stopped on his muscles as his mouth devoured me. I may have loved him more than I hated him. I just wasn't sure it was enough to make me jeopardize everything I'd worked so hard for.

His hands cupped my breasts, but I shoved them down. The last thing I needed was for him to find Noah's finger in my bra. This moment wasn't about Noah. It was about us. And I needed this. I desperately needed this.

Aiden's hands settled on my thighs. When his fingers slid up the inside of my thigh, I stopped thinking. And when they dipped beneath my Mrs. Claus costume, I lost all reason. I was done for. It didn't matter that the cops were probably hot on our trail. It didn't matter that I might end up in jail. All that mattered was this one good moment. I kissed him back like my life depended on it. Like it was my last chance at truly living.

***

I wasn't sure how long we lost track of time. But it was enough to have a layer of snow on our windshield. And it was long enough to make up my mind. It was easy to fall for Aiden. He had my husband's face. And I had loved my husband. If I hadn't, I wouldn't have been so jealous when I'd found out he was cheating. There was such a fine line between love and hate. I'd danced that line when I shoved Noah down the basement stairs. Just like I'd been dancing it this whole time with Aiden.

But I wasn't a dancer. I was a murderer. Different from the other serial killers in Windy Park. I wasn't Violet Clark. Or Adeline Bell. I didn't risk my future for a chance at love. I was Ensley Collins. And I was going to get away with murder. Even if it hurt. And it did hurt. Because I wasn't dancing the line with Aiden anymore. The emotions I was feeling were real. And I knew that they were real for him too. He'd made love to me in the car. Noah never had. Noah had used me. He'd used me until he was done with me. But I wasn't disposable.

When Aiden climbed out of the car to remove the snow from the windows, I dropped a pill into one of the bottles of Gatorade I'd packed. I stepped out of the car. "Do you mind if I drive?" I pretended to take a sip of the Gatorade.

"Whatever you want." He smiled at me.

I ignored the way the action made my knees weak as I pretended to take another sip. "Thirsty?" I held it out to him.

He grabbed it and took a huge gulp. Then another. I pulled it away before he could have any more. He just needed to be knocked out for half an hour or so. Not all night. I watched the snow fall peacefully around us. I'd remember this moment always. I'd wonder if I made the right choice. But once I made my mind up, it was hard to change it.

I'm so sorry, Aiden.

CHAPTER 33
Monday

Once we were back in the warm car, I leaned over the center console and kissed him again. I kissed him until his lips started to go slack.

He leaned away from me. "Again?" He tried to lift his hand but couldn't. "Why?" he asked.

"Because you're A."

A tear trickled down his left cheek. He tried to lift his hand to wipe it away, but he couldn't. "I'm not A."

Maybe. Maybe not. But it didn't matter now. He was my get out of jail free card. And I had done too many terrible things not to use it. I leaned over and wiped his tear away with my thumb. "The evidence against you is shaky. They'll hold you for a while. Maybe it'll go to trial. But they'll let you go. When they do, you can come find me. I'm not going to Mexico. I'll be in Canada. This doesn't have to be the end."

"You're fucking crazy." His eyelids started to close.

He didn't mean that. I couldn't let him mean that. I'd fix this. I'd fix it for him.

"No. I'm not crazy." I grabbed both sides of his face. "I'm crazy in love with you. And I need you to trust me. I'm going to get you out of this. I promise." So many people had made me false promises. But I wasn't like them. His last words to me weren't going to be *you're fucking crazy*. Not in a million years. "Do you hear me?" I shook his head. "I'll be in Canada."

His eyes closed. His chin dipped down to his chest as he finally fell asleep.

I wasn't sure if he'd remember what I'd told him. I eyed the gun on the floor of the car. Aiden was a loose end now. But I wasn't going to kill him, even if it had been my original plan. Framing him when I wasn't positive that he was A was one thing. But killing him? I wasn't a monster.

I put the car into drive. "You okay back there, Snuggle Muffins?"

He sighed.

"It's okay." I pulled the car back onto the road. "You were right. All we need is each other. We're going to be okay." My voice sounded shaky. I wanted to believe it. But it hurt.

The silence felt loud as I retraced our path back up I-95. But I couldn't play cheery Christmas music right now. If anything came on about love, I might risk ruining everything. I kept glancing over at Aiden. He was snoring lightly. A soothing sound. *I could still fall asleep in his arms every night. I could still... Stop.*

I knew it was risky going back to my neighborhood. But the Christmas light competition was in full swing. There would be a million Mrs. Clauses roaming the streets during the party. I'd blend in just fine.

When I was only a few minutes away, I called Sally.

"Ensley? Is that you? I just saw Detective Torres leave your house. But when I knocked, no one answered. Is everything alright?"

I didn't have time to answer her questions. "Can I still borrow your car?"

"Yes. Of course. I'm out rating the Christmas lights. But I left the keys in the ignition for you just in case. You're all set."

"Thank you." I hung up before she could ask any more questions. Although, I had a few of my own. Who left keys in their ignition when there had been multiple serial killers in the neighborhood? Sally was more trusting than she was gossipy. And that was really saying something. "You almost ready, Snuggle Muffins?"

He sighed as I pulled into my neighborhood. I did a U-turn and parked the car to make it look like we'd been leaving the neighborhood. And I parked it over the curb to look like it stopped in a hurry. Snuggle Muffins hopped onto my lap and looked up at me.

"You can't change your mind now, Snuggle Muffins. I've already drugged him." I shooed him to the side as I lifted the backpack off the floor. I pulled Noah's finger out of my bra and shoved it into the backpack. And then I pulled out Detective Torres' phone. I didn't have much time. It was important that I left it with Noah, but I still found myself dragging Detective Torres' finger along the screen one more time.

I was missing something. What if Aiden really wasn't A? I looked at Detective Torres' emails again. His texts. His phone calls. I opened his map app to see if I could figure out if he'd visited Sophia Tremblay while he was in Canada. He'd only entered two Canadian addresses into his GPS. And neither of them was the address Aiden had given me for Sophia. I quickly wrote them down. I was out of time.

I shoved Detective Torres' phone and finger into the backpack and then tossed it onto Aiden's lap. A perfect pouch of evidence. Too nicely wrapped up. I knew that. And I truly did think he'd get out of jail eventually. But it would give me enough time to disappear.

The gun and Snuggle Muffins were all that I needed. *I hope.* I looked once more at Aiden. I'd waited so long for a knight in shining armor to save me. But I wasn't a damsel in distress. I'd saved myself instead. I leaned over and placed a kiss on Aiden's lips. This didn't have to be goodbye. He could still find me one day. But it sure as hell felt like a goodbye. Like my heart cracked in half. But it could have been worse. I could have killed him.

I put the gun in my jacket pocket, grabbed Snuggle Muffins, and disappeared into the Christmas festivities.

None of my neighbors suspected a thing. They drank their spiked eggnog and rated each other's Christmas lights like it was the most important thing in the world. This party was usually a perfect night. Fake smiles as we all silently judged each other. I hated suburbia. And yet…I loved it too. I loved that someone like me could hide in plain sight. Everyone's smiles were fake. Mine just happened to hide something more sinister.

I practically ran down the street, looking for the perfect hiding spot. But everything was lit up in spectacular fashion. White lights covered every bush. Icicle lights dangled off rain gutters. Even the lamp posts were wrapped in lights. *Damn it! Why did my neighbors have to be such great decorators?* It was almost impossible to hide with how bright my neighborhood was. I turned in a circle and smacked right into another Mrs. Claus. So hard that I almost dropped Snuggle Muffins.

"Watch where you're going," I said under my breath. Even though it had been me that wasn't looking.

"Ensley? Is that you?" Charlotte grabbed one of my shoulders so that I'd turn to look at her.

Oh God. The last thing I needed right now was to be noticed. Especially by freaking gossipy Charlotte.

There was a half empty mug of eggnog in her hand. Maybe she was drunk. "Ho, ho, ho," I said. "Nope."

She laughed. "You're an odd duck. You know that?"

I'm a fucking swan, Charlotte. I just smiled through the witty comeback that wanted to come out. Had she forgotten about my sick burn earlier today? I thought she'd be avoiding me.

"It looks like you'll be spending Christmas alone." She patted my check.

Yup, definitely drunk. A mean drunk at that. One that remembered my sick burn and was looking for revenge. But if she was trying to insult me, it wasn't working. The only thing worse than spending Christmas alone would be spending it with her.

"How tragic," she said.

I glared at her.

"Oh, by the way…you have a little something on your outfit." She gestured toward the front of my costume.

There was a blood stain right between my breasts. I hadn't thought Noah's finger would be an issue because my costume was red, but there was a little white fur trim at the top. "Spaghetti." I lifted Snuggle Muffins higher to hide my chest. "I had spaghetti and tomato sauce for dinner."

"Mhm. Looks like I'll be winning the costume contest *and* the lighting display this year. Again. I should go practice my speech." She waved and started to walk away.

Your Christmas lights look pretentious. And I wore it better. I didn't have to say it out loud to be true. I looked down at Snuggle Muffins who was licking the white fur trim of my dress. "Stop it." I pulled him away from the blood. "And help me find a hiding spot."

I turned in another circle. There was literally nothing.... *Wait.* Perfect. There was a row of bushes in a nearby side yard where the lights had just gone out. I nestled between them and a light-up reindeer like the one I'd gotten Aiden. I wasn't completely hidden, but everyone was so drunk that it didn't matter. All that mattered was that I could see my car. I was even close enough to see Aiden through the passenger's side window. He was still knocked out.

I placed Snuggle Muffins down. "Stay right by me, little man."

He plopped his butt down in the snow and stared at my chest. Apparently my dog lusted for blood. Or maybe he just liked my boobs... *Men.*

I pulled out my phone and dialed 9-1-1.

It only took a few seconds before someone picked up. "911, what's your emergency?" the dispatcher asked.

"My husband's been murdered," I cried, pretending to be hysterical. "I thought he was just missing but...oh God, he cut him up into little tiny pieces and hid him in my garage attic." I gave her the address, without waiting for her to ask. "He had an accomplice who even knocked out a detective," I sobbed into the phone. Detective Torres couldn't be certain that it was me who'd kneed him in the head and cut off his finger. And I needed to plant as much doubt as possible. "He threatened to kill me too, but I fought him off. I think he's unconscious. He's in a black SUV in the south exit of Windy Park. If you get there soon you might still catch him!"

"Ma'am, where are you right now? Are you safe?"

"Oh God, please get him before it's too late! I don't want him to get me too." I hung up and tossed the phone into the snow before stomping on it. The screen shattered. Hopefully that was enough so they couldn't track it. Hopefully I'd said enough on the phone to wrongfully accuse Aiden. Hopefully they'd get here fast enough. Hopefully they wouldn't ask too many questions. Hopefully I had enough time to escape.

I stayed in my hiding spot, staring at my car. I could hear music somewhere off in the distance. *Baby it's Cold Outside* came on, drifting through the air. I remembered Christmases past. Walking through the festivities hand-in-hand with my husband. Drinking hot chocolate. Laughing. But today, I was knee deep in snow and straining my neck around a bush to watch my lover get arrested. It wasn't what I had in mind for the holidays.

"When we get to Canada, we'll have a real Christmas," I whispered and patted Snuggle Muffins' head. "With presents and multi-colored lights. It'll be just us for a while. Until…" My words froze in my throat.

Aiden stumbled out of the car, the backpack in his hands.

No. It was too soon. I'd told the police he was in the SUV. If they didn't get here right now, Aiden could disappear. All my hard work framing him would be ruined. It felt like my heart was beating in my throat. I looked around to see if there was anything I could use to fix this. But a glowing reindeer wasn't exactly going to help me. Rudolph couldn't fix Mrs. Claus' problems like he could fix Santa's. *Stupid reindeer.*

I watched in horror as Aiden turned in a circle. He shook his head like he still thought he was dreaming. And for just a second, I swear he looked over toward the bushes I was hiding in. I threw myself down, the snow biting at my exposed skin in this stupid costume. *God, this plan sucks.* He was going to escape. I could still get caught. I should have gotten up and ran. But my whole body was frozen.

Aiden scratched the back of his neck and looked down at the backpack.

No.

And then he slowly unzipped it.

Stop.

And pulled something out.

Fuck!

He held it up and looked at it. *One of the fingers.*

And that's when the lights in the neighborhood turned more multicolored than pristine white. Red and blue lights lit up the sky as the police cars surrounded Aiden.

Neighbors started screaming. Cups of eggnog and hot chocolate were thrown into the air as everyone started running around. Kids ran toward the lights. Parents ran from them. It was complete and utter chaos, decked out in Christmas decorations. It was magical. Better than I had even planned.

"Drop the bag!" yelled one of the cops. "Hands in the air!"

Aiden tossed the backpack and finger into the snow and raised his hands.

The cop slowly approached him. "On your knees."

Aiden fell to his knees and the cop cuffed him. Another cop grabbed the backpack. When he looked through the contents, he hunched over like he was going to be sick. And a third cop found the finger Aiden had dropped in the snow.

I was relieved when they holstered their guns and pulled Aiden to his feet. He was ushered to the closest police car and shoved into the backseat.

I'd watched longer than I meant to. My plan had worked. I slowly stood up and brushed the snow off the front of my costume. Aiden getting arrested would give me plenty of time. After all, Aiden's fingerprints were all over my house. He'd thrown up next to the plastic container. He'd also touched the container. He had Noah's finger. Along with Detective Torres' phone and finger. Oh, and Aiden also had my husband's face. That was suspicious all by itself. But all together? It was a nice, neat little Christmas gift for the police department.

I held Snuggle Muffins tight as I snuck behind my neighbors' houses, taking the fastest route to Sally's. The snow was beautiful, but I hated that it left a trail of my footprints. Not that anyone should be looking. I'd already given them the murderer.

I ducked past lit up trees and bushes, almost knocking into more people in the chaos. When I got a few streets over, everyone seemed calmer. You could barely see the red and blue lights over here. The chaos hadn't struck yet. I slowed down, pretending I was just another observer of the light display. It was a nice night leading up to Christmas. Filled with family, friends, and laughter. I hummed to myself, holding Snuggle Muffins close. And for just a second, I felt it. Christmas magic was in the air.

I hurried my steps as I saw Sally's car in the distance. When I was only a block away, I saw Sally herself. It looked like she was about to call it a night and head in early. But her night wasn't over yet. I had one more idea running through my head. One last set up.

"Sally!" I called and ran over to her, ignoring the fact that Snuggle Muffins was now licking the front of my costume.

She turned to me with a smile on her face. "Oh good. You got here okay. Did you get a chance to vote?" She dropped her voice. "I think Charlotte's winning. But every vote counts. I'm still rooting for you."

"Actually, Charlotte is the reason I wanted to talk to you before I headed out. She's the one that's been stealing your lawn gnomes," I lied.

Sally gasped. "No. Not Charlotte."

"I saw it with my own eyes. She's been swiping them for months. And burying them in the woods so no one would find them. She's really the worst, huh? I think she has a screw loose in that blonde head of hers."

Sally shook her head and then frowned. "If you'll excuse me. I need to go have a word with her." She bustled off. I could practically see steam coming out of her ears, mixing with the falling snow.

Merry Christmas, Charlotte. Framing her for stealing lawn gnomes was almost as satisfying as framing Aiden for murdering my husband. Almost.

I climbed into Sally's car, a huge smile on my face. The key was in the ignition, just like she'd promised. I made sure Snuggle Muffins was comfortable, and then drove away as fast as I could, being careful not to hit any of my neighbors.

There were so many things that could still go wrong. I didn't know if I'd be able to cross the border. I didn't know if any of this would work. But I had to try. For my sake. For Snuggle Muffins' sake. I just needed one more Christmas miracle. An easy drive through the Canadian border tonight. Well, maybe two Christmas miracles. I'd promised Aiden I'd get him out of jail. And I didn't have an actual plan on how to do that.

But I had a long drive to figure it out.

I looked in my rearview mirror, the blue and red lights growing more distant by the second. *Merry Christmas, Detective Torres.* Giving him a clean arrest was the least I could do after cutting off his thumb.

I pressed my foot down harder on the gas. I needed to cross the Canadian border tonight. Just in case my plan failed and it was my face all over the news instead of Aiden's.

CHAPTER 34
Wednesday

I couldn't look away from the TV in the dingy motel room. My murder had made national news. Scratch that. I'd crossed the border into Canada two days ago, which meant it had made the *international* news. But it was Aiden who was getting all the credit. He was becoming notorious for my crime. My plans. My brilliance. I would have felt cheated, but he was also taking the fall for me. And it was hard to feel cheated when all I felt was guilt. I regretted turning him in. We could have just escaped together. I hated how much I missed him. I hated how the guilt made my stomach feel like it was twisting in half.

He's A. Stop it. You couldn't trust him.

But that didn't mean he deserved *this*. My plan had been too good. They were already talking about the death penalty. And I couldn't let that happen. I'd made him a promise, and I was going to keep it.

The sun was peeking through the blinds. This wasn't how I wanted to spend Christmas morning. I'd promised Snuggle Muffins great things. And I was going to keep that promise too. But first, I had to fix what I had broken.

Originally I thought I might kill Aiden once I got my answers, but then I'd switched gears and framed him. And now that I'd framed him so well? I was switching gears again. Aiden had given me the greatest Christmas gift of all – my freedom. I wanted to give him his freedom back too. It was Christmas, after all.

"Wake up, Snuggle Muffins." I rubbed his tummy. "It's Christmas morning!"

He blinked up at me and wagged his little tail.

"I got you a present. I promise more will come later." I placed the neatly wrapped gift down in front of him.

And he bit it. Almost like he knew he was going to hate what was inside. He shook his head back and forth, really getting into destroying his only Christmas gift.

"Stop it." I grabbed the present away from him and tore the paper off. It was an adorable little Santa costume.

He growled at it.

"Don't be that way. You already agreed to the plan. And you're cute, but this will make you extra cute."

After several attempts, I finally wrassled him into the outfit. I flicked the little jingle bell on the end of his hat and he sighed. "See. You look adorable." I peppered his face with kisses and he looked considerably less upset.

"It's go-time."

I lifted him into my arms and took one last look at the crappy motel room. If today went as planned, we'd be in a nice hotel tonight. And a permanent residence in a few weeks. A new life. A fresh start. I closed the door behind us and made my way down the rickety steps.

Christmas morning was always eerily quiet, no matter where you were. Families were tucked inside their homes, cozy and warm. It felt like Snuggle Muffins and I were the only ones in the world outside this early on Christmas morning.

We got in the car and Snuggle Muffins watched me silently from the passenger seat.

"It's going to work," I said.

I still felt him staring.

"Fine. It'll probably work. Happy?"

He sighed.

I didn't know why he didn't have more faith in the plan. It was Christmas, after all. And if anyone deserved a Christmas miracle, it was us.

I pulled the car out of the motel's parking lot. We'd already hit all three addresses in Canada that were on our list. The first two from Detective Torres' phone had been useless. One was a police station, where he'd probably listened in on Sophia's questioning. The other address was in a neighborhood similar to the one I'd left behind. A house with a "sold" sign out front. A cute little place on Cherry Lane. And a complete and utter dead end.

But the third address? The one that Aiden had given me? I'd only had to stake the place out for two hours before I realized I'd hit the jackpot. It was Sophia freaking Tremblay's new place. And I mean *brand new*. A custom home. Enormous. Gorgeous. And…bought with my money. It was easy to figure that out with a quick Google search. The only owner's name on record was Dr. Noah Collins. He'd used my money to buy my replacement this house. Months ago. He'd been planning my death for months. The only question was…had she already given up her old identity? Was she already me? Did she have my money tucked away somewhere in her ginormous home?

Those were all questions that I couldn't find the answers to online. I needed to get inside. I stared at the huge house. There were still Amazon packages piled at the front door that had been there yesterday. Sophia apparently had no worry of theft or anything malicious happening in her fancy neighborhood. She was just spending my money all willy nilly, strutting around with my face and my bank account without a care in the world. Well, she was in for a rude Christmas surprise.

I looked down at Snuggle Muffins.

He sighed.

"You got this boy. It'll be the performance of a lifetime."

He yawned.

"Keep it up, cutie." I pulled down the hood on my black hoody to hide my identity as much as possible, slipped Detective Torres' gun into the back of my black leggings, and grabbed Snuggle Muffins.

The plan was simple. Snuggle Muffins adorableness was going to distract Sophia. I placed Snuggle Muffins down next to the Amazon packages. "Stay," I said. "Look cute. Be You."

He wagged his tail.

Such a good dog. I rang the bell and then ran as fast as I could to the back of the house. Which took a stupid amount of time because the house was so freaking huge.

I pulled out a bobby pin and went to town on the back-door's lock. I wasn't an expert. But I'd been practicing picking locks in my cheap motel room. The lock clicked in record time. I smiled as I opened the door. No squeak, thanks to the brand new hinges. I tiptoed through the laundry room, down the hall, and peered toward the entranceway.

Sophia had her dirty hands all over my sweet Snuggle Muffins. It was one thing to touch my husband. And my money. But my dog? *Hell no.*

I tiptoed up behind her, looked both ways to make sure all the neighbors were still snug in their beds dreaming of sugar plums, and whacked her in the back of the head with my gun. Snuggle Muffins jumped out of her arms before she was able to fall on top of him.

"Good boy." I patted his head and looked around the neighborhood again. The coast was clear. "You grab one ankle. I'll grab the other."

Snuggle Muffins sat down instead of assisting me. But it was okay. He'd already done his part. I pulled her unconscious body into the house and closed the door.

After making sure she was tied securely to a kitchen chair, I stared down at her. Just like I'd seen through her kitchen window the other day, her face wasn't covered in bruises like the picture Detective Torres had shown me. Her face was perfectly fine. Exactly like mine. Almost. It was like staring into a mirror. The question was…why had she worn makeup that looked so much like bruises? I could only think of two possibilities. Either she wanted to trick the local police station with a great makeup job. Or Detective Torres was trying to trick me. I was banking on the first option. My plan depended on it.

"Let's split up," I said. "You search downstairs. I'll search upstairs." Snuggle Muffins and I went off in different directions to go find what we needed.

It didn't take long for me to find a duffel bag stuffed with cash. Stupid Canadian cash, but cash just the same. At least it looked pretty.

And Snuggle Muffins was waiting for me downstairs with Sophia's purse. Tucked inside her purse was both her ID and mine - the one she'd used to steal my money. The house was under my husband's name. She had my face. The only thing in the house hinting at her real identity was her old ID. *What an idiot.* I placed the wallet down on the counter.

I had everything I needed now. Except my answers. I slapped Sophia's face, trying to wake her up. It was strange hitting myself. But I knew she wasn't me. I slapped her again.

She slowly opened her eyes. The shock on her face was price-less. One of my favorite Christmas presents ever.

"I like what you've done with the place," I said and looked around the kitchen. There were Christmas decorations galore. Everything was so perfect. Overly perfect. She reminded me of Charlotte.

She stared at me, her eyes glued to my face. *My* face. Not hers.

"Ensley," she said slowly.

"Oh good, you know who I am. So I can skip the question where I ask if you were sleeping with my husband."

"He didn't love you." She tried to move, but I'd tied her up pretty tightly to the kitchen chair. "He never did."

I thought she'd be at least a little regretful. I was kind of ex-pecting an *I'm sorry*. Weren't Canadians supposed to be super polite? "I'm not so sure. He at least loved me more than he loved you. Why else would he make you look like me?"

She glared at me. "You better untie me. Noah's coming home this morning. We're going to spend Christmas together. He'll be here any minute."

"Sounds like fun. I'll be out of your hair as soon as you an-swer a few questions for me."

She didn't agree. But she didn't disagree either.

"What happened to the bruises on your face?" I asked.

"You have no idea what's going on," she said.

"I think I do. I think you didn't want the local police to know you looked like me until I'd been disposed of. Because...that would be suspicious if there were two of me walking around."

She looked surprised.

And her surprise made me feel relieved. It seemed like I had gotten it right. "You were waiting for Noah to tell you I was dead before you let anyone see you. Right?"

She glanced toward the hallway, like she was hoping Noah would come in and rescue her.

I'd actually felt sorry for her a few days ago. I thought my husband hurt her too. But she was just…faking it? Faking my pain? Faking being me? "Were you working with Detective Torres?"

"Who?"

Her accent fell out of her mouth weird. *My mouth.* My mouth was never meant to talk with a Canadian accent. It grated on my nerves. "Detective Damien Torres. Were you working with him?"

"No. I literally have no idea who you're talking about. I swear to God, Ensley, if you don't untie me right now, you're going to regret it."

"What about A?"

"A?"

"A stands for Aiden. I know you were working with him."

"I don't know what you're talking about. I don't know any Aidens. Noah was going to make it painless, you know. But when he finds out about this? He'll make your death so slow. Unless you untie me right now. I'll tell him to kill you fast if you let me go."

This woman was seriously bad at negotiating. "Are you T?" I asked, ignoring her.

She shook her head. "My name is Sophia."

I swallowed hard. *I know your name, you idiot!* But I didn't know if I believed her. She looked like she was probably a natural blonde. Her breasts were too big. Oh, and she had my fucking face and had slept with my husband. She was clearly an idiot.

"Look, I'm sorry, okay? You can have your money back. It's all here. In the basement. Just over there." She gestured with her head behind her.

Wow. This bitch seriously thought I was going to willingly go in her basement while she tried to free herself? I'd already found my money underneath her bed. And her sorry didn't cut it. She wasn't sorry. She fucking stole my face. That wasn't something you do on a drunken whim and later regret. It was a huge choice. Sleeping with my husband. Robbing me blind? She wasn't sorry. "Last chance to tell me something I don't know already. Or I'm going to gag you." I lifted a piece of fabric. I didn't necessarily need the answers from her. I still had another way of getting them.

She started shaking her head back and forth. "You're going to regret this, Ensley. Boy are you going to regret this. Noah's going to be here any second and…"

"Noah's dead."

Her jaw dropped. "No." She shook her head. "He can't be. How?"

"Dead is such a gross understatement. He was murdered actually."

"What? You're lying. He said you were a liar."

I laughed. "I'm sure he said a lot of things about me. But I'm not lying. Noah's been murdered. Haven't you seen the news?"

"I don't watch the news."

Of course you don't. What had Noah seen in this woman? Oh right, he saw me. Because she had my freaking face.

"Who did it?" Sophia asked.

Dumb question. "It'll all be clear soon. I need to make a quick phone call. Do you mind being quiet?"

"Who killed him?" she said, her eyes staring daggers at me. They were one of the only things about her face that didn't match mine. And they looked stupid with my face.

I shoved a piece of fabric into her mouth and tied it around the back of her head. She'd given me nothing. But I'd still get my answers.

I picked up Sophia's phone from her purse and dialed Detective Torres' cell number. I wasn't sure if he'd have it back. Maybe it would be in evidence. Or maybe in the trash with his thumb. Who knew? But I wanted to talk to him. Dialing 9-1-1 didn't seem personal enough. I stepped away from Sophia as she screamed against the gag. I doubted he'd be able to hear her. But better safe than sorry.

"Hello?" said a groggy voice.

Thank God. "Merry Christmas, Detective Torres."

"Ensley? Is that you? Are you okay?"

I should have been the one asking him that. Wow, he really was a bad detective. He was worried about me. *Me.* "No." My voice trembled. It was easy to fake it when I was looking at my doppelgänger tied up to a chair.

"We got your husband's murderer. It's safe to come back now. You're safe."

"No." I kept my voice uneven and sobbed. "You have the wrong guy."

"What do you mean?"

"Aiden's innocent." I pretended to sob again. "I framed him. It was me. I killed my husband. Because he hurt me, Detective Torres. And you didn't help." No one had helped. No one had cared. *Until Aiden.* I glanced over at Sophia. She was straining against the ropes, trying to get free. For the first time since I'd tied her up, she looked truly horrified. "It was me."

All I heard was his breathing for a few seconds.

"Where are you?" he asked.

"It's...it's too late." I kicked the fake tremble of my voice up a notch. "And I don't regret killing him. But I'm so sorry that I hurt you. I'm so, so sorry."

"Ensley, where are you?" His voice sounded more icy than concerned. Probably because I'd cut off his finger.

"It doesn't matter," I croaked. "It's too late. I can't live like this." I pulled the gun out of the back of my leggings and stared down at it. "I can't. I can't."

"Take a deep breath. I need you to tell me where you are right now. We can have a nice long talk about all of this when I get there."

I shook my head, my eyes still on the gun. "I have your gun. I thought it would be good to call you. Have this recorded so that no one thought you were the one that killed me." I turned the gun toward myself. Just one click away. Would it hurt less through my forehead or heart?

"Ensley, put the gun down," he said.

I sniffled. "Will you answer a question for me if I do?"

"Yes. If you put the gun down and tell me your address. I'll answer whatever you want." He didn't sound upset anymore. He sounded desperate.

"Okay." I put the gun down on the kitchen counter. "Who is T? And who's A?"

"That's something we can talk about in person. If you tell me where you are."

"You said you'd answer my question first. I'm going to shoot myself in the head if you don't."

"Ensley..."

"I went through your emails, Detective Torres. Who are T and A?" I picked the gun back up. "I'll shoot myself unless you answer honestly. Do the letters stand for Tremblay and Aiden?"

"No. Now please tell me where you are. I can come get you. We can go down to the station to talk."

"I know you were working with them." God, I just wanted answers. Why did no one ever tell me what I needed to know? "Just admit it. What does the truth even matter now? I'll be dead."

"I wasn't working with Sophia or Aiden. Put the gun down, Ensley."

"Then who are T and A? I swear to God…"

"Tucker and Adeline."

Tucker and Adeline. The names seemed to roll around in my head until they stopped. Adeline Bell was the first suburban housewife serial killer. And Tucker Reed was the second suburban housewife serial killer's boyfriend. He was also Detective Torres' friend and former partner. It would make sense if he was still in contact with him. Asking for more supplies made sense. But the other email? That they had A and the plan was a go? *Oh my God.* "You found Adeline?" I asked.

"Yes."

"How?"

"Give me your address and I'll tell you…"

"How?" I screamed into the phone. It was easy to sound crazy when he was driving me crazy by withholding information.

"She just bought a new house in Canada. We're going to stop her before she strikes again. Now you promised me your address, Ensley."

Ah, the sold house on Cherry Lane. Not such a dead end after all. So T stood for Tucker. And A stood for Adeline. Which meant

Aiden hadn't been working against me. Neither had Detective Torres. It was good news. It meant I was about to make the right choice.

But it wasn't all good news. Detective Torres wasn't as bad of a detective as I thought. He was about to take down Adeline Bell. Maybe he'd even turn on Tucker and Violet next. He was actually a really freaking great detective. Which meant…he'd find me too. Eventually. Unless I pulled this off perfectly.

"You're a good detective," I said. "You don't need my address. You'll find my body soon enough."

"Ensley. Please just put the gun down. We had a deal."

"Oh, you mean like when you promised to help me? You of all people should know about empty promises."

"I can still help you. You can come down to the station and we can talk. We can work out something if you confess everything."

Did he not hear what I'd just said about empty promises? Maybe he was still a bad detective. And I was done with him. Done with this game.

Adeline Bell was about to be caught. She'd failed. Violet would probably get arrested soon after. Failure after failure. They were such a disappointment. I'd idolized them and they'd…messed it all up. Violet's boyfriend was literally talking to a detective. And Ben's escape probably hadn't helped Adeline. For all I knew, Ben had led everyone straight to her. Violet and Adeline had both fallen in love and ruined everything.

But me? I'd pivoted my original plan to successfully frame Aiden for murder. Now I had to pivot again to successfully get Aiden out of jail. Did I love him? Yes. Was I risking everything just to get him out of prison? No. I wasn't crazy. I was only doing this because my plan was flawless. I was done with this game because I'd mastered it. No one was better than me.

"Goodbye, Detective Torres. I hope you have a great Christmas. Make me look good on the news."

"Ensley!" He screamed into the phone.

I tossed it onto the counter. After all, I needed him to hear the gunshot. I needed him to know for a fact that I'd really offed myself. The gun trembled slightly in my hand as I walked over to Sophia at the kitchen table.

She was still struggling against the ropes. Trying to scream through the gag. It was like watching myself. That was the only reason why my hand was trembling. Because I sure as hell didn't feel sorry for her.

I leaned forward so I could whisper in her ear. "You asked who killed Noah. Sophia, you stole my face. My husband. My money. You have my ID in your purse. You're not Sophia anymore. Technically, you're Ensley Collins. Which means...you killed him." I pulled away and shot her in the side of her head.

Blood splattered on the table beside her, completely ruining her beautiful Christmas table setting. There couldn't be two of us in this world. Even my husband was smart enough to know that. Plus, her dying was the only way to save myself and Aiden. She looked just like me. Yet, she had a different name. I needed her name. I needed the life she was giving up. And I needed her to take the blame instead of Aiden. Because she looked just like me. She was trying to be me. And I was the one that killed my husband. When you try to steal an identity, you should make damn sure that person isn't a murderer.

I lifted her wallet off the counter and pulled out Sophia Tremblay's ID. That and the money were all that I need to start my new life. But I still had to do one more thing.

I checked to make sure Detective Torres had ended the phone call before I grabbed a few pillows from the family room. I removed the gag from Sophia's face and untied her hands. Then I wiped off the handle of the gun and shoved it in Sophia's hand. I knew it wasn't perfect. But…it seemed good enough. Besides, I doubted anyone would connect the dots. After all…Detective Torres had arrested the wrong person for murdering my husband.

I lifted the gun in Sophia's hand and pressed the trigger down with her finger. The bullet shot through the pillows.

Then I dropped her hand, the gun falling slightly out of her grip. It looked natural enough to me. A suicide spurred on by guilt.

I looked down once more at Sophia Tremblay. It was good that the bruises had been makeup. They'd never even suspect that this was Sophia Tremblay. She'd done her best to hide her new face from the police.

I smiled and grabbed my money, my new ID, and the holey pillows. Snuggle Muffins and I had better things to do on Christmas morning than to stare at a dead body. I had already planned out our whole day. We were going to bake cookies, sing carols, and hopefully make some snow angels. Snow angels were a favorite of ours.

"You ready to start our new life, Snuggle Muffins?" I asked as we walked down the hall together.

The little bell on his hat jingled.

"Aiden will know I'm not dead. He's the one that told me about her having my face."

Snuggle Muffins' bell jingled again.

"I agree. He'll find us soon. Until then, the two of us are going to have so much fun." I started humming *Baby it's Cold Outside* as I closed the front door of Sophia's house behind us. The snow had picked up. It was the kind of Christmas morning that everyone always dreamed of. Well, maybe not the murder part. That was just a special present for me and the man who had stolen my heart when I'd kidnapped him. *Merry Christmas, Aiden.*

WHAT'S NEXT?

For more crazy twists and turns, check out my bestselling romantic suspense series, *Made of Steel.*

I fell in love with the boy next door the first time I ever saw him. And he never said it, but I'm pretty sure he loved me too. Until suddenly...he didn't.

In the blink of an eye, I lost everything. But losing him hurt the most. Everyone I loved was taken from me. But him? He chose to stop loving me.

It's been ten years since he left me. I've gotten over him. Or at least, I think I have. Until I start college and realize he's living right down the hall from me. I try to tell my heart to listen to reason. Because I can't possibly still be in love with the boy next door.

And even if I was, it wouldn't matter. Remember how I lost everything? I'm pretty sure I wasn't supposed to walk away alive. Those people are still after me. The boy who broke my heart would never recognize the person I've become anyway. I barely recognize myself. He left me to the wolves. He's the reason my life fell apart. No matter how I feel, I can't talk to him. If I did, I could get us both killed.

A NOTE FROM IVY

Merry Christmas! After last Christmas, I got the idea for this crazy book. So I told my husband we had to keep playing Christmas music and keep all the holiday decorations up until I wrote it. So it was Christmas in our house until March. I don't think he minded, minus the constant Christmas music.

Fast forward to this year. I couldn't wait until this Christmas season so I could finally release it! This year I said we had to decorate for Christmas early because I wanted to get in the mood for the release. So my Christmas tree has been up since the weekend after Halloween.

Anyway…I'm driving my husband crazy. BUT at least I haven't murdered him. Yet. Love you, Ryan! <3

And I hope you all have a very Merry Christmas!

Ivy Smoak
Wilmington, DE
www.ivysmoak.com

ABOUT THE AUTHOR

Ivy Smoak is the international bestselling author of *The Hunted Series*. Her books have sold over 1 million copies worldwide, and her latest release, *Empire High Betrayal*, hit #4 in the entire Kindle store.

When she's not writing, you can find Ivy binge watching too many TV shows, taking long walks, playing outside, and generally refusing to act like an adult. She lives with her husband in Delaware.

Facebook: IvySmoakAuthor
Instagram: @IvySmoakAuthor
Goodreads: IvySmoak

Recommend *Crazy In Love* for your next book club!

Book club questions available at:
www.ivysmoak.com/bookclub